Return
From Darkness

Return
From Darkness

Graham Jones

First impression: 2017
© Graham Jones & Y Lolfa Cyf., 2017

Cover design: Sion Ilar
Cover illustration: Teresa Jenellen

ISBN: 978 1 78461 371 6

Published and printed in Wales
on paper from well-maintained forests by
Y Lolfa Cyf., Talybont, Ceredigion SY24 5HE
e-mail ylolfa@ylolfa.com
website www.ylolfa.com
tel 01970 832 304
fax 832 782

'Myths live in us all, in our darkness…'

Joseph Campbell

Contents

1	Swirling Waters	9
2	Expose an Ancient Tome	15
3	Uncovering Secrets	24
4	In Man's Hidden Mind	33
5	Flights	41
6	To Former Days	51
7	Will Help Guide You Home	61
8	Ghosts	68
9	Beneath the Mask	75
10	Show there's More to Find	86
11	Lost Souls	96
12	Opening the Doors	108
13	To Golden Mists	117
14	Return	124
15	To Reveal	130
16	A New Horizon	136
17	Deceit Destroys	145
18	Even Where Love Persists	154

19 Rebirth of Hopes   162

20 Unchain the Hawk and Lion   172

21 Beguiling Words   180

22 Hidden Beneath the Leaves   190

23 Save the Hunted   199

24 Amandlas Unleashed   207

25 The Chain of Life   213

26 Forged in a Web that Weaves   223

27 On Crossing Waves   234

28 The One at Last Released   245

29 The Road to Hope   255

30 Comes through the Mask we Raise   264

31 Untangled Forces   275

32 Symbiosis Blaze   288

CHAPTER 1

Swirling Waters

OUR ESCAPE ROUTE was covered so we retreated to the top of a grassy mound in the trees: two women, a paunchy clergyman, the old man and myself. I looked down into the worn, disfigured faces of men who thought and acted with their fists and boots. Their bull-like shoulders exuded power, they moved like lions warily circling an isolated prey waiting for the moment to pounce and kill. Their cold eyes showed an icy indifference to whatever they had to do to us. Six of them looked like professional thugs who hurt and killed for money outside bars and in back streets; they were directed by a seventh who had a bandage around his head where I had bitten off his ear a few days' earlier.

They paused momentarily below us to gather for the attack and, in that lightning flash of time, a quarter century of my life sparked out from my unconscious. It instantly disappeared but too late; it came, it went like a shooting star but in that mini-second those lost years darted before me as vividly as if they were being re-lived in the instant we call 'now'.

*

The bus was crossing the mile-long Severn Bridge. As usual I was sitting alone, my only companions the sad faces with downturned mouths I had drawn on the steamy windows; tears of condensation dribbled out of the crestfallen features before fleeing down the window into the puddle expanding on the sill. Suddenly seeing myself exposed on the glass, I swept it away with a sleeve before anyone else saw it. Below surged a wide estuary of muddy, swirling water, violently rushing to the sea on a fast ebbing tide like brown blood pumping out of a torn artery. Ahead, across the estuary lay a surly, colourless land, darkened at midday by layers of heavy cloud. The gloomy scene seemed familiar, as if I had been here before and seen it all, a long time ago. I felt a dread as if I knew I shouldn't have returned. I didn't understand.

My reward for failing the mock 'A' level examinations was a last-minute sixth form residential study course in Pembrokeshire with the very people I blamed for my downfall. For six years, my supposed school friends had bullied, teased and mocked me until I was unable to speak in front of more than two or three of them without stammering and bracing myself for their ridicule. All I could do was play the roles they cast me into.

'Mañuel.' A familiar voice called down the bus.

One of these roles was a dumb Spanish waiter, stooge to a bossy hotel proprietor in a TV sitcom that was popular in those days.

'Mañuel! Come here.' Jenkins, my persecutor in chief and one of the school's 'certs' for an Oxbridge place, was hailing me from his throne in the middle of the back seat. His pretence of friendship accompanying the humorous summons always prompted a string of cheap laughs from his courtiers, at my expense. I knew this but daren't refuse his invitation, not simply because he was popular and commanding, but also because he took notice of me and gave me a distorted sense of being under his protection. I needed to please him, so when he called I always played his game, even feeling a perverse pleasure imagining I was his Rigoletto and a willing accomplice in my own humiliation.

I shuffled across the empty seat next to me into the aisle where I slumped into a hunchback stoop and, with a show of confused urgency, stumbled towards the heart of inevitable ridicule.

'I coming Mr Fawlty, I coming.'

Jenkins was tall and rangy with scraggly ginger hair and a rapier tongue, which he used like a cudgel when he became bored. He wasn't cruel by nature, but liked to be the centre of attention, which he got by making people frightened of him; any one of them could be the next Mañuel.

'Mañuel,' he said. 'We're a little confused back here. We need you to explain the theory of relativity to us.' Everyone around him mindlessly convulsed.

'Que?' I asked. My tongue felt thick and heavy, and the more I tried to meet his wit, the more I tripped over myself pretending it was deliberate.

'Relativity Mañuel,' muttered Jenkins with exaggerated desperation. 'Ex… plain.'

'Ah, relativity.' I let my face light up. 'All my relativities in Barcelona, Mr Fawlty.'

Everyone laughed and I looked around laughing too, feeling a momentary spasm of happiness.

'You stupid, stupid Mañuel,' scoffed Jenkins. 'Einstein's relativity you dumb waiter.'

'Ah yes, I understand,' I said. 'Einstein's relativities in Austria, Mr Fawlty.'

'Germany actually, and you're talking about the war again, I told you not to mention the war. Go back to your comic.'

I was dismissed and returned to my seat with my agony accentuated because I didn't know if I was still expected to limp.

The bus took us deeper into the dark land and deeper into my sense of foreboding. Through the misted windows and driving rain was grey motorway, the spray from traffic, the roofs of hundreds of houses – each one looking like all the others – and confusing road signs, with place names in English and Welsh. I broke my obsession with self-pity by trying to read the Welsh names on the road signs, and discovered that after some practice they started to roll around my tongue quite easily. One word I especially remember was 'Aberdaugleddau', the Welsh name for Milford Haven. I couldn't handle the double ds but was drawn to the rhythm of the word, which I wrote down and learnt by repeating it under my breath like a mantra.

Gradually the scenery softened into a rural dampness, and by mid afternoon the bus stopped in the narrow lane outside our home for the next five days, a former rectory, now a youth hostel, standing alone on a Pembrokeshire cliff top surrounded by mud, damp vegetation and wind.

'It's smaller than I imagined,' said Miss Jellings, the female teacher in charge of the girls. 'I hope the toilets are clean.' She had weary, disappointed-looking eyes, which made her seem older and sadder than she probably was, so the girls felt they had to look after her.

'Professional virgin,' was Jenkins' profound assessment of her.

Mr Halliday, our young General Studies teacher, was still learning how a teacher should behave, and was trying out being 'one of the boys'. 'Ooooh, it's creepy,' he said, squelching his way to the main door. 'It must be haunted. Come on lads, let's see if we can rouse a ghost or two.'

*

The first few days were the waste of time I knew they would be. Examination cramming and question spotting in the mornings, rain sodden field trips in the afternoons largely spent in overcrowded, ill-ventilated coffee shops and, worst of all, team activities in the evenings when we had to report to our groups what we had learned during the day.

After three days of steady rain, clambering every morning into cold, damp clothing and having to endure the standard high spirits everyone seemed programmed to demonstrate from first light to long into the night, I felt suicidal, but the sun came out for the first time on the penultimate morning. The sea sparkled in an after-the-storm swell; wild flowers spread like a multi-coloured carpet along the cliff top and into the distance. I felt a rare sense of being at peace, as if everything ugly in the world had disappeared during the night.

We were eating breakfast when someone whispered excitedly, 'Ticker!' I looked up and saw our headmaster, Dr T.C. Lloyd, standing in the doorway. Pupils and teachers adored him, so everyone that bright morning was pleased to see him, and the room literally buzzed with anticipation.

He made his way to the teachers' table at the far end of the room, stopping on the way to exchange some light-hearted words and pat a few shoulders. Finally he sat down with the teachers.

'Something's up,' said Jenkins.

After a few minutes Miss Jellings, smiling for once, stood up with a dessert spoon in her hand and used it to rap the table for attention.

'There will be a change of plan today people,' she announced formally. 'As it's such a nice day, we're going to go out as soon as you've done your chores.' She looked around to emphasise 'chores'. 'Today Dr Lloyd is going to take you.' Her words were greeted by a muffled cheer and an expanding bubble of expectation.

'What are we going to do, sir?' someone asked.

'Aha.' He leant back in his chair with a knowing but

uncommunicative smile on his face and said, 'I'm going to take you on a mystery tour.'

'Where to, sir?' someone else asked.

He raised his right eyebrow which always warned us to be ready for a 'loaded' answer, tilted his head slightly to one side, smiled slyly and whispered a reply that would hound me for over twenty-five years.

'Into darkness – into your own darkness.'

CHAPTER 2

Expose an
Ancient Tome

Porth Clais is a tiny, disused harbour on a narrow inlet near St Davids. In the Middle Ages it had been the main port of Britain's smallest city and a busy trading centre, but today it is no more than a minor tourist curiosity and a sandwich break for walkers. The bus parked at the head of the inlet, and we tumbled out to follow Ticker along a narrow, ankle-twisting path, squeezed on both sides by encroaching branches of overgrown blackthorn bushes. After ten minutes, we came to a grassy cliff top overlooking a broad bay. Below us, the sea shimmered in the sunlight like thousands of liquid diamonds on the restless surface. To the left, waves lapped against a succession of undulating cliffs, alive with seabirds swooping and soaring and twisting in what were, to my envious eyes, expressions of pure joy and freedom. Beyond the cliffs, layer after layer of white, yellow and pink wildflowers extended into a horizon-softening haze that seemed to mark the limits of the enchanted world we had entered.

'Put your coats down here and sit on them,' ordered Ticker. 'You never know who's been here before you.'

Automatically I found a place where I felt inconspicuous, and looked up at the headmaster standing close to the edge with his back to the sea, waiting for the stragglers to settle. A tiny white sail bobbed across the bay in the far distance; a gull screeched overhead. Then, with the wind rustling his hair, he started speaking.

'We're all creatures with many faces.' He paused a moment so we could assimilate this obvious fact. 'Yet when we look at other people, we see only a mask and assume we know who they are.'

During countless morning assemblies for over six years I had looked up into this 'mask', firm and lean with strong bones, quick to smile, open and friendly. His eyes sparkled, yet what he was saying was true. I had never looked into them, had never seen who lived behind the benign surface.

'Also,' he continued before I could take these thoughts further, 'when we look at ourselves in a mirror we think we see ourselves, but how much of our true selves do we see?' He paused briefly again. 'Isn't it possible that at a deeper level we are even strangers to ourselves?' I thought sadly of poor Mañuel and wondered how deeply he lived within me.

'Can we assume that we don't even know ourselves?' he asked.

A few hesitant doubters murmured an uncertain reluctance to agree with him, which he dismissed by saying, 'Let's wait and see... Remember I'm going to take you on a journey today, ladies and gentlemen.' He enthusiastically rubbed his hands together, as if trying to make a genie appear. 'A journey into the unlit corners within each of you. At the end of this voyage, you may have firmer opinions.

'Just imagine this bay more than a thousand years ago. It is filled with hundreds of brightly painted wooden ships, each with huge white sails full and pulling in the breeze, some with the great crimson cross of St George, others with dragon heads or eagles. Can you see the long pennants and proud standards tugging from the mastheads?'

He gave us a moment to picture the scene.

'Look inside the boats, what can you see? Hundreds of knights in bright armour and high plumes on their helms. Listen!'

He paused and strained to hear a sound from the sea.

'Can you hear their great chargers snorting and stamping on the decks, unnerved by the movement on the water? All around them, see the men-at-arms sharpening axes, spears and swords. Hear the bowmen laughing and shouting boldly to each other across the water. Listen! I can hear a signal trumpet blowing a command and another responding.'

He put his hand to his ear, straining to hear something. 'Can you hear it?' He looked around, daring us not to. 'I can hear singing too, as the fleet pulls away. Perhaps it's a hymn, perhaps it's a song of battle, perhaps merely a lament for a lady lost or left behind. Or is it just a trick of the wind blowing through the sails?'

Many times during our regular Friday afternoon sessions with him in the school library he would tell us stories – unusual, often outrageous stories, invariably with a hint of mystery and surprise. Some came from familiar sources like Kahil Gibran and Hermann Hesse; others were historical mysteries, like the mysterious disappearances of Giovanni Borgia in Renaissance Rome, or Agatha Christie in Istanbul. As a storyteller he was compelling, although his aim was not to entertain but to get us to think about the story, its underlying meaning and how it affected us. His abiding message was always, 'Read between the lines, my friends. All words are lies... only between the words will you find the truth... that's where your minds have to penetrate.'

He'd sometimes pick up a book and hold it up for us to see. Then he'd shake it in the air like a terrier shaking a rabbit, saying, 'Every book tells the truth... even if the author is a damnable liar – but you have to shake the truth out of it. And where do you start, form six?'

'Between the lines, sir,' we'd reply obediently.

'Today's story comes from the *Mabinogi*.'

'What's that, sir?' asked Kelly Chambers.

Kelly was the 'mystery woman' of the sixth form. Her figure was almost fully developed when she entered the school as an eleven year old, and she appeared to be a fully developed woman at thirteen. Although many of the other girls had now caught her up and she joined in all the school activities, the years of physical 'separation' had created a social gulf between her and the rest of us that seemed unbridgeable; she was friendly but had no bosom friends, and none of the boys had dared try to date her. She certainly showed no interest in any of us and had built a social life around students from the local university.

'Long, long ago Kelly,' he said gently, 'long before anything was written down, stories were passed down from age to age by professional storytellers. They tell us that Celtic Britain was inhabited by an assembly of larger-than-life people and beasts. Kings ruled the land with superhuman wisdom and power. Warriors massacred their foes with greater regularity and brutality. Lovers loved with greater passion and purity, and the beasts were larger and more ferocious than any before or since.' Two seagulls swooped down beneath the cliff. Ticker watched them go but didn't stop talking. 'As time passed, fact and fiction got mixed up, so we now call them myths.' Kelly nodded, Jenkins yawned.

'Of course, the *Mabinogi* was written originally in Welsh, and only translated into English in the nineteenth century. The stories tell of princes going on impossible quests; of interfering wizards defying the laws of nature; of shape shifting and spells, and of the complex relationship between man and nature when animals and trees could talk; of men interacting with the supernatural, and of a parallel dimension that existed alongside us.'

Abruptly he looked at us as if surprised to see us. 'You all have a relationship with nature today. I'm sure you can feel it… with the sea and wind, the gulls and the cliffs, but perhaps we can no longer feel a parallel dimension alongside us.

'The stories are not to be taken literally,' Ticker continued, without explaining the 'parallel dimension', in spite of some puzzled faces. 'But "between their lines" lies a wealth of ancient wisdom and memories of things long forgotten. Or perhaps they are not forgotten, but temporarily out of sight… languishing in the depths of our unconscious.' He paused before adding mysteriously, 'Or somewhere else.'

'In a parallel dimension?' suggested Kelly.

'Why not?' he said impishly.

'Today, I'm going to tell you about an evil king who was changed into a boar called Twrch Trwyth.'

Suddenly I wasn't sitting on a cliff top, but seemed to be running alone through a wood, blundering through undergrowth and bumping into trees. I was fleeing from something, something terrifying. It lasted but a heartbeat before I was back in the sun and the wind and fidgeting classmates; barely enough time for my senses to register it as he continued the story.

'There was once a wicked king who ruled a small kingdom in the middle of Britain.' I tried to revive my spasm of terror, but it was already dissolving like a fading dream. 'His depravity and the atrocities he committed against his subjects and his neighbours were so great that the gods finally lost patience and punished him by turning him into a giant boar.'

He then told us how, as a boar, the wicked king became even more evil, rampaging over central Britain, destroying everything and everyone he came across. He quickly attracted other forms of evil to him, until soon he was leading a huge malevolent army, transformed after his image into wild boars.

Eventually, with most of central Britain devastated, he led his army westwards into the sprawling kingdom of the great and just King Arthur. Even this powerful king was not strong enough to protect his territory, so he sent envoys to all the kingdoms in western Britain, and gradually assembled a massive army to pursue and destroy the boars.

'It wasn't long before the two armies met, and became embroiled in a series of angry battles and blood-soaked skirmishes fought across the hills and valleys in what is now called Wales. Slowly, the Christian forces forced the boar army back through the mountains and across the wild moors, until Arthur cornered it along on a narrow strip of land a few miles up the coast from here.' He pointed his eyes over our heads to the north.

'The boars escaped by swarming into the stormy waters of the Irish Sea and swimming across to Ireland, where their appetite for wanton destruction continued unabated as they trampled the whole country beneath their cloven hoofs and razor-sharp tusks.'

Ruth gasped 'Oh!' at the mention of cloven hoofs. She was the 'Miss Prim' of the year because of the ground-sweeping hemline of her skirt, thickness of cloth in her blouse and a sanctimonious attitude to anything remotely raunchy.

Ticker didn't pause. 'The Irish were too weak to resist and fled before the merciless hoard. Finally, in desperation, they had little choice but to call on their traditional enemy, Arthur, to come over from Britain to rid them of their tormentors.' Ruth looked huffily disgusted.

'Now, Arthur wasn't interested in helping Ireland, but he did have one serious weakness,' Ticker continued. 'A weakness common to many kings: an insatiable appetite for more and more power. He knew that ultimate power was symbolically represented by a comb, a razor and a pair of shears, which lay concealed in the coarse hair on the top of Twrch Trwyth's head between his ears, and the longer the conflict lasted the more obsessed he became with possessing them until in the end nothing else mattered to him. So, he gladly mobilized his allies once again, assembled an enormous fleet of fast ships and set sail for the beleaguered Ireland.'

'From here?' prompted Jenkins.

'From here,' Ticker concurred, before telling us of the glorious fleet sailing out of the bay and across to Ireland where the armies of Ireland and Britain, united under Arthur, finally confronted Twrch Trwyth across the river Boyne.

I was starting to feel sorry for the boar and to take his side. Perhaps it was sympathy for an underdog, but more it seemed that, like me, the world was against him, and we shared a firm bond in a brotherhood by being the 'odd ones out'. Ticker went on relentlessly, 'Before either side had completed their preparations or arranged themselves into effective battle formations, a curtain of bloodlust descended over them and they rushed at each other pell-mell screaming and bellowing in rage and fear. A chaotic frenzy of killing and maiming followed, as iron and tusk tore into flesh and bone. Horses were disemboweled, knights beheaded and pigs dismembered. The Boyne ran red into the sea many miles away, and the hillside became strewn with the tormented remains of the slain and mutilated. The once-proud banners lay torn and trampled in the greasy red mud, while streams became blocked and overflowed because of the bodies, the entrails and the gore.

'After nine days of slaughter, Twrch Trwyth knew he couldn't survive another day on the battlefield; so, after moonset on the ninth night, the surviving remnants of his army slipped away into the darkness. Next morning Arthur glumly surveyed his empty triumph; he had won the battle, but not secured the three symbols of power that had become his main objective and already sacrificed so much to gain.'

My sympathy was now completely with the wretched boar, and while I felt relieved that he had escaped, I knew Arthur would not be satisfied until he'd destroyed him and usurped his powers.

'Twrch Trwyth and the surviving boars had fled to the sea once again,' Ticker continued. 'They swam back to Britain and came to landfall in this bay.' With a slow sweep of an arm, he brought our minds back to the coastline beneath our feet. My eyes were drawn to a tiny shingle beach at the foot of a red cliff; there was something familiar about it.

'There's more, very much more! Follow me,' he ordered, abruptly striding off in the direction we had come without waiting for us.

*

Back at the little harbour he sat on a large, flat block of limestone and we gathered around him.

'Power, ladies and gentlemen. What can it do to us? Why do we crave it so?'

'It corrupts absolutely,' said Ruth.

'That's absolute power,' said Jenkins, politely for him.

Ticker broke into their little dialogue. 'Power may or may not *tend* to corrupt, but today I'm not interested in King Arthur's psychology. I don't care if he had become a bad guy. Whether he was doing his Christian duty or had become crazed with the dual lusts for blood and power. Today we are looking into our own darkness. Daniel Defoe wrote on the subject, "All men would be tyrants if they could." So I want you to consider how *you* would have behaved in Arthur's place.'

Another inconsequential discussion started which he

immediately stifled. 'Oh no, no, no, you have to dig deeper my young friends.'

He hopped off the rock and stood with his back to the sun so we were forced to squint at him. 'After supper tonight, you will tell me what you would have done if you had stood in Arthur's shoes. Was Defoe right? Until then my curious young *fiends*, think about it.'

He now brought us back to the story. 'The return voyage was very different from their first exultant crossing.' His voice and body language mirrored the hopelessness he was trying to convey. 'Silently, weary men and beasts, many carrying wounds and dragging nightmares in place of the gaudy banners they set out with, slumped into their boats, allowing the wind to drag them back across the grey sea to the final showdown. No-one looked with any enthusiasm towards the approaching land, and no boasts or songs could be heard across the water as the lifeless fleet approached the coast of Wales and silently crept into this little estuary.

'Come,' he whispered gently, moving slowly towards the waiting bus, 'The silent men are disembarking all around us. Let's not intrude on their nightmares any longer.'

CHAPTER 3

Uncovering Secrets

THE BOARS FLED forty miles northwards through a stony, pitiless land, until they came to a labyrinth of narrow, intersecting valleys which today is called Nevern. The whole area was densely forested of old oaks, with branches reaching the ground and tangled undergrowth providing a dense shadowy habitat for wild creatures to hide from pursuit and to ambush a prey bold or desperate enough to enter. They merged into its protection, and must have believed that at last they were safe in an environment that gave them so many advantages. Ordinarily, a victor would have called off the chase here and returned home to bask in the heroic glory heaped on him by his court bards, but Arthur was not an 'ordinary victor'. Power, not glory, had become his driving force. He followed the trail to the edge of the forest, but even he dare not enter such a viper's nest without preparation, so he withdrew to the high ground around a prominent tor dominating the surrounding countryside, called Carn Ingli – Hill of Angels – to consider his next move.

We merrily followed the same trail to the Hill of Angels; most were chatting and laughing about going home next day, a few arguing about ideas Ticker had strewn around Porth Clais; I sat alone fretting about Twrch Trwyth. Ticker hadn't taken a seat, but slowly moved down the bus, stopping to talk briefly to individuals and pairs, sometimes squeezing in with them to squash three bottoms into seats made for two. I hoped he would pass me by, but no such luck: he slipped into the vacant seat alongside me.

'David,' he chirped, apparently delighted to see me. 'On your own?' After a few generalities he asked me how many times we had spoken, one-to-one, over the years.

'Three, sir,' I said.

'That's right, our paths haven't crossed much. You seem to be an expert at keeping below the parapet, is that how it is?' He spoke in a quiet, disarming way, but I didn't want to be disarmed or to meet him above the parapet.

'I don't know, sir,' I answered defensively.

'Even so, I don't miss much, young man, and over the years I've come to know you quite well. Does that surprise you?'

I mumbled, 'Yes sir.'

'You seemed to be interested in my story today, am I right?'

'Yes, very much.' I momentarily dropped my defenses and even looked at him. If we talked about *his* story we wouldn't have to talk about me.

He outsmarted me by bringing both me and his story into one question. 'Who do you identify with David, King Arthur or Twrch Trwyth?'

'Well…'

'Yes.'

'I think everyone in the world is picking on Twrch, making him out to be bad when all he wants is a place to be left alone.'

'Right?' He seemed delighted. 'You're the first to show any sympathy or any understanding for Twrch, good for you.' A mini surge of pride swallowed a chunk of my diffidence. It returned with the next question.

'So you feel that the Twrch and David Tanner have a lot in common?' he asked quietly.

I didn't reply. The question was too close for my insecure comfort.

He stretched an arm along the back of my seat. 'I can see how difficult life is for you at the moment, my boy, but I know you very, very well.' I looked down at my hands and dug my calves painfully against a metal bar under the seat to help prevent my bungling emotions from tearing away my flimsy protective façade.

'Stick it out, young man. The difficulties you're experiencing are only part of growing up and finding out who you are.' He shrugged his shoulders rhythmically, like a cobra about to strike. 'I already know who you are; I see nobility and strength in you… Once you have put Mañuel to rest, others will see it too, and your life will change.'

'How can I do that, sir?' I grimaced.

'It will simply happen… Soon, I believe.' He stood up and slipped like a shadow into the aisle. 'One day you will flower into the glory of who you are.' The cobra had struck, but injected balm, not venom.

'Yes sir,' I said quietly.

He squeezed my shoulder as he moved away. I snuggled into the comfort of the few moments I had spent exclusively in his commanding presence, and watched the friendly countryside gently slip by my window.

*

We made two more stops that day. The first was in a lay-by at the foot of Carn Ingli, which rose six hundred rocky feet above us. We chased him, wheezing and complaining, through the stony foundations of an Iron Age village and clumps of shoulder-high bracken, to the top. It wasn't a fair contest; Ticker was still an athlete. He had been a double blue, a member of the UK Olympic sprint relay squad, and for six seasons a fixture on the wing for the Harlequins. Even in his late thirties, he turned out in the annual Staff v School bloodbath, giving as good as he took, whenever his long, wiry frame got into full stride; even our 'fliers', who wanted nothing more than the glory of overhauling 'the old man', couldn't get near him.

He waited for the stragglers to settle around him on the top of the hill, balanced himself on the highest rock like a patient eagle, calmly and without haste surveying its doomed prey, then swung an arm towards Nevern, little more than a mile away. The valleys were still quite heavily wooded, and patchy copses of oak still extended out of them into the rising open land beyond; it must have changed little over hundreds of years.

'It's likely Arthur came up here to survey the situation,' he said, looking down into the trees, then northwards towards the sea less than a mile beyond. 'This is the closest thing to a spotter plane they had in those days.'

Jenkins asked why Arthur hadn't sailed directly to the Nevern estuary instead of dragging tired legs forty miles over such a painful landscape.

'He probably sent scouting parties in many directions, Bill,' he replied, looking squarely at him. 'But he couldn't have known the boars would come this way. He may also have sent a few boats into the haven and up the river Cleddau, we simply don't know. All we can reasonably assume is that, for a few brief hours, the boar army disappeared into the valleys below, and Arthur was determined to find them and root them out.'

'Cleddau.' I rehearsed the name silently in my mind, but somehow the word came out of my mouth.

'Yes David, did you want to say something?'

'No sir, well I wondered…'

'Go on.'

'If the river Cleddau had anything to do with Aberdai cleddai?'

'The same, David,' he replied, adding a literal translation and finding a 'g' somewhere in the middle before continuing.

'Arthur may have seen something from this very spot. I don't know what it could have been, perhaps a careless boar rooting for food, or other woodland creatures fleeing from them, but soon he ordered his exhausted warriors to attack once again, and once again the boars were routed.'

He pointed at the retreating boars; everyone but me followed his finger. I was snatched for a moment by my imagination at the 'mouth of the two Cleddau rivers' – Aberdaugleddau – and seeing a magical waterway once used by men in longships, nature spirits, and long extinct water creatures. I felt the journeys they must have made into the mysterious hills sulking on the horizon beyond the range of Ticker's finger. Perhaps it had even been a route into Ticker's 'parallel world'. Perhaps those hills were part of his parallel world?

Another heartbeat and I was back following Ticker's restless finger, this time pointing down to dense clusters of trees with small clearings, and a stunted tor showing above the canopy. 'Thousands of years ago, that grove covered everywhere you can see, and was the druid's equivalent of Canterbury cathedral. Perhaps the boars felt its sanctity, and may have felt in their confused state that this was where they had to stand and die.'

'Perhaps Twrch Trwyth found what he had been looking for there.' To my surprise, the words came out of my mouth.

'What would that be, David?' asked Ticker encouragingly.

'I... I... don't know,' I mumbled. 'Peace perhaps.'

'Well done, Mañuel,' someone scoffed under his breath.

'Peace?' Ticker thought for a moment. 'Why not!'

Jenkins looked at me quizzically as if he was trying to make sense out of something.

'Anyway,' Ticker continued, 'regardless of how Twrch may have felt or thought, he had very little time for introspection.

Or peace,' he added, for my benefit. 'Arthur's mounted knights grimly scoured the forest, and cornered the demoralized boar army for one last soul-wrenching assault.' Ticker's descriptions had lost their gory detail, and became more contemplative, even despairing.

'Again, the boars fled. Past the great stone portal at Pentre Ifan, and the sacred tors you can see on the hill behind the wood, and into the magical heights of the Preseli hills over there.' The sulking hills now had a name and came within the range of Ticker's finger.

'Portal? What's a portal, Dr Lloyd?' asked Kelly.

'It's a gateway or an entrance, Kelly,' he replied. 'The word is often used for the way into the Otherworld.'

'What's that?' someone asked.

'It's a parallel dimension,' I said, 'Like Avalon in the Arthur legends.' For once I didn't feel stupid because I seemed to know.

'Yes, it's an idea that's used a lot in legends, isn't it sir?' For once Jenkins was agreeing with me and sparing me his measured scorn.

'Wouldn't it have a guardian?' he asked.

'Yes it would, Bill,' Ticker enthused. 'Usually spirit guardians, often in the form of animals, and there's a secret ritual or word the traveller must produce before he can pass through.'

'Like "Abracadabra"?' asked Jenkins.

'Perhaps. Or "Open Sesame"... But we must get on, the action is moving away from us.'

He indicated the Preseli hills again. 'That's our last stop.'

He jumped down from his perch, then, as a carefully measured afterthought, reminded us of the things he wanted us to think about on the way: the truth between the lines of the story, what Arthur and Twrch Trwyth were really like behind their masks. What made them tick? Was it only a lust for power in one and an evil nature in the other? 'Some of you I know have already sensed more than appears obvious.' He skipped down onto a patch of grass and took a few steps down the path, but turned once again. 'And, oh yes, form six, if you had the absolute power Arthur enjoyed, how would *you* have used it. Keep mulling it over and tell me tonight.'

*

We re-assembled at the highest point of the main road crossing the Preseli hills, gazing all around. To the north-west lay Cardigan Bay, blue, clear and sunlit with the shark's-teeth-like outline of the Wicklow Mountains on the horizon. Further round, the massive mount Snowdon lay like a crouching wolf watching an approaching rabbit. To the south spread the entire county of Pembrokeshire, hazily shimmering in the bright sunlight like an Avalon: much later I learned that the Welsh call it a land of 'mystery and enchantment'. In lazy repose across the middle distance, like a gleaming snake of light, lay the magical waters of the two Cleddau rivers.

Ticker nodded to rising ground just visible over the top of a spruce plantation. 'That's the top, shouldn't take much more than half an hour.' We did it in forty-five minutes.

'Below us is Cwm Cerwyn.' Ticker looked into the valley. 'Here, the remnants of the boar army, too exhausted to flee further, came to die.' I saw a treeless expanse of wiry brown grass with a few lonely boulders standing like small children lost in the terror and the beauty of a crowd of strangers. My strongest feeling was of desolation, which grew more awful as Ticker gave us the bloody details of the last stand.

'Many of Arthur's most valiant knights and some of his sons perished on this barren mountain. Arthur himself had his thigh sliced to the bone by a slashing tusk; all the boars except

Twrch Trwyth himself were killed. Finally, he stood in breathless defiance, his flanks covered in blood and quivering with nervous energy.'

My mouth had become dry with pity, and I was trembling. 'Run, run,' I silently implored.

Ticker was becoming more subdued as he spoke. 'He opened his cavernous jaws and let out a thunderous lament that echoed around the cwm like a stampede of wild horses. His adversaries froze, and some simply sank to their knees in submission. Then he turned and fled from this dreadful place.' Ticker slumped and hung his head for a moment before racing on with the story.

'Arthur had won a victory, but the boar still lived and still possessed what the great king prized so dearly. He ordered his blind-weary knights into pursuit and not to return without his prizes. They blundered after the boar across the rivers and valleys for a day and a night, until they caught him as he was about to cross the river Severn, not far from where you had crossed the previous Monday.' I remembered the dark whirlpools and racing currents I'd seen from the bus, and pitied even the strongest swimmer caught in them.

'The knights caught him at the crossing and snatched the shears and razor and placed them into Arthur's clawing hands. He gazed at them in disbelief and delight, then snarled with rage, forcing them to chase Twrch into the dervishing waters. "The comb, the comb, I must have the comb!"

'We've come to the end of the story,' Ticker gasped with exaggerated relief. 'The pursuit continued past the mound and tower at Glastonbury, and across two great moors to the very end of the land in Cornwall. Here the bedraggled warriors finally cornered their quarry. Twrch Trwyth stood trembling, bleeding and panting on the top of a high cliff overlooking the grey, cold Atlantic. The antagonists were barely able to stand, let alone raise a weapon; they simply stood and stared at each other. As if it had its own will and knew that it was time to change masters, the comb slid from the boar's head onto the grassy cliff top. He looked down at it as a sigh came from deep inside him. He then turned and plunged into the water, never to be seen again.'

CHAPTER 4

In Man's Hidden Mind

D URING TICKER'S TIME, the school's examination results had been good, though not exceptional. What was exceptional was the sense of enquiry that developed over the years, so that successive waves of young people went into the world unable to pass a stone without turning it over, a corner without looking around it, or a mystery that couldn't be solved.

During an early session with him the previous autumn in the school library, he asked us what we were searching for. The answers were confused, but he suggested that they amounted to 'the truth'. The truth about the world we found ourselves in and the truth about the meaning of our lives.

'Would you believe me if I told you that I know where you can find it?' he asked.

'Between the lines?' someone suggested.

'That's a good place to start, my friends, but I'm searching for a deeper truth that is not "out there" but "in here".' He pressed both his hands over his heart. 'Don't believe anyone who claims he can tell you what *your* personal truth is. Many will try; politicians, clergymen, used car salesmen, authors, and worst of all headmasters. Your truth, my young friends, is in yourselves, and each of you has to discover it for yourselves, and for each of you it will be different.'

I remembered these words as I tried to make sense of Twrch Trwyth. Why did I feel such an affinity with him? Why did I believe that Land's End was not *his* end, but that he would return? His gratuitous evil didn't sound authentic to me, so I wondered if the original myth had been altered at a later date. If so, by whom, and why? However, amid all this uncertainty, I was sure of one thing: I would keep these meddlesome thoughts to myself.

After supper, Ticker presided over a lively debriefing of the day. Many opinions were expressed about the effects of power on people; most agreed that it could corrupt even the noblest individuals, but we were too immature in worldly cynicism to believe that it was inevitable. Coming from staunch middle-class backgrounds, only a couple thought Daniel Defoe could be right to suggest we were all potential tyrants, so that particular 'hornets' nest' was shelved for another time while our attention was drawn back to the story of Twrch Trwyth. With the prissy exception of a few girls like Ruth, all agreed that it was more than a 'ripping yarn', and 'between the lines' lay deeper meaning. But no-one admitted that it was a route into their darkest corners; I certainly kept such implications securely locked away. Ticker seemed to expect a more positive response from us, so he resorted to what he called 'rapid fire questions'. He demanded instant answers coming spontaneously without thought, regardless of how stupid they may sound. 'They all mean something. The truth may sneak out when you're not thinking,' he'd declare. 'Let rip and see what comes out. Remember, young ladies and gentlemen, I want your immediate reactions, not your thoughts. Responses, not opinions, please.'

He started by asking us to tell him the story of Twrch Trwyth in one sentence.

Jenkins started, 'Good and evil are always at war but ultimately good will win.'

'Lyn!' He pointed to Lyn Tyrrell, a Gollum-like acolyte of Jenkins.

'Oooh… er… A pig goes ape…'

'Yes, go on Lyn.'

'King Arthur chases him into the sea and… er… gets his power.' He glanced at Jenkins for approval that wasn't forthcoming.

'Kelly!'

'Err… let me think…'

'The first thing, Kelly… don't think.'

'Oh… King Arthur rescues the world from evil but at the cost of his own innocence.'

'Some nice answers coming. Ruth!'

'It's an allegory like the *Pilgrim's Progress*, Arthur is "Mr Great Heart" who frees the world of "Giant Despair" who is the boar.'

Ticker nodded thoughtfully. 'What character are you, Ruth?' She blushed. 'Perhaps Piety from the house of beautiful maidens?' he suggested with an impish shrug.

Several more single-sentence synopses were given before he said, 'So now we have some idea of the story. Let's hear now what it's about, what it means to you.'

'Power corrupts,' suggested Jenkins.

'Evil must always be confronted regardless of the cost,' came from Ruth.

'You didn't mention the word "love" today Dr Lloyd,' said Kelly. 'What the story taught me was that without love we are all losers.'

Even Tyrrell saw his own philosophy of life in the story. 'Let those who want to get themselves killed do so, the wise will stay under cover.'

'The martyr theory, eh?' Ticker acknowledged each contribution with a light smile, a slight nod, sometimes a brief comment, but he was ready to go to a deeper level.

Then Ruth spoke up again. 'I think it tells us of something that really happened, sir.'

Ticker opened his eyes wider and tilted his head a little to one side, encouraging her to go on.

'It tells of how Christianity came to a heathen land and replaced the cruel Pagan religion.'

'Tell me more, Ruth.'

Ruth was the only child of elderly academics who were enthusiastic members of an obscure evangelical sect and vigorous weekend door-to-door campaigners of their beliefs. She had a plain face, short straight hair that looked as if it had been chopped, not cut, and even came to school parties as if she was, in Jenkins' words, 'dressed for chastity'.

'Well Dr Lloyd, my father says that everyone in Britain were pagans until Christianity came with the truth. The Pagans believed in human sacrifice. In their ignorance they worshipped goats and wild animals, rivers and springs... Evil and wickedness was everywhere, and dwelt in the hearts of the people. The boar represents this wickedness.' Her answers came pat, as if she had heard them repeated hundreds of times at home.

'So what's Ruth saying?'

'She's saying that it's an apocryphal story telling us how Christianity is the means of protecting us from darkness. Imagined or real,' said Jenkins.

'You're thinking too much,' declared Ticker. 'I want you to show me the unrevealed. What is said without the burden of words.'

He moved back into his quick-fire mode, with staccato questions about individuals' feelings, and reactions producing snappy, sometimes outlandish answers; but they gathered momentum, to his clear approval. All this time my thoughts were vaulted deep inside me, until Ticker looked at his watch.

'Well folks, it seems we still have a lot to think about, but at least this is a start. Before we finish does anyone else have anything to say?'

Apparently they had not. We'd had a busy day and were going home the following morning, so most minds were starting to turn away from Twrch Trwyth and his problems. 'OK,' said the headmaster. 'Thank you, form six. Once again you've given me a stimulating and enjoyable couple of hours. Would someone like to sum up for us?'

'I will, Dr Lloyd,' said Ruth, her evangelical ire well and truly roused.

'Off you go then, young lady.'

'This is a story,' she said, 'that was told by the Christian Celts and passed down from generation to generation. It tells how Christianity came and swept away the cruel old pagan religion...'

'I can't listen to any more of this.' The demon had broken out of the padlocked vault.

I heard an impassioned voice interrupt her neat little speech. To my horror, the voice was coming from me, and every eye in the room was turned on me like pointing fingers of scorn. I wanted to creep away and hide but was standing on my feet, in a place I'd never been before, listening like the rest of the room to the words coming from my mouth.

'Can I please say something?'

'Of course, David. You're just in time. What do you want to say?'

'Well sir. I don't know... I don't think...'

'Take your time David.' The smile had returned to his voice, and its warmth encouraged me to keep plodding on. 'Well, it doesn't sound right to me... I'm sorry but I think perhaps the story is not... perhaps it's wrong.' My mind was too busy stemming what little fluency my words possessed. Why hadn't the others started hooting and mocking me yet, I wondered? Hadn't I better sit down before they did?

'Indeed David. In what way?' My mind blanked out

completely but my voice kept talking. The kind way he said 'David' encouraged me. 'In every way.' Words were pouring from my mouth as if a tape recorder was playing inside me.

'For a start, I wonder if we understand why the story was told in the first place.' A strange sensation of calm seemed to be replacing the customary blur of dizziness I felt when eyes were turned on me.

'It seems important to know…'

'Go on, Da…'

'Has the boar always represented evil?' I asked, forsaking his attempt to help me. 'No! To the old Celts who lived here before the Romans came, the boar represented the power and energy and strength in the land.' I was falling in love with the strange words I was uttering. 'It was the force… the power that supported all the people who lived on it, and all the crops that grew on it. To them, the boar did not stand for destruction and chaos. To them it stood for their sustenance and fertility… It was their hope.' I stopped to look around. The room seemed full of faces all turned in my direction, listening to my words, although a couple of the lads were grinning as if they were expecting Mañuel to fall into a bowl of custard. Tyrrell whispered 'Idiot', but was instantly hushed by Jenkins, of all people.

'When the boar dies his blood and his carcass is taken back into the land and the land is replenished. The people of the time needed to know this, and originally the story told them so.'

'That's interesting, David,' said Ticker quietly. 'Go on.'

'Why was the story so horribly distorted?' I answered my own question. 'I believe the original story was changed and retold by the early Christians. It was their version, not the original version, that was later written down and told to us today. It's obvious why they did this and it makes me so angry!' If I'd ever felt anger before I would never have allowed anyone to know about it, for fear of punishment and appearing ridiculous.

'It was an attempt to give Christianity the power over the people of the land that the boar had held. Arthur, a metaphor for the Christian religion, was the one who was corrupted, not the boar.' All the doubts, vague feelings and uncertainties I had felt during the day were coalescing into a fluent flow of words; I was contemptuous of who I offended or what values I attacked. The anger I felt was real and irresistible.

'That's blasphemy,' blurted Ruth, jumping to her feet. But I hadn't finished.

'What I am saying is the only objective way of interpreting the story.' I looked at the poor fuming girl and said as gently as I could, 'Subjectively, like Ruth's, is I'm afraid only a smokescreen; a smokescreen to conceal what is between the lines.' I looked at Ticker, who allowed the hint of a twinkle to flirt with his eyes. 'And we all know that is where we should look.'

I sat down feeling, for the first time in my life, strong and unafraid.

'That's just a horrible lie.' Ruth jumped up belching more anger than coherence. A few consoled her with some weak support, but the general atmosphere was one of surprised silence.

'Say your piece calmly please my friends. Disagree yes, name-call no,' Ticker said firmly.

'But sir, how does he know all this stuff?' Ruth called, almost in tears. 'Has he got a hotline into the minds of people who have been dead for almost two thousand years?'

'Well David, have you?'

I had no doubts now and answered, 'Yes sir, I have. It's there for everyone to use if they want to. It's loud and clear between the lines in the story you told us, sir. And we hear it *here* as you taught us.' I pointed my index fingers at my heart. The room seemed to be slowing down to a standstill, like a slow-motion film with a subliminal message veiled within curtains of clouds. I waited for a chorus of disapproval; to my intense disappointment, I was not challenged. There seemed nothing more to say, and Ticker quietly closed the meeting with a brief and fairly neutral summary. He then left the room without speaking to anyone.

*

During that evening, more individuals than usual spoke to me. All were friendly, but only one spoke about my 'outburst'; that was Lyn Tyrrell.

'I felt exactly the same way as you,' he said. 'If you hadn't said what you did, I would have.'

'But you didn't, did you Lyn?' I said.

'I wonder what Ticker thinks about what you said,' he mused.

'I don't think I care.'

We would never know; none of us ever saw him again.

CHAPTER 5

Flights

Entering the bus for the homeward journey was like
waking up in Outer Mongolia. Everything was different.
Halliday, who had not spoken to me all week, gave me a wink;
the back seat brigade looked warily at me; some girls sheepishly
smiled; but most of all *I* felt like a different person. It was as if
I now owned myself, and had no need to play roles for anyone.
Jenkins also took me by surprise. I was one of the last to get
on the bus; he was sitting on his own near the door apparently
waiting for me.

'Dave, sit here.' I obediently dropped into the seat beside him.
The bus door hissed closed, and Miss Jellings counted heads
before turning to the driver. Even she seemed different; fresher
somehow.

'We can go now, driver.'

'What came over you yesterday?' he asked without preamble.
Already a few others had tentatively raised the question, but
none so directly. 'I'm not sure, Bill,' I said slowly. 'It seemed as if
I knew there was something… not right about Ticker's story.'

'How did you know?' He sat half-turned in the seat so he
could see my face. 'What made you so certain?'

There was nothing more I felt able to say so I asked him,
'Why do you want to know? Why is it important to you?'

'It's not,' he said quickly. 'It's just… oh I don't know… you
got me thinking.'

'Isn't that exactly what Ticker wants us to do?' I asked. 'You for yourself, and me for myself.'

He pondered this until we got on the main road before surprising me again.

'My thoughts are not about Twrch Trwyth or King Arthur, Dave. They are about you. The way you changed as the day went on was much more interesting that all that myth guff. I wonder what happened to you.'

Now it was my turn to ponder on his words.

'I haven't changed, Bill,' I eventually replied in a whisper that forced him to lean over to hear me. 'It seems like I've become… how can I say it, more myself.'

'Don't say Ticker's mind game about bringing light into our dark corners worked on you?' He was trying to sound flippant but I could see he was earnest.

'Perhaps it did, I honestly don't know.'

Neither of us was satisfied with our chat so far but we sank into another short spell of thought watching, then he said in a faraway voice:

'This isn't going to end.'

'What?' I had heard him but not understood.

'Myths never have endings,' he said mechanically as if reading the words from a prompt. 'Now we have been sucked into a living myth, we are caught in it forever.'

'What do you mean?' His words made no sense to me.

'All myths are true, Dave.' He spoke as if being aroused by a faded memory. 'They are revelations of what has always existed… to those who can understand them. You understood this one, now you've forced me to try to understand it too. Damn it.'

This still made no sense to me, perhaps not to him either at the time. We spoke no more on that subject but many years later I marvelled at how one so young could have been so perceptive and wondered where he had travelled to during his silent moments on that bus.

He sank into a private daydream staring straight ahead, so I took the opportunity to study him closely. Little frowns puckered his forehead as if his thoughts were sending coded messages to the outside world. His downy moustache flattened onto his lip in time with his breathing; there was dandruff on his collar and wax in his ear. I gazed fascinated at the God I had created, who was only human after all. Later we briefly small-talked before he opened a book and disappeared into it.

I looked out of the window which was full of the spring green and fresh light. I tried to remember poor Mañuel. He seemed like someone I knew a long time ago, in another life perhaps. I was already finding it difficult to bring him back and knew I had said 'goodbye' to him forever.

*

Ten days later I walked through the school gate for the start of the summer term. Lyn Tyrrell sidled alongside me. 'Done much swotting, Dave?'

'A little, Lyn,' I replied, more interested than pleased to receive such a friendly greeting from someone who had previously heartedly enjoyed my humiliation. He addressed me with the obsequious familiarity he had previously reserved for Jenkins, but I had other things on my mind. All my senses were on alert for a glimpse of one particular young lady.

'Come and get an eyeful of this, Dave.' One of a group of lads, furtively huddled in the corner of a cloakroom, called to me. I recognized the sidelong glances and conspiratorial smirks and guessed there was a 'girlie' magazine hidden away inside the huddle.

'Ever seen anything like this mate?' Groves, a dark, curly-headed lout and front row forward in the first XV, furtively pushed a handful of photographs towards me; they showed naked girls in various 'acrobatic' positions, leaving nothing for my imagination to complete.

'My brother got them in the States,' he explained.

'Quite graphic,' I said as calmly as a trembling falsetto could. 'Can't see Miss Jellings doing that.'

Groves returned them lovingly into a wallet and walked away with his smutty crew in search of further amateur voyeurs.

The 'acrobats' were still cavorting in my mind when I came face to face with Ruth in the corridor; she seemed excited. 'Have you heard the news?' she gasped breathlessly.

'What news?' I tried to picture her as a Groves 'gymnast'; I couldn't.

'Dr Lloyd has flown.'

'Flown?'

'Yes,' she said hopping up and down with excitement. 'He didn't turn up for the governors' meeting last week or a staff meeting yesterday.'

'Perhaps he's sick,' I said, looking down at her voluminous skirt, unable to believe all girls were the same 'underneath'.

'That's what my father thought after the governors' meeting, and he went round to his house, but his housekeeper told him that she hadn't seen him since he left for Wales.'

'Maybe he's had an accident.' I'd never looked closely at her mouth before; it was wide with full shapely lips.

'No, my father rang the police but they'd not heard of one.'

'Oh, he'll turn up, you know Ticker.' I walked away thinking about her lips. She took them in the opposite direction to spread the news of the missing headmaster.

*

The mystery buzzed around the school, but to me it seemed a fuss over nothing. I knew he'd turn up soon. I was more fascinated by the way the school seemed to have changed. It was completely different to the place I had left two weeks' earlier; it had lost its hostility. Relationships were different, sunlight seemed to shine into the dark corners, and for the first time in over six years, I felt safe there. I hadn't even noticed that I had stopped stuttering.

Weeks passed, and he still hadn't shown up, so school life had to go on without him. A new regime took over and started to impose its control, a temporary replacement headmaster appeared after a month, and inexorably the memory of Ticker became submerged beneath the merciless countdown to the 'A' level examinations – and, for me, merciless hormones. I had discovered a delightful alternative to exam swotting: Kelly and I had become close friends.

It started when she came up to me during a stop at the Severn Bridge services on our journey home from Wales.

'You've had enough of Jenkins. Come and sit with me for the rest of the journey.'

'What for?' I asked

'I want to talk to you.'

'What about?'

'You'll see.'

In fact we talked about nothing important – family, places we'd been to on holiday, books and films – but we did get to know each other. She had lots of furtive admirers of both sexes but no friends, and in many ways was as isolated as me, so inevitably the conversation came around to being a 'loner' and our difficulty in connecting with the people around us.

'I've made lots of friends at the university,' she admitted with a wry shrug of her shoulders. 'But most of them are still like school kids, not one of them is half as interesting as you.'

'Me?' I said surprised and a little embarrassed.

'Yes, it came as a shock to me too,' she said laughing. 'But you have surprising depths, David. Depths that are well hidden... and not obvious at first sight.'

'Oh.' I felt pleased, but didn't want to unravel her opinion by saying anything stupid.

'I find them exciting,' she said.

'Oh,' I repeated.

She took hold of my hand and said, 'I want to see you.'

'What d'you mean?' I asked disingenuously.

'David!' she said with mocking admonishment still holding my hand.

Yes,' I murmured quietly, 'Me too.' I took my hand back and sat on it so she wouldn't feel it shaking.

During what was left of the holiday we went to the pictures twice; the first time she held my hand again, the second time I held hers. We also went for walks around the city; sat for hours in coffee shops, and a few days before going back to school I plucked up the courage to put an arm around her and kiss her lightly on the cheek in the deserted cloisters of the cathedral. She responded like a tiger with a soft, moist mouth forcing my lips apart and pushing her body hard against mine. I felt the ecstatic inconvenience of sexual arousal, which I tried to conceal by half turning away from her, but she laughed and impaled her hips hard into mine.

I was pushed back against a thousand-year-old column and almost demolished it. Then we heard voices as a guided straggle of tourists appeared on the far side. We shuffled apart, breathless and laughing as they slowly passed between us, scanning the old stones like surveyors, photographing everything inanimate and holding their guide books like perambulating monks hold their psalters. They discreetly took no notice of two disheveled local school kids looking hungrily at each other, the girl standing tall, the boy bent double like a cockroach.

That brief moment of passion in the cloisters was as close as we got to the ultimate sexual experience but, as far as I was concerned, it had made us lovers and I adored her with the temporary intensity of first love. In my inexperienced but optimistic eyes, her 36 bust became 46, and each night I imagined her slipping into my bed beside me, although I never managed to imagine what we did.

The flame that had burnt so fiercely during the holiday seemed to go out once school restarted. We saw nothing of each other during the first two weeks of term because we were in different sets and worked at opposite ends of the building, so I assumed she had grown tired of me.

One afternoon, at the start of the third week, I had a late interview with the careers' master. When I left his room the school was almost empty, but on my way out I turned a corner and came face to face with her. For a moment we stood welded to the floor, looking into each other's eyes unblinking and unspeaking, mesmerized into immobility by uncertainty and renewed desire. Like a slow-motion reflex, I stretched out my hand and lightly touched her breast for a moment then quickly removed it, anticipating a stinging rebuke or a slap or scream, I didn't know what. She merely said, 'Leave it there.'

Then she was kissing me with open lips and pressing herself against me with a vigour I tried unsuccessfully to match.

Until then, despite the incident in the cloisters, I harboured the belief that in matters of sex boys had to do all the leading, while girls remained passive and inscrutable; it was a great boon for me to discover at that early age that this was not so.

We drew apart as we heard cleaners clattering buckets and gossiping their way down the corridor, but what we'd started we had to finish.

'Come,' she said leading me towards the gym, in search of somewhere we could be alone.

Breathlessly and with great incompetence I lost my virginity on the dusty coir mats in the gym store. As the term proceeded, we revisited the gym store at every opportunity, and extended our operations to include leafy sections of the 'Pilgrim's Way' and study bedrooms of her former university friends. By the end of that term my competence had improved immeasurably, and Groves' contortionists were relegated to the nursery.

*

Meanwhile, the mystery of the 'disappearing headmaster' remained unsolved. The local paper reported that after leaving us he had attended a short holiday course at Swansea University. At the end of the course he'd bought a return ticket for the Swansea to Cork ferry, but was not recorded boarding, seen during the voyage, or getting off in Ireland. The Garda had gone through the motions of looking for him, but didn't break sweat over one missing person who may or may not have visited their country. Back in Kent the police were more vigorous, searching his home, contacting friends and acquaintances, and scanning his past in their efforts to find an explanation for what had happened. His life seemed to have been open and straightforward. The only thing that puzzled investigators was that, despite being a moderately wealthy man, they only unearthed a modest current account with no trace of investments or other stashes.

A lecturer at Swansea University remembered that he had become friendly with an Irish woman during the course, but on checking the records discovered that she was a last-minute applicant who simply turned up on the first day and had registered without giving a home address. Someone on the course said that there had been bad feeling between the two, but this was contradicted by others, and soon it became apparent that this was yet another blind alley that led nowhere. His hire car was eventually found, over a month after his disappearance, in a lock-up garage in Swansea. A three-month rental had been paid, but the car had not been returned after it had expired.

Rumours flew around cheerfully like summer swallows. Falling overboard from the Irish ferry was a favourite, although no luggage or clothing was left behind – it was never conclusively established that he had even boarded. Amnesia was seriously considered but no-one answering his description had turned up in hospitals, police stations or guest houses in either the UK or Ireland. Being kidnapped or murdered were tested but had no credibility. He had no close relatives and had been a bachelor, so once the various authorities had exhausted all reasonable lines of enquiry there was nobody interested enough to keep the kettle boiling. After a month, the only policeman left investigating the case was diverted to deal with an outbreak of obscene graffiti in Maidstone bus shelters, and that signalled an end of the search for Dr Lloyd. He had become yesterday's news, and the case quietly slipped into the cobwebs of a musty police storeroom.

We talked about him from time to time during our last weeks at school, and remembered him with affection and good humour; but these were important times in our young lives, and we had little appetite for dawdling in the past. The relentless approach of responsibility, adulthood and the terror of poor examination results demanded precedence over everything else.

*

I failed all my exams to the disappointment of some teachers and my long-suffering mother, who seemed to believe that entrance to a university was the ultimate goal of mankind, but it came as no surprise to Kelly and me.

'Tough luck Dave,' said the radiant Jenkins sporting three As like Olympic gold medals. 'Are you going to resit?'

'Not a hope,' I said.

We had not become close 'mates' and never talked about the trip to Wales, but a broad equality and unspoken respect had developed between us.

'Good. I think you'd find university boring and not for someone of your talents,' he grinned. 'Don't take offence.' I didn't. It seemed a fair comment and was kindly meant.

My results mattered to me for one reason only. If by some miraculous process I could have been rewarded with 2 Cs – even a D for spending every spare moment with Kelly and hardly opening a book during the month before the exams – I may have found a place at one of the new universities who sucked up 'A' level flops. I briefly luxuriated in the fantasy of spending three or four idle years drinking during the week and seeing Kelly every weekend, but even these universities wouldn't look at me. With my ill-formed plans confounded, my father took my future in hand. He knew a Bournemouth hotelier, and within two weeks of receiving my results he'd packed me off to the south coast to start a career in what he portentously called, 'the tourist industry'.

Kelly passed all her exams but with poor grades, so her parents bought her a place in an obscure privately owned university in Oregon. Although we wrote for a while, our relationship was about feeling and touching, not words and air miles. Soon, all I had left of her was the memory of our sweet, breathless, exciting gymnastics on those dusty mats and beneath the horse chestnuts of the North Downs. Even that was brusquely put to rest when she wrote to tell me she was married. Our brief flight into the heights of discovery was over, but I had learned to fly, and nothing could stop me taking to the air again.

CHAPTER 6

To Former Days

A T LAST I had found something I loved and did well as I embraced a new mistress – my work. I had bold ideas and was prepared to take risks; my judgements were usually sound, and I instinctively seemed to know how to motivate and satisfy the people I worked with – bosses, colleagues and customers. Because I loved the work and was successful, I never counted the hours; the harder I worked the more energy I seemed to have; it was like playing endless games of chess insatiably and winning them all. More than anything else I was lucky, and looking back at the blunders that turned out for the best, I still find it difficult to believe how anyone could walk through so many minefields unscathed.

At twenty-five I owned a flourishing little private hotel in a popular south coast resort. By my thirtieth birthday, I'd expanded my holdings to the West Country, and included upmarket caravan parks and exclusive apartment blocks in my empire. I celebrated my fortieth birthday in one of my Caribbean resorts, but the celebration was muted. The thrill and excitement had gone; the challenge was no longer stimulating; but above all, winning all the time was no longer any fun. Success was no longer a mountain top to plant a flag on before moving on, but an enormous rut that I was sinking deeper into and couldn't see out of.

Soon after my birthday, I visited Vancouver on business. One fine afternoon I went for a walk in a leafy park by the water. Across the sound I could see mountains in the misty distance, their snowy peaks winking in the sun. Sea birds owned the skies, and a mile off, a whale languidly took possession of the vastness of the world's greatest ocean. This was a paradise, yet I saw no beauty and felt no joy. I thought grimly of my life which was only half over, yet I had nothing more to strive for and no dependants to care for. What would I do with the rest of my time on this earth? With these crushing thoughts still chasing me, I met Kelly again.

With a few hours to kill, I decided to lunch in one of the city's famous Chinatown restaurants. The room was full, but after a short wait I was shown to an empty table where I sat down and looked around for a waiter. There didn't seem to be one near, so I beckoned to someone pushing a trolley loaded with bamboo baskets. 'No order,' he said, 'Take off trolley.'

There was no way of telling what I was getting, but everything tasted delicious, so it didn't matter. Soon a pile of empty baskets was rising in the middle of my table. I had noticed a plump, homely-looking middle-aged woman sitting across the gangway; she was engaged in an animated and laughing conversation with an attractive young couple in their mid twenties. She kept looking at me then turning away to speak to her companions, who also started to cast furtive glances in my direction. I tried to take no notice, and was opening another basket when I felt a tap on my shoulder. I looked up to see the young man smiling down at me.

'Excuse me sir,' he said in a confident, natural way, 'But is your name David?'

'Yes it is.'

'And do you come from Canterbury, England?'

'Originally, yes I do. How…'

'Well that's really neat.' A huge grin appeared on his face. 'My mom says she knows you.'

I looked across at the woman and the moment our eyes met I recognized her. The lean, well-boned face I had known over twenty years earlier was now fleshy; the pert figure had spread, and the mass of cornfield blonde hair had darkened to deep auburn, but the eagerness and devilment that lit up her features and the come-to-bed dare in her eyes hadn't changed.

'Kelly!' I called, making even the polite Chinese diners turn and stare. Noisily scraping my chair back I loped across to her table. 'How wonderful.' I kissed her on the cheek, and in an instant all the years that separated us sloughed off and the old excitement at being near her returned, as fresh and as exciting as it had been during our youthful awakening.

'Have I changed so much?' she laughed. 'You looked through me twice. You've hardly changed, David.'

'Can I sit down?' I asked. 'I've gone quite weak at the knees.'

I had eaten enough but joined them for a drink. I don't remember what we drank or how much, but I'll not easily forget the next hour, when we returned to the passionate oasis we had once shared together. This time we shared it with her children, who joined in, apparently delighted at the possibility of discovering some secrets from their mother's 'murky' past.

'She hardly talks about her schooldays David,' said Mark, leaning forward confidentially. 'I do hope you're a skeleton that's escaped from her cupboard. Tell us all about her.'

'How long have we got?' I asked.

'Teasing is one of the ways we show love,' said Sally, her daughter. 'Sometimes we go too far… but not often.'

Between interruptions from the young people, she told me that she had left university when she became pregnant with Mark, and married his father, who was a Canadian salmon fisherman.

'He's really a poet,' she said, with a look of contented pride adorning her face. 'But only in his thoughts and words and actions and looks. He never writes things down.'

'He's barely literate, Mom,' said Mark, laughing.

I felt a sting of jealousy. It would be wonderful to have someone talking about me like this, I thought dolefully, but it's too late now.

'Most of all he loves like a poet,' she added, with a wicked smile. Sally giggled and I loved them all.

The little family settled down in Bliss Landing, a small fishing town a hundred miles or so north of Vancouver, and Sally came along two years later. Kelly didn't have to tell me that she had really followed and found *her* bliss. I bitterly realized that, at that moment, I would have given all my success to have what she had. I hadn't felt so completely empty since before the school trip to Wales, and for an instant, the bitter memories of those days crept into my bones like a dark winter. I felt deeply alone and hollow.

The conversation inevitably turned to my life since we'd parted. Compared with hers, it seemed like years spent pounding a treadmill that hadn't moved me from where I started.

'Are you married? Do you have any children?' Kelly asked, and looked surprised when I shook my head.

'Oh my dear, you don't know what you've missed,' she blurted, then realizing she'd gone too far, adding, 'Disrupted nights, never having enough money, a damp draughty cabin, endless winters…'

'It sounds wonderful Kelly,' I said, recovering. 'But I've followed a different star, and by and large I've no complaints.'

I described in more detail my life which, until recently, had seemed perfect, but she looked pensive.

'Isn't there anyone special in your life, David my dear?' she asked tenderly. 'Isn't there anyone who warms you when you're cold, soothes you when you're fretful, lies with you when you're lonely? And lies *to* you when you feel insecure?'

'Well, yes,' I said, looking around the room at the other diners, mostly Chinese, laughing, interacting with each other and eating. 'I've got plenty of girlfriends and quite a sophisticated social circle I fit into…'

'But no-one special?'

'Not really… I've never had the time… I've never even thought about it.'

She looked down at her bowl but couldn't hide the sadness in her face.

'It's fine, I like it,' I said defiantly.

'I'm sure you have a wonderful life and I'm happy for you David.' Her face was once again open and smiling, and she looked into my eyes confidently as if she meant every word. 'Most people would hate to live the way we do.'

'I apologize for my mother,' Mark said, still smiling. 'If she has one fault it's smugness.'

'Oh Mark!' she pouted. 'Don't remind me.'

My mind flashed back to the cloisters and two excited children learning to fly. I felt both joy and a depth of sadness that vibrated down to my roots.

They eventually had to leave, but before we parted I asked her a question that twenty plus years before I had been too preoccupied to ask.

'Do you remember the day we met in the corridor after school?'

She nodded and glanced guiltily at her daughter.

'Was it by accident, or did you plan it?'

Sally looked up eagerly. 'Oh, this sounds interesting.' She

leant towards her mother and put a hand on her arm. 'What happened, Mom? Was David your boyfriend?'

'I believe in fate, David,' said Kelly with a wicked smile. 'But sometimes it needs a leg up.' Sally looked puzzled, but I was content.

We exchanged addresses and vowed to keep in touch, but I felt our business together was over. She had, however, given me one last priceless gift that would ultimately save my life.

*

I returned to my various businesses and tried to muffle the echoing void seeing Kelly had opened up by working even harder, but there no longer seemed to be any point. In a manic surge to allay the pain I took even greater risks, both business and sexual. I ran a gauntlet through lovers who came and went in a blur of hotel rooms, frantic weekends and hollow one-night stands. Twice I came close to being hoodwinked into wedlock by bimbo gold-diggers, but even *I* wasn't that desperate or empty. Months ticked by; the feeling of discontent grew; the sense of emptiness expanded in me; the rut deepened and the tiny seed sewn by Kelly slumbered in a warm, safe place; waiting, as seeds do.

In a futile attempt to give my life more purpose I started supporting charities, and for a few months flirted with a project to bring water to an African village, but despised myself for my opportunism and indifference to the success or failure of the projects. In desperation, after living for over two decades with hardly taking a real break, I started going on a succession of extended holidays. I went trekking in Nepal, caving in the Pindos mountains of northern Greece, and whale-spotting in the Norwegian fjords. Each briefly assuaged the pain as I became engrossed in a new activity and challenge, but the unyielding emptiness always returned stronger than ever, as if a dark shadow was standing behind me whispering, 'Find your true self, David Tanner, or die!'

*

One January I went to South Island, New Zealand, with a girlfriend and chartered a forty-five-foot ketch to explore the western seaboard. About a week into the cruise I had to stay below to send some e-mails and didn't come on deck until mid morning. We had entered a deep fjord with steep, heavily wooded slopes rising thousands of feet on both sides. The tops were covered by a sullen cumulus, and an aura of Tolkienesque gloom hung over the place which I found strangely comforting.

'Is this the way to Mordor, skipper?' I enquired pleasantly, rubbing my shoulders for warmth.

'Dunno,' he muttered.

Surly sod, I thought. 'Is it going to clear up?'

'Maybe.'

'Are you going to let me steer, Mike?' Trish, the American woman I had brought along, emerged from the forward cabin, swathed in a lurid tapestry jacket and a pink Angora scarf wound around her like a boa constrictor. 'Hi David, finished your work?'

'Not quite.' I had, but was already tired of her and was withdrawing as graciously as I could. Mike had no such problem.

'Like to steer, Trish? Come and take hold of it… you've got to be careful, the wind's a bit fluky.'

'Oh, don't leave me then,' she said, in her teasing, flirty way.

Trish was a trainer for a personal development organisation called EST and the perfect partner for me because she took my curmudgeonly manner as being all part of a day's work. Her strongest expression of annoyance was, 'You don't get it do you, David?'

In the early days of our brief time together I would ask, 'Get what?'

'Ah… if you knew that you would have it?'

'Well put me out of my misery and tell me.'

'Oh no fine sir, the whole point of "it" is that you find it out for yourself.'

I soon got tired of this nonsense, but as a farewell gift before we split she finally told me that 'it' didn't exist. That was 'it'. This perfectly summed up our relationship.

'Actually, I don't mind this weather.' I re-engaged Mike. 'I like the darkness. It's mysterious. I bet there are lots of Maori legends of monsters and dark lords lurking in the shadows.'

'None that I know of,' he grunted, making barely enough room for Trish to squeeze past him and take the wheel.

'What's the name of that huge mountain straight ahead?' Trish asked with a giggle.

'It's Mitre Peak,' he said standing close behind her. 'Hold the wheel like this… good, now fix your attention on something prominent and head for it… you're a natural.' She giggled again.

I glanced at a conical mountain rising straight out of the water and cutting into the soft underbelly of cloud a few miles away.

'Umm, it seems awfully big,' she said deviously. 'How high is it?'

'One thousand, six hundred and ninety metres,' he said proudly. I shivered, as much with the double entendre as the cold, and went below without another word.

I pulled on a fleece, brewed some coffee and sat down at the chart table to drink it, warming my hands around the mug and idly looking at an open chart. Through a window I could see the cloud clearing from the top of Mitre Peak; it looked like a massive canine tooth in a black liquid gum. All around, the cloud was lifting, and the pointed tips of more and more peaks were emerging on both sides. We seemed to be sailing into the jaws of a great salivating monster.

I wondered where we were, so looked down at the chart and read 'Milford Sound'. There was something familiar about the name. Looking closer I found Mitre Peak; it had two rivers flowing into the sound on either side. I sipped the coffee and idly traced the rivers back on the chart to see what they were called. Their names were 'Cleddau' and 'Arthur'. A tremor of memory shuddered me from head to toe. I knew those names from a story I'd been told many years earlier at school. Fragments of the story jolted into my head: King Arthur, a wicked boar, the corruption of power, a sparkling sea, my strange empathy with the boar, even how my life was somehow different afterwards.

Eagerly I looked out of the window again. Mitre Peak was now completely clear of the cloud but still shadowy and forbidding. It was less than a mile away, and I had to move closer to the window and lower my head to see the top. There was enough light to pick out shapes and features, but it was too gloomy to see them clearly. The trees looked like coarse hair; something amongst them glinted which seemed like an eye staring unblinkingly at me. I saw a muzzle and a tusk, then the head of a massive boar seemed to appear, glaring malevolently in my direction. Its back was arched and bunched into a posture of belligerence. Mesmerized by the apparition, I watched the 'beast' as it came nearer and nearer. I imagined it grunting and snorting and sensed it wanted to communicate with me. I heard nothing, but the words 'Come home' entered my head. 'Come home, you're needed now. Now!'

*

One evening in early April only three months later, I was taking my boots off in the 'wet' room of my delightful new home after a muddy trudge along the north Pembrokeshire coastal path when the telephone rang. I laughed to myself as I struggled with the laces. 'Don't go away, I'm coming pal,' I called.

I skipped around a chair, catching a stockinged toe on the corner of a leg.

'Bugger… OK, OK, I'm coming,' I called, hopping my way towards the telephone, 'If the furniture doesn't kill me first.'

I lunged for the receiver and flopped backwards into a sofa, rubbing my toe with one hand and pressing the receiver against my ear with the other.

'Hello. David Tanner,' I panted.

'David.' I heard a confident, slightly overbearing voice. 'Guess who this is?'

'Sorry. I don't have a clue.'

'We were at Chaucer's Grammar School together. Do you remember Bill Jenkins?'

CHAPTER 7

Will Help
Guide You Home

'JENKINS! GOOD HEAVENS! Of course I remember you.'
I remembered him as I would the pattern on a broken plate, shards of fragmented incidents mixed up with each other without forming a single meaningful picture. They were isolated pieces, some bitter, many sweet; some meaningless, others significant; most distorted, but striding about them all like an invisible colossus was the feeling that we had unfinished business. What the business was lay far outside the range of my imagination.

'How are you after all this time?' I asked warmly, recalling the last time I saw him, by the school gate, when he gave me an embarrassed bear hug and wished me well. It had been utterly out of character for him to show his feelings this way and he broke away before I could react. 'What are you doing now?'

'Look old friend, I've got a place down here… We're almost neighbours… How about coming over for a drink? I'll reveal all to you then.' As he spoke I saw his absurd downy moustache, wild hair, the clever smirk of self-assurance; I even saw the dandruff on his shoulders. I felt a nostalgic tweak for the days of innocence and uncertainty.

'Good idea,' I said, 'When?'

'Can you get over in half an hour?'

'Make it an hour. I've just come in from a walk and need a bath. I look and feel like a hippopotamus.'

'That's great. Bring your wife along if you've got one, she can keep mine out of our hair.'

'Don't have one, I'm afraid,' I said gaily, although the joy I had seen on Kelly's face as she spoke of her poet husband still stung, and I didn't feel as light-hearted as I tried to sound.

'What, a man with all your money, still free?' I wondered how much he knew about me. 'How about girlfriend? Mistress?'

'Only a dog, I'm afraid.' I lied, I don't know why. I didn't have a dog either.

'Listen Bill, I'm getting cold.' I was wet through and starting to shiver. 'Give me your address and I'll be around as soon as I can.'

I dozed in the bath amidst the purging scent of Radox 'muscle soak' as earlier, more painful memories of Jenkins sidled in and out of the mists. Mañuel returned as an amorphous ghost. The years of humiliation flickered on and off like a loose light bulb; I vaguely remembered my unhappiness, but more compelling were the last few months of school, the new respect he had shown me, and the curious way I caught him looking at me when he believed he was unobserved. Until this moment I hadn't fully appreciated how profoundly his attitude to me had changed after our trip to Pembrokeshire, when I first met the boar. Quite abruptly, I remembered that I had promised him an hour, so splashed out of the bath and grabbed a towel. He had said something on the bus about us being forever trapped in the myth with the boar. I couldn't remember everything; it hadn't seemed important then, but after my recent experiences with a boar flitting in and out of my life and actually being responsible for my eventual move to Wales, the coincidence was too compelling for comfort.

*

The beast I had seen emerging from Mitre Peak had been as real to me as my own face in the shaving mirror, and the instruction to 'return home' because he 'needed me' as emphatic and unambiguous as a New York traffic cop. Yet three days later, after curtailing my holiday (to the clear satisfaction of Trish and Mike), I stood in Christchurch international airport quite convinced that I was mad. Only a madman would chuck an expensive holiday, dump his 'paid for' girlfriend in the lap of a taciturn sex manic, jump on a plane and fly around the world because he imagined a mountain had turned into a boar and spoken to him.

Although my original plan had been to go directly to Wales, by the time the 747 touched down at Heathrow, I'd changed my mind and decided to spend a couple of weeks in London completely on my own, without any commitments, until reason returned. I bought a *Time Out* and, as the taxi crawled into London, took the time to consider my options. There was so much to do and see in this exciting city; shows, exhibitions, architecture, history. I was still undecided about where to start when the driver announced, 'We're 'ere mate.'

For my infrequent stays in London I had a room in the Primrose Hill flat of an old friend. The room was small and minimally furnished, but this was all I needed. I normally only used it for a night or two for 'getting my head down'. The shared kitchen and bathroom were compact but well fitted, while the living room was spacious and comfortable; it was the perfect bolt hole for a tight-fisted recluse. An added attraction was that the owner lived in New York and only used it a couple of times a year, so I rarely bumped into him and hadn't seen him for five years.

A benefit of flying business class on long flights is the separate sleeping cubicle that helps eliminate the effects of jet lag. It didn't work for me this time, because although

I'd slept well on the flight, by 2 a.m. I was sitting up in bed, wide awake, staring at the blank wall. My mind seemed to be alive with maggots restlessly crawling over each other in a directionless frenzy. I got up and shuffled into the icy kitchen to make a drink, but the cupboards were empty; I cranked up the heating and went into the sitting room where I vainly trawled through the TV channels for something to calm me down. I viciously killed the screen and lurched over to the bookcase where, to my delight, I found a Dashiell Hammett. After a dozen pages my brain surfaced, and I had no idea of what I'd just read. My eyes may have followed the words, but my mind was wallowing through a maze of instantly forgotten images and thoughts that came and went like raindrops on a leaf.

The flat seemed claustrophobic, the heating was inefficient and there was nothing to eat. I shivered over to the window and looked out through the curtains. Ice had formed on a puddle, not even a cat moved, and the street lamps gave off frosty halos. I turned back towards the bedroom and the haven of a well-togged duvet, but changed my mind and got dressed, climbed into a duffle coat hanging by the door, wrapped a long college scarf around my neck and slipped outside into the wintery night. The idea of moving on to Wales had dissolved like a snowflake on my cheek.

I strode out along the empty streets in the general direction of the 'Hill'. Lazy snowflakes drifted through the eerie, spectral light to settle on the pavement, the road, the bare branches of the trees, and my shoulders. They brushed against my face like soft breathing, and I felt warm despite the chilly air stinging the tips of my nose and ears. I walked briskly, surrounded by a cascade of wild, empty thoughts, paying no attention to my direction or distance. I remember looking into shop windows on the Finchley Road and passing the Swiss Cottage, but nothing else until I came to a set of high iron railings which I recognised as the outer perimeter of London Zoo.

I kept walking until, midway along the railings, I heard something on the other side and stopped to listen. The noise was of an animal – or animals – snuffling and grunting in a clump of trees. I peered into the trees, but there was only darkness and the impression of unusually great depth. I was outside the wolf enclosure, where I had stopped before from time to time to admire the silent menace of these wonderful creatures; yet I didn't remember the trees being so dense. Then something, even darker than the shadows, moved in the wood. I stared into the blackness trying to see what it was. It was too big to be a wolf. The noise became louder and more insistent then. Although there was no wind, the trees started to shake and snow hushed down to the ground off the branches. My eyes slowly adjusted to the darkness; it seemed that all the trees were moving, stretching and flexing, like a sleeper waking up after a deep sleep. Gradually the movement became slower and more subtle until, finally, it silently calmed the trees. I waited timelessly, gaping through the railings, hoping whatever it was would come back but all I saw was a deep, black stillness. Whatever had been there was gone, leaving the trees empty and me alone in the mute world of snowflakes, street lamps, iron railings and the empty white park, with just two words – come home – in my head.

I returned to the flat with the words still nagging me, and felt irritated by the sheer boredom of their repetition. They followed me in through the door and into the bedroom. Shivering, I climbed under the duvet, curled into a ball and closed my eyes, but they wouldn't let me sleep. Angrily, I flounced into the main room with the duvet wrapped around me and stood briefly watching stale news on television, then sought sanctuary in the bathroom. But the words followed me like a hound of heaven, up and down wherever I went, until my resistance capitulated and I lifted the telephone.

The blackness of night had turned to pre-dawn grey before I slumped into a peaceful sleep, sitting in a chair fully dressed with bag packed and the telephone on my lap. A hire car was delivered at 8.30, and ten minutes later I was easing my way through the busy, slushy streets of north London, towards the M4 and Wales.

The rigours of the night soon wore off and I drove west along the motorway, relaxed and humming to myself, free from anxiety, doubt or the need to understand rationally what I was doing. Automatically, I turned away from the new Severn Bridge, built since I last came this way, and took the longer route across the old bridge. Passing through the cage-like structure of the suspension wires was a different experience this time; the sun was already high in the cloudless sky behind me, highlighting a multitude of colours in the gently rippling water below and glittering on the friendly, snow dusted hills ahead in the distance.

My destination was Pembrokeshire and I headed for the only name I remembered – Aberdaugleddau, where I found a hotel overlooking the haven. Although the town claimed Nelson and Brunel as former residents, I found it cheerless and run-down, so checked out next morning and headed over the Cleddau bridge into south Pembrokeshire. This is a pretty, rural area with winding waterways, an exciting coastline and interesting little towns and castles, but I didn't feel comfortable there. Everywhere seemed to be locked and shuttered, the people polite but aloof, and not interested in a lone winter traveller.

Next day, convinced that I was chasing wild geese, I decided to take a quick look in the north of the county before heading back to London. Once across the main A40 road, I seemed to enter a different country. The land was rough, hilly and wild, studded with granite tors and deep wooded valleys, but the greatest difference was that I felt welcome and wanted there. People in the lanes and little towns stared at me as I passed, and always waved back if I waved first. If I called into a shop to buy a newspaper or ask for directions, the transaction was always followed by shy questioning about where I was from, why I was there and what I thought of the county. The soft, lolling hills were like reclining girls, gentle, saucy and friendly, but most of all I loved the wild coastline with rocky cliffs, vigorous waves and inaccessible coves. It was a land made for wreckers and myth.

Within a week I'd found the perfect place to live. It was a medium-sized house with two acres of land on the north coast near Newport. I liked the large windows with views of the sea, and the gate at the end of the garden leading onto the coastal path. Stepping through it was like entering another world of elemental forces and impulses. I could feel fine, wind-borne spray from waves breaking over the rocks a hundred feet below and subtle tremors in the ground when a particularly large wave thundered in.

'Look at that.' The estate agent pointed out into the bay at a violent hailstorm. It was so intense that the waves in the sea beneath it were flattened into a spitting angry pawprint. 'We get some strange contrasts in the weather, but I've never seen the sea flattened like that before,' he said. 'The waves all around it must be three feet high.'

We walked around to the front of the house and I noticed an outcrop of rocks on top of a hill.

'What's the hill called?' I asked.

'Carn Ingli,' he replied. 'It means…'

'Hill of the Angels,' I said. 'I'll take it.'

I had come 'home', and moved in six weeks later.

CHAPTER 8

Ghosts

JENKINS ONLY LIVED a few miles away from me, but his house was at the end of a succession of narrow lanes, steep hills and tight corners, so I arrived a few minutes late. I parked and crunched over the gravel drive towards his front door with the obligatory bottle of red in one hand, and a small posy of wild flowers (mainly bluebells I'd collected from a hedgerow) for Mrs Jenkins in the other. His 'place' as he called it was a determined looking stone farmhouse with traditional double glazing, satellite dish and burglar alarm. A barn had been converted into a garage with a remote controlled up-and-over door, and the cowshed into lock-up storage space with a self-contained visitor flat above. A light showed in the flat. It all stood in little less than an acre of land, on the side of a hill looking down onto the wide spread of Cardigan Bay barely a mile away. Over the sea to the south-west, heavy clouds were jostling in the fading light, promising another wet night.

The door opened before I reached it and Jenkins emerged sedately to greet me with a full frontal smile. Perversely I had expected to see him as I remembered him, tall and gangling with a mop of uncombed red hair and a weak ginger moustache; it was a shock to see what the years had done to him. I was confronted by a rotund, shiny-bald, red-cheeked stockbroker type, dressed with immaculate informality down to the straight creased slacks, cashmere sweater, paisley cravat and loafers. While we were shaking hands he took the flowers.

'For me? Oh you shouldn't have,' he laughed. 'Come in, come in, my dear chap… It's so nice to see you again. I've often thought about you.'

'How did you find me?' I asked, following him into the house. 'Aha,' he turned with a mischievous twinkle. 'I have special connections.' He tapped the side of his nose, looked heavenwards and ushered me deeper into his kingdom.

During the next hour I changed my mind several times about whether I thought the intervening years had been kind to him, or a sick mockery of his youthful promise and energy. He completed a summary of his life since leaving school, and I must have spoken no more than half a dozen sentences in reply. He had swept majestically through his university career, which he left with a wife, two children and a doctorate in theology. The fast-track of a Church career beckoned, which he skipped along like a smooth pebble skimming over a flat pond, barely touching the water, barely making a ripple. By the time of our reunion he was the Dean of a large Midlands diocese. 'My job is to wipe the Bishop's backside,' he claimed. 'I'm a glorified lavatory attendant.'

Whatever he was, he was well rewarded for it, and could afford 'little places' in Pembrokeshire and Brittany; and a monumental smugness.

During that hour he found a moment to tell me that his daughter was 'still' at university and his son lived in a sub-let bedsit in Brixton; he was a 'chef' at the local McDonald's. He spoke about them with brevity and disinterest, as if they were boring books he'd read long ago. I nodded and smiled from time to time to show I was still awake, and felt genuine happiness for his success and apparent satisfaction with his life, but not once did I envy him as I had Kelly in the embrace of her cheerfully loving family. Despite his good fortune and complacent pride, I started to feel sorry for him. The old enthusiasm and intelligence was still there and lovely to see, but I also detected an empty cynicism which his career and probably his marriage were unable to fill. After little more than an hour, I'd decided to make an early exit, and never return.

'I'm surprised you went in for the Church,' I said, just to remind myself that I still had the power of speech. 'I could have seen you as a writer or academic, yes, even a civil servant, but never a clergyman.'

'That's the way the cards fell, my friend,' he said, beaming. 'It's only a job after all, and I've no complaints. Look around you.' He waved a hand around the room. 'Life seems pretty good and the prospects even better. I should say there's a good chance of a bishopric within the next few years. All I have to do is keep my nose clean,' he laughed and winked, 'And up the bishop's arse.'

I'm no prude, but the sentiment shocked me; the man seemed to have no principles and his values only of self-gain. I tried to form a picture of the woman he had married from the many clues around me. He hadn't mentioned her once, which suggested there were very few points of contact between them and a marriage of suitability rather than love. The inside of the house told me a great deal about her. It could have come out of the pages of *Ideal Homes*. Fresh cut flowers, most arranged with evening class creativity, garlanded every flat surface without a grain of pollen out of place and where dust feared to settle. Ornaments and fittings were thematically arranged; I decided the dining room was the Turkish room, the living room the Indian room, and the kitchen a homage to steel and plastic.

Taste and affluence gleamed from every corner, yet there was no joy or spontaneity and beneath the immaculate façade I could 'hear' the screams of the poor woman who had put it all together. It seemed obvious to me that she was just one of the many stepping stones lying along the path of her husband's ambitions, and was as dry as a dead stick. I counted six picture frames containing photographs of Jenkins looking important in various regalia, two of his children taken during their self-conscious teens, coyly grimacing into the sun, but nowhere could I see a picture of Mrs Jenkins.

'Tell me about your wife,' I said.

'Oh, you'll see her for yourself... she'll be home soon.'

'Good, I look forward to that.' I was curious but not enthusiastic. 'Where's she gone?'

'Some woman's thing, I s'pose. She probably told me but it didn't sink in.'

'I can see her influence in the house. It's immaculate,' I said.

'It should be. The "help" comes in three times a week,' he said coolly.

I started to plot my escape. The reunion had been interesting and filled in some of the gaps of the intervening years, but we clearly had nothing in common, so now I felt ready to leave him for another twenty-five years, and with luck after minimal small talk with his wife.

'Do you ever see anyone from Chaucer's?' I asked, getting up as a preliminary notice of my departure, replacing a wayward cushion I'd knocked out of alignment and noticing a duster concealed beneath it. I mentally gave the 'help' a pat on the back.

'We got married very young,' he said slowly, ignoring my tactical change of subject and not rising with me. 'Do sit down... Then the kids appeared before we knew what had hit us...' He tailed off, not seeming to know what happened next in his marriage. I lowered myself onto the edge of the chair but not into it.

'What are their names?' I asked.

'Whose?'

'Your children.'

'Oh, them. Ben and Naomi. They came along during my O.T.

period,' he said with a dry laugh. 'Did I tell you I'd written a couple of books?'

'On religion?' I asked.

'Naturally,' he smiled condescendingly. 'I have high hopes for the second... It's ready for the publisher. The first was crap but still made the non-fiction top twenty, which pleased the Bishop.' His ebullience returned as he plunged enthusiastically into explaining his theory about Jesus having visited India and being influenced by both Buddhism and Hinduism. 'The evidence is all there for anyone who cares to read it,' he said. 'And there is a convincing argument to suggest that Christianity and Buddhism are different branches from the same tree.' As he got into his stride, my mind wandered away from the banks of the Ganges back to Mrs Jenkins. I pictured a cold, thin-lipped, desiccated woman, desperately trying to ignore her dehydration by hiding behind a life of trivia and the make-believe importance of a clergyman's life, with its teacups and sub-committees. The clatter of a garage door closing interrupted my reverie. Jenkins heard it too.

'That's her now... no don't get up... she knows you're here... we'll be able to eat now.'

My heart sank. I didn't want to stay for a meal, so revived my escape plan.

'I'll just say hello then I must leave,' I asserted, getting back on my feet. The front door opened and closed softly, almost timidly I thought, poor woman. Light footsteps in the hall, then the swoosh of the living room door being pushed across the carpet. Jenkins reached across for my glass. 'Another?'

I ignored him and turned to greet her as she came in.

The bundle of energy and life that exploded through the door almost caused my spontaneous combustion. She was above medium height, with an athletic set of her shoulders and a firm stride. Her dark hair, cut a mite too short for my taste, framed an open smiling face with full lips. It was not a beautiful face, but it had a pert cheekiness that I found captivating. A radiance glowed out of her that destroyed all my sour preconceptions about her. To cap everything, she wore a brick-red tracksuit and trainers with more elegance and bravado than many fashionable women wear a Dior gown. All my reserve and resolve to retreat at the earliest possibly moment instantly dissolved.

'David… how wonderful to see you again… it's been so long.' She came over and kissed me warmly on the cheek.

'Again?' I blurted.

She stood in front of me, hands lightly holding my elbows and smiled impishly. 'You don't remember me, do you? And I can see Bill hasn't told you.' She lowered her hands and looked across at my bedraggled bluebells that Jenkins had left on the sideboard. 'Oh, these poor things.' She skipped across the room, swept up the flowers, ignoring a few wayward leaves her sweep had scattered, and strode off into the kitchen.

She called through the open door. 'Think back, David. I'll be terribly offended if you don't remember me.' Jenkins grunted, trying to act invisible and deaf. She quickly returned with my pathetic posy drooping limply from a small porcelain vase.

'They'll perk up,' she said, sliding them onto the coffee table, leaving a trail of spilt water which she deftly spread with a swipe from a sleeve.

'I much prefer wild flowers to nursery poseurs, although they don't last as long. Thank you David.' She grabbed my shoulders, pulled herself up and gave me another little kiss.

'They're a bit woebegone,' I grunted, ungraciously.

'They'll be fine in an hour,' she said. 'Now young man let me have a good look at you.' She leaned on one hip, folded her arms and eyed me up and down in undisguised critical appraisal.

'Sorry,' I said, enchanted by her total lack of inhibition and the way she didn't walk but danced around the house. 'I still can't place you. You'll have to give me a clue.'

'You've worn fairly well.' I couldn't read the full meaning of 'fairly'. 'We were in the same year at school,' she said, brimming with furtive amusement.

I searched back in my mind to those days, but apart from Kelly, none of the girls had half this woman's poise and physical wit. My face remained vacant. Jenkins' looked up and yawned.

'Remember Ruth?' she asked mischievously. 'Ruth Pierce? That was me!'

CHAPTER 9

Beneath the Mask

T HE GREAT THRILL of any surprise is that it takes us totally unawares, giving us no time to rationalize or gather thoughts before we react. My reaction to the lady's pronouncement would have been the same if she had appeared with two heads or if Jenkins had turned into John the Baptist with his head tucked under his arm. My eyes seemed to leave my head and my jaw hit the ground.

This couldn't be that dowdy, self-righteous little prude with the plunging hemline I remembered. 'Were there two Ruth Pierces?' I slurred, trying to rescue my wits. 'You're not the one I remember.'

She beamed. Jenkins looked up and winked at me while I dumbly stared in disbelief.

The next few hours passed in a dream of delight as we peered back at our schooldays and the years in between through a fluffy pink filter, with laughter, exaggeration and some creative forgetfulness. Jenkins hardly talked about himself in front of Ruth so, as the evening wore on, he loosened his psychological vestments and produced some raunchy stories of 'goings-on under the vestry table'. Ruth demonstrated her domestic talents by producing a 'magical cold collation', as Jenkins called it, and we gently munched and wined and reminisced our way far into the evening.

It was quite late when a doorbell rang.

'Who can that be?' asked Jenkins.

'You'd better go and see, darling,' Ruth advised, with perhaps a hint of irony on *darling*.

'I still can't work out which bell is which. Was that the front or the…'

'It's the front, Bill,' she interrupted wearily, as if this was a familiar routine between them. 'The side door has chimes.'

She turned to me, looking skywards and shrugging her elegant shoulders in exaggerated exasperation. 'We've been coming here for three years and still he can't tell a ping from a dong.'

Jenkins shuffled off into the kitchen. I noticed, for the first time, how awkwardly he moved.

'He's got a bit of arthritis,' she said, reading my thoughts. 'May have to have a hip replacement one day, the way he's going. He doesn't look after himself.'

All evening I had been captivated by the feline way she curled her legs beneath her in the soft cushions of her chair, and the baggy tracksuit blouse which couldn't conceal the generosity of her curves from my surreptitious sideways glances. She had a deep contralto voice with resin in her vocal chords, which gave it a sexual huskiness that didn't fit with my image of a clergyman's wife. What miracle, I wondered, turned a sexless little frump into this voluptuous woman? It was enough to make me believe in God.

With Jenkins out of the room, a few links broke in the chain of restraint I'd put around myself.

'I can't get over how much you've changed, Ruth.'

'Changed, David?' she looked straight at me with wide, mockingly innocent eyes. 'How have I changed?'

'Well, er… you have a lot more confidence and poise.'

'Confidence. Poise. In what way, David?'

Am I crazy? I thought. Surely she can't be flirting with me.

'Oh I don't know… in little things, like the way you express your personality in the house, and handle Bill, and oh… you know… your general deportment.'

'Deportment?' I had meant the way she ruffled her hair with two hands when she was thinking, or wiggled her hips and shoulders when she moved into a more comfortable sitting position.

'Yes, deportment… you know… your posture… the way you stand and move… the way you pour coffee,' I added lamely. 'Your non-verbal language tells me you're at ease with yourself which is not how I remember you.'

She looked at me steadily as if inviting me to blunder on. Was she really so innocent? Could she be so unaware of the effect she was having on me?

'You're a flatterer, David,' she laughed. 'What a disappointment, I thought you meant it.' If she was fishing, I didn't have the courage to take the bait.

Voices from the kitchen came to my rescue. Jenkins' quick and light, the other deeper and slower. 'Seems that it's someone he knows,' I said, eager to divert attention from the morass of messages I was getting from Ruth.

'How do you think Bill looks?' she asked.

'Not too bad,' I said evasively, 'A bit older… a little slower perhaps… but still plenty of oomph.'

'Poor Bill,' she said, trying to hear the voices in the kitchen. 'It's Mr Verres. I wonder what he wants.' She turned back to me. 'But how have *you* changed, David?' Her thoughts flitted like a butterfly, moving to the next idea before all the nectar had been taken from the one it was on. Was she playing with me? I still wasn't sure. Well lady, I thought, let's see if two can play.

'Me? I haven't changed at all. I'm still shy. I won't say boo to a goose and I'm still scared stiff of girls.'

She threw her head back and spluttered with laughter. 'Pull

the other one and you'll hear the Westminster chimes… have you seen Kelly lately, by the way?' she added slyly.

'Bit of a character, that old boy,' said Jenkins, returning before the floor swallowed me up.

'Mr Verres?' she asked.

'That's right. Came to return my book. Said it was quite interesting.'

'Only quite?'

'Yes,' said Jenkins with a short dismissive laugh. 'He said it had too much head and not enough heart.'

'What did he mean by that?'

'He said that my suppositions, as he called them, were well argued, and what few facts I had, bloody cheek, were presented cleverly, but it would convince no-one because I didn't seem to care. And if I didn't care, he said, no-one else would. Cheeky devil.'

'And you disagree?'

'Of course I do. Don't you?'

'Everyone else seems to think it's a winner, darling,' she said, sidestepping his question.

'I told him that, but all he said was that only people who wanted their thinking done for them would buy it.' He sat down heavily, and a puff of air escaped from the cushion.

'Is he right?' asked Ruth gently.

Bill pondered for a few moments before reluctantly grinning. 'Of course he is,' he said with a dry laugh. 'If people could think for themselves we wouldn't need clergymen. It's just a bloody cheek of him to say so.' After a pause he added with a hefty guffaw, 'I didn't think it was so obvious.'

'It's a bit late for returning a book, isn't it?' I suggested.

'Not for our Mr Verres, it isn't.' Ruth laughed. 'A law unto himself is that gentleman.'

'Who is he? Where does he live?'

'He's renting the glowty,' said Jenkins.

'Glowty?'

'It means cowhouse,' said Ruth. 'If you're going to live down here, David, you'll have to learn some local Welsh dialect.'

'He's been there for almost a year,' continued Jenkins, still thinking of his tenant.

'Closer to six months actually, Bill.' Ruth gave me a direct look full of meaning.

Jenkins had first met him at the St Davids Music Festival the previous year. 'I thought a Welsh Black bull had strayed into the cathedral,' he said, with a half smile. 'It was after the concert and I was waiting for Ruth by the door when this huge creature loomed up in front of me.

"Dr Jenkins," he asserted, as if he was nailing me to the door. "Verres." He didn't offer his hand. "Did you enjoy the concert?"

"Very much thank you," I replied, "And you?"

"Can't stand Bach," he replied bluntly. "Wasted his talents. His music stayed in the same rut all his life. I understand you have a flat to rent."

I looked up into his eyes.'

Jenkins' own eyes narrowed to slits as he spoke. 'They were not hostile, but he seemed to see right through me. They were thatched with eyebrows that met in the middle, with an aggressive tuft that seemed to look at me as keenly as his actual eyes. I've never seen eyes so savage yet so strangely gentle.

'"That's right," I said. "Just holiday lets, as a rule."

"I want to stay for a year, perhaps longer."

I found his directness intimidating, but refreshing. I'm used to church committees who measure a successful meeting on how many decisions it's put off and how many issues it's avoided altogether.

"I don't deal with the bookings myself," I said but gave him the address of the agent.

"Thank you," he grunted, studying the address. "I'll get in touch with him tomorrow. Excuse me for interrupting your evening. I expect we'll meet again soon, Dr Jenkins. Goodnight."

I wasn't sure what to make of his formal familiarity but before I could say anything he had turned and was walking out through the main door. I noticed he was amazingly light on his feet for such an ox. And I'll tell you something really strange, David,' he leaned forward, wagging a finger at me, 'All the way home I thought only of his smile and the warmth and pleasure it had given me. Poor Ruth wanted to talk about the concert and the scandal she'd picked up afterwards, but all I could think about was Verres.'

'That's true,' interrupted Ruth, 'He was so quiet in the car that I thought he was ill or had had some bad news. More coffee?'

'No thanks.'

'Yes, I'd seen him from a distance, talking to a large man rather intently, and I wondered who on earth he was. From behind he looked almost deformed; his back and shoulders were round and powerful and his head seemed to have no neck, as if it had grown out of his shoulders. Only when he moved… he seemed so… so…' She faltered for a moment as she looked at him again in her mind's eye, searching for the right words to describe him. 'He was graceful… like a dancer.'

'Like Nureyev,' I suggested, unable to think of a more recent example.

'In the way he moves, perhaps, but… how can I put it?' She tilted her head a little to one side and puckered her lips as if the lucky words were stuck there. 'Nureyev's beauty was external. Mr Verres' appearance is decidedly off-putting, but he exudes an inner glory.'

Their tenant seemed to have an inordinate effect on their lives. 'How does it show?' I asked.

'The old bugger has a refreshing candour at times.' Talking about Mr Verres seemed to bring a streak of brusque humanity out of Jenkins. 'I must say I find it a pleasant change from the barrage of servile platitudes I live under most of the time.'

Ruth put her hand on her husband's arm, 'More than that Bill, I think he cares… He's got a good heart.' Jenkins shrugged, as if such a concept was beyond his understanding.

'When did he move in?' I was uneasy about the influence this man had on my friends.

'About a month later, I think,' said Jenkins.

'Why did he choose you?' I asked suspiciously. 'There must be hundreds of other apartments to rent in the county.'

'I asked him that when he first arrived,' said Ruth. 'He said that he'd seen this place while walking and its solitary position was exactly what he was looking for.'

'How did he know who owned it, who you were, what you looked like and where to find you?' I felt protective of my friends and blurted out my anxiety for them.

Jenkins looked at Ruth. 'Asked around, I suppose.'

'Are you sure he's OK?' I asked. 'I've some experience in the letting business, and have met some dodgy types who I wouldn't let within miles of any property of mine. Did you get references?'

'I assume so. That was the agent's business,' said Ruth. 'We simply got a phone call saying that he would be moving in and asking us if we wanted to be here when he arrived. Bill couldn't get away, so I came down on my own. I didn't have to but was curious to meet the man who had won Bill over in five minutes flat. Usually Bill hates on sight.'

'Clergymen don't hate on sight,' Jenkins chanted with mock piety. 'They leave that to God; we come along to cash-in on the fear it generates.' I liked his irreverence, but did wonder if a bolt of lightning would strike him at any moment.

81

'Anyway I found him charming,' she continued, ignoring the interruption. 'His luggage arrived in the morning. He came about midday. I did the usual welcoming landlady things like putting flowers in the hall and living room, some fruit in a bowl and lit essential oils in strategic places. Of course I had a good old 'nose' at his luggage too, but didn't learn much. Most of it seemed to be books tied up in cardboard boxes. There was also an expensive looking laptop, two rucksacks packed tight, walking boots and a large suitcase.' She put her hands behind her head, arched her back and pressed her elbows back. I saw an inch of tanned midriff and thought 'sunbed'.

'I'm getting stiff from sitting,' she said, looking at me with studious innocence. 'Anyway, I waited for him upstairs like Lady Muck when he arrived and acted surprised when he appeared at the top of the stairs. Heaven alone knows why, I'm not usually so disingenuous.'

'I've noticed several times,' interrupted Jenkins, 'that we tend to behave differently when we're with him.'

'Yes, that's right,' agreed Ruth, vigorously tousling her hair with both hands to my delight. 'He seems to see straight to the core of things… it's lovely in one way and disconcerting in another.' Those were exactly my thoughts. She smiled tenderly, stretched again, and I looked away to conceal what felt like a lusty leer etched on my face.

'He came into the room and the first thing he did was to thank me for not coming down to meet him. "Formality is overrated," he said. I felt about an inch tall, but proceeded with the formal welcome, "Welcome Mr Verres, I'm Ruth Jenkins."

"Yes I know," he said, smiling warmly with his mouth and eyes. "I feel at home already. This room is very… thoughtful." He seemed completely at ease, as if he was the host and I was the visitor. "Would you mind very much if I replaced the books on the shelves with mine?"

"Please do," I said. "I'll move them out."

"Good," he said. "That would be kind of you."

Without asking or inviting me to accompany him he proceeded to inspect the flat. He looked hard at the nondescript modern pictures on the walls of the living room. "Do you like these?" he asked.

"Well er… not really," I replied.

"Good. You won't object if they go with the books?"

"Not at all," I said. "Let me tell you how the hot water works."

"Let's not," he said. "I'm sure I'll be able to work it out. Tell me about yourself, Ruth. Do you mind me calling you Ruth? Or must it be Mrs Jenkins?'"

Abruptly she leaned back pulling her irrepressible tracksuit blouse back down over her tanned navel enabling her breasts to find the space to express themselves.

'More coffee, David?'

'No thanks,' I slurred.

'Bill?'

'I don't think so, caffeine is coming out of my ears.'

'He seems a real oddball,' I said, attempting to restrain my lustful thoughts.

'I wouldn't call him that,' she said, stretching again and bringing her navel back into the unspoken part of our conversation. I still couldn't decide whether she knew the effect she was having on me, or was completely guileless. It had been many years since I had been so delightfully flummoxed.

'But he certainly isn't bound by the normal rules of social intercourse,' she continued. 'I'm not normally a babbler, but it seemed that for the next hour I talked non-stop and eventually came away having told him far too many of my secret thoughts.'

Bill got up, and out of habit poured himself another cup

of caffeine. Ruth looked straight and hard at me while he was turned away from her. There was a question in her eyes but she didn't stop talking.

'Yet I still knew nothing about him, except that he was obviously well educated, he seemed to be comfortably off, and spoke several languages including Welsh and at least one other Celtic tongue.'

'I didn't know you had any secret thoughts,' said Jenkins pleasantly, returning to his chair.

'You'll be surprised my boy,' she said, turning towards her husband. 'Everyone has secrets. I'd like to know Mr Verres.'

She looked back at me. Her eyes were alive and eager and deviously honest. 'Every time I speak to him I always tell him too much about myself, yet when I ask him about himself he simply smiles, replies lucidly and says nothing.'

She put her hand on the coffee pot. 'It's gone cold. I need another.' She picked it up and took it into the kitchen. I heard her fill the kettle and turn it on.

'This morning I came out directly and asked him to tell me about his past and who he was,' she said from the kitchen door. 'All he said was, "My future is much more interesting than my past, Ruth." Perhaps I imagined it but I thought there was sadness in his eyes. He looked wistful but I didn't have the courage to ask him why.'

'I'll have another, Ruth,' said Jenkins. 'This has gone cold. David?'

'No thanks,' I said. 'I must go.'

Despite my earlier misgivings, the evening had been brilliant. I liked Jenkins a lot more after Ruth's arrival when he'd stopped trying to impress himself. She intrigued me; perhaps in my opportunist bachelor eyes, all attractive women were seductresses and in my imagination I had created another one, when all she'd been was a considerate hostess. I liked what I had seen, but put a mental cross against her name; an involvement with her would be too complicated. My thoughts, as I drove home, drifted away from the convivial company of the Jenkins' to the mysterious Mr Verres. I felt both uneasy and fascinated by the man, especially his cryptic words, 'My future is more interesting than my past.'

CHAPTER 10

Show there's More to Find

THREE DAYS LATER I received the telephone call I had been hoping for but dreading.

'David, hello. This is Ruth.'

'Good morning Ruth. This is a pleasant surprise,' I said, hoping my lack of surprise did not sound too obvious. 'How are you?'

'I'm very well, thank you,' she answered primly. 'David, I'm calling you for two reasons. First, to say how nice it was to see you again after all these years.'

For a few minutes we whitewashed each other with shameless platitudes expressing our mutual pleasure at meeting again. For the sake of protocol I mentioned her husband's health and career, and we observed all the rules of propriety. Round one, even, I thought. Let's see what happens in round two.

'And the second reason?' I asked.

'Oh yes,' she said, as if she would have forgotten about it without my prompting. 'Bill bought tickets for the Mid Wales Opera in Cardigan tomorrow night, but something came up and he had to go back home this morning. Now I've got a spare ticket but no-one to go with…'

'I'd be delighted if you'd let me take you,' I interrupted on cue, oozing oily testosterone, certain now that despite my earlier uncertainty we were playing the same game with the same timeless rules.

'Would you? That's awfully nice of you David!' Yes, isn't it, I thought. 'I know it's a terrible cheek to ask you, especially at such short notice, but I was so looking forward to going and wouldn't go on my own.'

You went out alone the other night, I thought. 'I wouldn't dream of letting you go on your own. It will be my pleasure… thank you for asking me.' Then adding as an afterthought, 'What opera are they doing?'

'Oh! It's… um… you know, I've quite forgotten.'

I grinned to myself as a fox would grin when seeing his supper waddling towards him. 'And what in God's name is Mid Wales Opera?' I asked. 'How many people in Mid Wales know anything about opera?'

'Now I won't have you disparaging Mid Wales my boy. You have to live here for forty years to earn that right.' My rising heart rate almost shook the phone out of my hand, but not the grin off my face. 'You'll be surprised what they know about in them thar hills.' The twinkle in her voice seemed like a musical box; my metabolism pirouetted to its tune as I primed myself to throw caution, better judgement and foreboding to the winds. 'Anyway, you struck me as a man who would try anything once.'

'More than once if I'm lucky…'

A roar like the start of the Tour of Hell car rally came down the line. I held the phone at arm's length until the sound faded away.

'What in heaven's name was *that*?' I asked.

'That was our Mr Verres going off on his motor bike. It *is* a bit noisy, isn't it?'

'One way or another *your* Mr Verres certainly makes his mark. Are you absolutely certain that the man's kosher?'

'You'll have to meet him,' she cooed, 'then you can decide for yourself.'

'Yes, I'll have to.' I instinctively sensed the need to be on my toes if we ever did meet.

The spell cast by our suggestive sex game had been broken, so we chatted for a few minutes before she gave me instructions for collecting her. She then contrived a well-worn excuse for hanging up, leaving me with my reckless anticipations. I caught a glimpse of my face in the mirror as I walked away from the telephone; it was like a cat that had eaten the cream, then the saucer.

*

'No tracksuit tonight?' I asked with rehearsed nonchalance, even before my eyes adapted to the dark outline opening the door.

'Come in, young sir,' she said with an exaggerated sweep of her arm. 'I'm ready – just have to put my coat on.'

She was dressed as one would expect a modern clergyman's wife to dress, with a loose-fitting, sexless dark brown trouser suit over a white cotton blouse with a wide, pointed collar fastened at the throat by a small brooch. I instantly knew that my expectations of a low-cut, figure-hugging dress and dangly earrings had been wildly unrealistic. Once inside in the light I could see she wore hardly any make-up and apart from gold ear studs and a wedding ring, no jewellery. I couldn't even detect perfume. It's just as well I haven't shown my hand, I thought. Perhaps I misread the signs.

I properly helped her on with her coat and she properly thanked me. Then I stood to attention by the car as she locked the front door, then opened the car door for her and received a civilized 'Thank you' for my gallantry.

We crunched off down the gravel drive, and the ice seemed

unbreakable. All my well exercised, spontaneous double entendre banter had been killed off by the deadly correctness of our behaviour, and I had no contingency banter to fall back on.

For five minutes or so we forced polite conversation about the weather, Jenkins having to be called away, what we'd done since we last saw each other – anything to avoid an uncomfortable silence. Inevitably, the trivia dried up, and we slumped into a sterile silence punctuated with the occasional unnecessary advice like, 'Turn right here' and 'This is a tight corner'.

She broke the impasse. 'Your waters are running deep tonight David Tanner.'

I didn't answer but slowed down to pull into a lay-by we were approaching on the left. I rolled the car to a halt, braked, switched off the engine, undid my seat belt, turned on the interior light and swivelled round to face her.

'Ruth,' I said.

'Yes, David?'

'You're right, my waters are running deep, and they are also swirling round and round.'

'Oh dear, that sounds painful.'

'Are you laughing at me?' I asked.

'Only a teeny-weeny bit David,' she said. 'Please don't be offended.'

'Well, what's so funny?' I *was* offended. I felt like a child caught playing at grown-ups.

'You are, David.' She undid her seat belt and twisted round to face me, at the same time moving back against the door to keep a space between us. 'You obviously have something on your mind… you're bursting to let it out, yet you talk about the weather, the state of the roads, everything except what you want to talk about. Now isn't that just a wee bit funny?'

I tried to relax and forced a sheepish grin into the concrete lining my face.

'Are they worth a penny, Mr Tanner?' She was still playing the game.

'That depends, Mrs Jenkins,' I said, trying to match her lightness.

'Depends on what?'

'On whether you like what I'm thinking. Perhaps it will be a waste of money.' That's better, I thought.

'I can probably afford a penny.' The light wasn't good enough to see her face clearly but I thought I saw wickedness in her eyes.

'OK,' I said, setting my shoulders. What could I lose?

'I came over tonight looking forward to having a date with a beautiful and exciting woman, and what have I got? Escort duty with the wife of the Right Reverend Dean of wherever it is.' She remained silent and showed no reaction. 'I'm sorry if I've offended you.' I added, 'But...'

'There's no Dean's wife in this car, my dear,' she said simply. 'And a Dean is the Very Reverend. Bill is a *Very*, not a *Right*.' I looked at her and she returned my gaze from behind shadows. I leant over to take hold of her 'Very Reverend' body but she held me at arm's length.

'Opera first,' she said, laughing. 'Then... who knows?'

Undeterred, I pushed my lips towards hers, but she gave me a cheek and firmly planted her hands on my chest. I knew now that she'd played this game before; so had I. The playing field was now level.

'OK,' I said. 'Mid Wales Opera had better be good. What are they doing, by the way? Have you remembered?'

'*The Magic Flute.*'

'Oh,' I grunted. 'Verdi, isn't it?'

'David!' she said aghast, then with an expletive that questioned my parenthood punched my shoulder. It hurt, but I was now sure we were rolling the same dice and they were loaded. I waltzed the car out of the lay-by and twenty light-bantered minutes later we were squeezing ourselves into the tiny theatre.

*

The opera was fun. The auditorium was cramped but cheerful with hard, bottom-numbing seats, no legroom, and within spitting distance of the singers. We were able to see a dragon having a 'cuppa' with one of the three witches in the wings while the hero and heroine endured their monumental trials with the elements by walking in circles on the narrow stage. The show had all the ingredients of village farce. In a major opera house the audience would have been in uproar, but here the intimacy and the spirit of 'all hands to the pump' was delightful. The principals had ordinary voices but they sang their hearts out, and we applauded them as passionately as we would have Domingo at Covent Garden. At the final curtain I got on my feet and clapped and 'bravoed' like a rutting bison, unaware that only polite applause was coming from everyone else. Ruth remarked that she was relieved no lady bison was in the audience.

On the way out through the tiny foyer I made a cradle with my arms to protect her in a bottleneck and 'accidentally' allowed myself to be pressed against her by the throng. She appeared not to notice. Even her keep-your-distance business suit that earlier in the evening had deflated me so effectively now seemed to invite and excite me, and the heat of the crowd brought the perfume she had subtly applied in the 'ladies' during the interval into bloom and me into arousal.

'Drink?' I suggested, more out of habit than need.

'Let's wait until we get back,' she said with a smile as breathtaking and revealing as the morning sun rising over a great city.

I was melting with desire, and wondered if being a civilized animal was preferable to being a wild animal that did what it wanted when it wanted to do it, without having its nature suppressed by decorum.

'Ruth, I thought it was you.'

I hadn't seen Verres before, but needed no introduction. He seemed to appear out of nowhere, but even in the mêlée a space appeared all around him; nobody jostled *him*.

'Oh, Mr Verres,' said Ruth, breathless at the abrupt encroachment into her cradle. 'I didn't know you were coming tonight. Did you enjoy it?'

'Enjoy it?' he mused. 'I don't usually think about things in terms of enjoyment,' he said, a little pompously I thought. 'There seems to be so much more to an experience than mere enjoyment. Tonight was an utter delight. I don't think I've met this gentleman.' He scanned my eyes. Not unpleasantly.

'Tanner,' I said, 'David Tanner. You must be Mr Verres. I was in the house the other night when you returned William Jenkins' book.'

'I know. I saw your car,' he said. 'Expensive! Are you in business, David?'

He assumed an instant intimacy which alerted my caution; yet there was something appealing and tender about his manner. Despite my reservations and his inopportune intervention, I was in danger of liking him on sight.

'It's alright to call you David, isn't it?' he demanded.

'Y-yes of course,' I stammered. 'What can I call you?'

'Verres is fine,' he said. 'What business are you in, David?'

'I was in the holiday business, but I'm semi-retired now.'

'What do you do now?'

'Nothing really,' I said. 'I still travel quite a lot and have recently bought a house down here.'

'Why?' he asked, hunching his huge shoulders as if he was about to charge me. 'What made you move down here?'

'Well,' I said hesitantly. 'It's a long story, I'm sure you wouldn't be interested.'

'Oh I would, believe me – you must tell me, but perhaps some other time.'

'Certainly,' I said, feeling miffed at being unable to get *my* questions unloaded onto him.

'And has life improved for you now that you've moved down here?'

'Well it's early days yet.' I didn't want to be over-charmed by him, but my curmudgeonly resolve was rapidly dissolving. 'But I'm amazed how quickly I've adjusted to the slower tempo of life and how little I miss airports, meetings and making a dozen life-and-death decisions before lunch.'

'What challenges do you have in your life now?' he asked.

'None. Isn't that the point of retirement?'

'I wonder,' he said dreamily. 'Is that what you *really* believe?'

He turned to Ruth without bothering to wait for my answer. 'And what did you make of this evening's entertainment, Ruth?'

'I enjoyed… For what it was, I thought it was wonderful.' She smiled at her correction.

'Why?' he asked. His stone-melting gaze had moved off me, and I took the opportunity to study him. His shift of attention was total, and now completely directed at Ruth as if I no longer existed, and the foyer was empty.

'I love the opera anyway, especially *The Magic Flute*, and would go to see it even if it were staged in a barn by a school choir,' she replied, gazing straight back into his eyes with open confidence. The instant intimacy they had established was total and beautiful; she returned his gaze with equal intensity and assertion. I looked on with the soft delight I feel when contemplating a Giorgione nude or the revealing, enigmatic face of Rembrandt's last self-portrait.

'Perhaps that would be the purest way to witness the rites of this particular masterpiece performed,' he said, with a smile in his voice. 'Without trappings. Without clever tricks of lighting and scenery.'

'Yes, I agree,' she said.

'What character impressed you most?'

She thought for a moment and he waited in front of her, stroking his beard. 'The dragon,' she said defiantly.

'Wonderful.' He clapped his hands with spontaneous delight. 'Why the dragon?'

'Well,' she thought for another moment, 'because he was the only character who was truly himself and not pretending to be what other people wanted him to be. He was what nature intended.'

'You're very perceptive, my dear,' he said. 'And what about you, David?' he asked, riveting his eyes once again into mine.

'I liked the bird catcher,' I said.

'Is he you?'

'Is he me?' The question surprised me and I had to think for a moment before answering cautiously, 'Perhaps he is.'

'In what ways?'

'Well, I don't want to put birds in cages but...'

'Perhaps it's not birds that he's catching?' he interrupted. 'What would you want to catch and put in a cage, David?'

'I hate to stop you,' Ruth interrupted. 'But I think we should go. Almost everyone's gone and they'll be wanting to lock-up soon. You can finish this conversation at home, if you like.'

'Why not?' I said. 'I'd like to answer your question, Verres.'

At first I had felt crotchety by his incursion into our space, but I liked the blunt intensity of his manner and found his questions interesting. I felt comfortable with the effortless way he took me down to unexpected levels of thought and looked forward to the next time, much as a child would look forward to anticipating a surprise birthday present that is no surprise.

'Would you like to come round for a nightcap, Mr Verres?' Ruth asked.

'Perhaps not for a nightcap, but I'll come for your answer David.' Without another word he turned towards the door gracefully, sliding an enormous leather coat over his great shoulders as he moved. We looked at each other, smiled and in one voice said, 'Phew!'

The car park was almost empty and we sat in the car for a minute or two without speaking but wrapped in a comfortable silence of expectation.

'Perhaps I should drop you off and not come in,' I said quietly, looking into the dashboard.

'Why not?' she whispered turning slightly towards me.

'Because… I… Are you sure this is what you want?'

My wavering was not out of a sense of loyalty to Jenkins. The night had started with the hope of a casual sexual odyssey without sentiment or attachments. During the evening I had found a shard of honour, and started to care for Ruth and the possible repercussions casual infidelity could have for her.

She didn't reply, but simply looked into my face passively and waited. I twisted my body and reached out for her, cupping my hands softly around her face as if holding a newborn kitten – helpless and blind. The blind kitten closed her eyes and tilted her head gently up towards my face. I stretched forward and kissed her forehead, trembling with desire as I did. I heard her inhale deeply as if in a dream, then raise her face towards mine and I kissed her sweet lips. I felt her arms slide like silk around my neck and shoulders; she pulled me close and the tattered remains of my lukewarm scruples blew away in the moment.

Suddenly a headlight swept across the car park and into our faces. We guiltily flew apart.

'Let's go home,' she said softly. 'You will stay tonight?'

'Of course.'

CHAPTER 11

Lost Souls

I'D NEVER HAD time for a conscience in either my business or my love life. On the rare occasion when it appeared, I contemptuously dismissed it as the first refuge of the timid and an escape route of the indecisive, but tonight my conscience troubled me. We were out of the town and away from the invasive orange lights of the bypass before I spoke.

'Are you alright?'

'Perfectly.' Her conviction was impeccable. 'Are you?'

'I'm not sure. Are we heading for trouble?'

'You're not getting cold feet?'

'No, but you have responsibilities and a position,' I grumbled. 'I have none.'

I felt her body stiffen. 'Pull into this lay-by.'

I obeyed; she turned on the interior light and eyeballed me. 'What gives you the right to take charge of *my* responsibilities, mister? What pathetic little miss do you think I am? What…'

'Enough, enough… I apologise.' My flimsy conscience made a hasty disappearance and I reached over to grab her like a clumsy octopus.

'Oh no you don't,' she snorted with *fairly* light-hearted menace. 'I'm angry and it's going to cost you.'

Still unable to tune into her mood, I got behind my Maginot

line by acting deflated and contrite. 'Alright I'll pay. What's it going to cost me?'

'Lots, my boy. Just wait 'till we get home!' I felt reassured by this and restarted the car eager to take my punishment.

After a mile and still feeling the need to reinstate myself I spoke again. 'When I saw the Mrs Respectable Clergyman's wife tonight I thought I was being told to keep my distance.'

'Good,' she said with a tight laugh. 'Too many people around here know me… and Bill. What do you think they'd imagine if I turned up in public with a strange man and a deep cleavage or tight sweater?'

'I understood that… eventually.' I ruefully rubbed my jaw. 'Guess I'm a bit slow on the uptake at times.'

'I wouldn't say that, exactly,' she said slowly. 'Although I think I've been way ahead of you my boy, from the start.'

I asked her what she meant.

'When did you first think that something might happen between us?'

'Oh quite soon, perhaps half an hour after you came in the other night.'

'I knew instantly,' she said. 'Your eyes undressed me the moment I walked into the room and didn't stop all night.'

'God! Was it that obvious.' I was truly aghast. 'I thought I was being discreet.'

'Discreet?' she laughed. 'You were about as discreet as a fox in a chicken coop.'

'Didn't Bill notice?'

'You were safe there. He wouldn't have noticed if we'd got undressed and made love on the rug at his feet.'

'I'm sorry if I offended you.' I was humbugging and knew it. Phoney contrition isn't one of my stronger attributes.

'Offended? Not at all. I loved it. If I can't have a lover's hands on my body then his eyes are the next best thing.'

I remembered her athletic navel and mobile hips and the natural way she had them perform before me. 'It sounds to me that you've had your fair share of that,' I said.

'Perhaps.' I sensed her smile in the darkened car. 'Would that surprise you?'

'I'd only be surprised if you hadn't.' I ached so badly to hold her, it hurt. 'Let's stop for a minute.'

'Keep driving,' she commanded. 'And keep both hands on the wheel.' That put her ahead on points but I looked forward to catching-up soon.

Twenty minutes later we stopped outside the house. Verres glided over from the glowty. 'Damn, I'd forgotten about him. He moves like a shadow,' I said. 'And not a sound.'

We crunched noisily over the gravel drive towards him. 'Come in, Mr Verres.' Ruth opened the door then disappeared upstairs, leaving Verres to close it and follow me inside. We automatically made ourselves comfortable and sat facing each other across the spotless room.

'Well, David,' he said as soon as we were settled, 'Have you decided what you will put into that cage of yours?'

'To be truthful Verres,' I said, 'I've been talking to Ruth and haven't thought about it since we parted. What was the question again?'

'You identified with the character of Papageno, the bird catcher, but unlike him you didn't like putting real birds in a cage.' He carefully moved a cushion out of his way. 'So I asked you what the birds represent to you?'

All interest in his banter had long gone; my thoughts were upstairs but I had to say something out of politeness. 'Well,' I began, 'I suppose they represent something small and helpless and inoffensive.'

'Go on,' he encouraged.

'Perhaps it's…' I struggled on trying to say something I

thought he would like to hear. 'Perhaps it's aspects of his own personality he doesn't like and wants locked away from view.'

'Such as?'

For heavens sake, I thought, doesn't he ever stop?

'Like... inadequacy, timidity, uncertainty, lack of achievement, self-doubt... oh yes, and loneliness.' Words, any words, flew out of my mouth whilst I wondered what she was doing upstairs.

'But you're not lacking in those things, David. You're a successful man of the world, you know your way about, you must be used to controlling and manipulating people to get where you are.'

He got up and went into the kitchen. 'Can I get you anything, or will you wait for Ruth?'

'I'll wait, thanks.' He returned carrying a bottle of spring water and two glasses.

'What do you think of the idea David that, instead of trying to conceal things about yourself that you don't like, you're doing the opposite.'

'The opposite?'

'Could the birds you're trying to catch and keep in your cage represent qualities that you don't have but wish you did?' When did the dialogue move from Papageno to Tanner? We were now talking about *me*. 'What would you like to catch and keep in a cage, David? Something you need. Perhaps something you've lost.'

'Peace of mind I suppose, unfulfilled dreams, self-knowledge...' I reluctantly pushed 'upstairs' aside and looked up into his face. It was a worn face, it was a wild and untamed face, it was a face capable of crushing rocks and creating terror in the hearts of his enemies. Yet to me at that moment, despite my irritation, I only saw the face of a wise and caring father. Upstairs started to fade.

'Does that mean then David that you have fears, unfulfilled dreams and doubts? If so, where do they come from?'

'Come from?' I asked, now listening carefully. 'What do you mean, come from?'

'Do they come from outside you, or from within?'

I'd never thought about it before so I replied, 'Outside, I suppose.' His voice was almost lulling my senses to sleep, but my mind was becoming alert. 'From habits, experiences, fears, events, the media, other people...'

The mat of hair above his eyes crinkled quizzically. 'What about from your psyche, your intuition, your unconscious?'

A message coming from 'within me' was a novel concept but as I considered it the more reasonable it seemed to be. 'From my unconscious? I'm no psychologist, Verres.'

'Are we talking psychology or are we talking feeling. Instinct?' he asked so quietly I was compelled to listen closely. Somehow the suggestion was appealing and it insisted on steadily percolating in my mind until it seemed so simple and so obvious. 'I think you must be right.' I remembered of how profoundly I envied and still envy Kelly – deep down inside so I had to agree. 'All my fears, my self-doubts, lost dreams must come from somewhere inside me. Yes... somewhere very deep inside me,' I whispered.

He emptied and refilled a tumbler of water. As he drank he seemed to change shape, his outline become somehow softer. I felt giddily at ease.

'Do you feel alright about going in there?' He handed me a glass of water.

Into myself? Impossible! 'Yes.' I sipped the water. 'If I can.'

'What's this place inside you like, David?'

'Sorry, I don't understand.'

'Is it full of things, or empty? Is it light and airy? Or dark and stuffy?'

'Oh, I see.'

'Well?'

I closed my eyes. 'I can only see darkness.'

'Keep looking.'

I still saw nothing but darkness and I didn't know what I was supposed to see anyway but each time I told him so he just repeated, 'Keep looking'.

I'd never scratched about in my imagination before but with his steady insistence I eventually began to feel more and more at ease until, after a while, images started to emerge. First just light, then vague shapes, finally, 'I see a room,' I said.

'Yes. What else David?'

'It seems full of things.'

'Go on.'

The room became clearer. 'It's full of bundles and boxes... even rucksacks and suitcases and, wow, even some of my old things... I can see my old bike.'

'Move around the place. Look everywhere. Tell me everything you see David.'

In my imagination or mind's eye or daydream, or whatever I was experiencing, I moved around. It was like exploring the attic of my past which I enthusiastically described to him in detail. Then suddenly, 'Oooh.' I froze. 'I've come across a huge space where there's nothing. It's a total void.'

'How do you feel about that, David?'

I looked into the space and felt lonely and unutterably sad.

'Terrible. It's a desolate place. I don't want to look at it.'

'Come away if you want to David, but just tell me one more thing before you do, OK?'

'OK.'

'Breathe deeply, feel safe.' I obeyed and felt at ease again.

'What was in that empty space? What has been taken away?'

'It was me.' Now totally focused I knew instinctively that

what was missing was part of me. 'A piece of me should be there but it's gone.'

'Go on, my boy,' he urged.

'I left a long time ago.'

'What part of you is missing, David?'

I looked into the void again and felt its emptiness. It wasn't a physical emptiness, it was more like a moral or spiritual one. 'It's like a part of my soul has left me.' A long moan left my mouth and I felt tears welling up from somewhere in my throat. 'Part of my soul has left me, Verres,' I repeated, opening my eyes. 'How could that happen? Has it gone forever?'

A smile covered his gentle, ferocious face. 'No soul fragment leaves forever David, although you may have to bribe it to return. Can you tell me when it left you?'

I closed my eyes again and returned to my inner attic. 'When I was at school,' I said.

'What made it go?'

'I c-could... I c-could... I c-couldn't speak...' I stammered.

'Tell me David, what have you got to promise it before it will come back?'

A child's voice I didn't recognise replied from deep inside me. 'Run with the wolves through the trees and across the mountains. Be wild.'

'Can you do this?' he asked.

I knew I had to. I had no choice! I sat up and looked at him. We smiled at each other from a deep level like travellers bidding farewell before setting out on a long journey, but said nothing.

*

'Well boys, what have you been talking about?' Ruth chortled, refreshed and perky in a long dress that promised more than a respectable woman should, but still revealed nothing. She had tidied her hair and wore a little more make-up than she had to the opera, and wore a different perfume than demanded more attention.

'David's been telling me why he identifies with Papageno,' Verres said. 'I like the scent.'

'Oh, thank you,' she beamed. 'And why does he?'

'Because they have both lost a part of their soul and want it back,' he said simply.

'Oh,' she said. 'That's nice.' I thought she looked gorgeous, despite being in a place a million miles away from us.

'What about you, Mr Verres?' she asked. 'What character did you identify with?'

'Yes, tell us Verres.' I was still mentally breathless but relieved to be shifting into her flighty mood. I knew he would surprise us.

Of course he agreed and of course, true to form, he asked us a question first.

'What do you think will be my answer?'

Ruth and I looked at each other and answered in unison, 'Sarastro'.

Sarastro was the wise and virtuous leader of the priest's order whose wisdom and morality was the hub around which the opera revolved. It was impossible to imagine Verres being anyone else.

'Interesting,' he said. 'Interesting too because neither of you chose a heroic character, yet you assume I would.'

'Heavens,' screeched Ruth, 'I'm forgetting my hostess' duties. What can I get for you? Hot drink? Whiskey?' He held up the bottle of water. 'I've helped myself,' he said. I showed her my half full tumbler.

'The problem I have with the heroic characters is that they are usually nothing more than cardboard cut-outs; they have no guts. The Queen of the Night is all bad, the Princess all pure, the Prince all virtuous and Sarastro all holy and little else.' He paused, then continued, 'You both selected characters with depth. Characters with weaknesses and strengths, with good and evil in them, with blood in their veins and faeces in their intestines. I think this is a great credit to you both, and it tells me that you too have these depths. Depths,' he added accusingly, 'that you have yet to fully explore.' Ruth looked puzzled. 'I think one day you'll be surprised with what's down there.'

'Well if you're not Sarastro,' I asked, 'Who are you?'

'Monostatos.'

'What?' He had surprised us again.

'The treacherous eunuch?' said Ruth in disgust.

'The guy who betrays the priestly order and almost destroys it,' I added.

'Aha,' replied Verres triumphantly. 'True, he behaved in an apparently cruel and self-seeking way, but his actions brought about the rebirth and reformation of the flagging priest's order.' He nodded confidently. 'And how else could the Queen of the Night's evil hold on the world have been broken if it hadn't been for Monostatos bringing it out into the open?'

'Yes, and for bringing the lovers to their destiny?' said Ruth eagerly.

'That's right,' said Verres. 'He is the fire that makes it possible for the phoenix to fly. The world needs people like Monostatos. Such people often unwittingly clear away the clutter and bring salvation, regeneration and enlightenment.' He hovered on his last words before asking, 'And their reward?' He looked at us with a shadow of sadness over his rugged face. 'Their reward is usually punishment, revilement, persecution and death. Judas was another such character. Without him, Jesus could have lived to a ripe old age and Christianity would never have happened.'

'Don't tell Bill that,' said Ruth, smiling impishly. 'He'd hate to think he owed his livelihood to Judas.'

'You'd be surprised, young lady,' nodded Verres earnestly. 'Your husband, despite appearances and despite himself, has broader opinions and more insight than many people would imagine. People would be unwise to underestimate his awareness and sensitivity.' He rose to his feet abruptly.

'That's enough for tonight. We'll meet again, David.' He squeezed my shoulder, spurning my outstretched hand.

'Goodnight Ruth.' He gently kissed her forehead as tenderly as if she was a dove. 'I don't think we met by accident tonight.'

Ruth led him to the door, then returned to light a couple of candles and put out the main light, before nestling next to me in the cushions on the sofa with the naturalness and ease of a cat snuggling into a warm lap.

'At last,' she said, turning towards me expectantly. 'He's a dear man, but I thought he'd never go.'

'Ruth.'

'Yes, David.'

'Who is he?'

'I don't know,' she smiled. 'He's our man of mystery.'

'But, he's so… I don't know… perceptive,' I said, struggling to contain his mystery in one word.

'Yes, not much gets past *that* gentleman.' She stroked my cheek gently. Her fingers felt like downy feathers floating in the air and brushing against my face.

'I love your hands,' I murmured. 'I love you close to me.'

'It's where I want to be.' Her hands slid like oil under my jacket and around my shoulders. 'Kiss me,' she whispered.

I put my mouth against hers but felt like a stone trying to kiss moss. My lips were dry and firm against her yielding moistness.

'I'm so sorry Ruth,' I stammered. 'I can't.'

'What's wrong?' She pulled back to look at me. 'What went on between you two when I was upstairs?' she asked, sitting up. 'You've been different since I came down. I noticed it immediately.'

'Yes I know, I don't know what happened. Somehow he made me see… no, he helped me to see myself, as I've never seen myself before.'

'And what did you see?' she asked coolly.

'I saw that I am empty.'

'Empty?'

'More than empty… disconnected.'

'Disconnected? From me?' she asked, looking concerned.

'No. No my dear, not from you. From myself.' My eyes pleaded for her understanding. 'In fact I feel closer to you now than ever before. I feel closer to you at this moment than I've ever felt to anyone before.'

Her face softened and she reached out to lay her soft hands against my cheeks again. 'What did he say?' she asked, gently snuggling back into my arms.

'It wasn't what *he* said. It was what he got to me to see within myself.'

'And you saw the disconnection?' she asked.

I nodded. 'I wasn't fully at home,' I said. 'A huge part of me seemed to be missing… I felt that I had been crushed from the inside.'

'Oh David, my dear.' She turned and put her arms around me again and pressed the side of her head into my chest. 'Will you always have this disconnection?'

'No, I know what I have to do to get back in one piece. I have to run with the wolves.'

'What? That doesn't make sense.'

'It does if you know that the wolves are the parts of me that have to run wild. I need to learn how to release them.'

'I don't understand David but is there any way I can help you?'

'Dear Ruth!'

'Yes my dear.'

'Please stay close to me for a while. Give me your energy. Empower me.'

She wriggled into me until it seemed that we shared the same body. We stayed that way, softly embraced, for a long time without speaking. The gentle movement of our chests seemed to become synchronized and our breathing spread over each other like a healing mist.

'I can't make love with you tonight,' I said quietly. 'I want to. I want to more than I've ever wanted anyone but… but I need to be certain I'm completely "at home" when we do. It would be a violation otherwise.'

'Shhhh. It's alright.'

'I want to love you with my whole being,' I said, 'not just the outside of me.'

'Do you want me to wait for you?'

'Yes,' I said.

'Then I will,' she said simply.

We didn't break our embrace and we didn't make love. We may have dozed. At about six o'clock I simply said, 'I'll go now.'

'Will you be alright, my dear?'

'Yes.'

'Do you mind if I go to the loo?' she asked. 'I've been ready to burst for the last hour.' She got up and moved in stiff haste to the door.

I'd left before she returned.

CHAPTER 12

Opening the Doors

THE CONCEPT OF soul loss and retrieval was utterly beyond my understanding, so to experience it happen to me was simply unbelievable. The hours spent with Ruth had anaesthetized me somewhat, but away from her the only way I could live with it was to sub-consciously shut down a large part of my nervous system. I remember little of the journey home until the car engine stalled outside my front door. I don't think I moved out of first gear or exceeded a walking pace; several times I seemed to be kept in line by a soft scuffing of the hedgerows and grassy banks against the wing of the car. Entering the house I levered off my shoes without undoing the laces, lurched into the bedroom, flopped face down onto the bed and dived into a deep, dreamless oblivion.

An aeon later, a sound came from far away in the blackness. It seemed to get nearer, and I crept out of the healing depths of sleep back into the world of telephones and confusion. My eyes flickered open and I looked around. Outside the sky was darkening, inside was shadow; a reflex stretched out a hand to grab the telephone and drag it towards my ear. Closing my eyes again I grunted, 'Tanner'.

'David?' rasped a deep, earthy voice.

'Hang on please, I've just woken up.'

'Take your time, David.' The voice was like no other. Its mellow coarseness was familiar. As I gradually returned to the world I remebered the owner.

'Verres?'

'Come back slowly, David.'

'Y-yes... sorry, I was knocked out. I'm OK now.' I rolled onto my back and peered at my watch. It was after seven o'clock.

'Good. I want you to meet me tomorrow morning. Got that?'

'Tomorrow morning,' I repeated.

'Ten o'clock at the Last Invasion tapestry in Abergwaun. Got it?'

'Yes.'

'Say it back.'

'Ten o'clock at the Last Invasion tapestry in... where?'

'Fishguard. When?'

'Err... tomorrow morning.'

'Good. Now go and write it down straight away, then get up and do something physical, like taking a turn on the coastal path. I think you'll feel marvellous tomorrow.'

He hung up without a farewell and I obediently scrawled his message on a pad, looking at the time again; I'd slept round the clock and felt as stiff as an ironing board. I slipped off the bed, undressed, took two steps towards the shower room; then stopped, returned to the bed, pulled back the duvet and flopped into another deep sleep.

During the black early hours of the morning, the first beast came to me. It was a wolf, loping out of the trees, its salivating tongue hanging limply from its jaws and a look of stark hunger on its face. Then a dragon ambled up to stare at me before moving away, swishing its tail and chuckling to itself. A line of silent men followed, each wearing priestly robes with their faces lost in the black depths of their cowls. After the priests came a fowler, laden down with a wickerwork cage, full of small birds merrily singing as if they were free in a forest. I followed the procession past fire-spitting volcanoes, into ocean depths swirling with kelp, then over a wind-shattered mountain where nothing grew. All the time we were accompanied by the same three maddening notes from an unseen flute. I vainly fought to wake up and escape the madness, but sleep enmeshed me in its twisted vines as I was dragged deeper and deeper into the dream. Suddenly, amidst the flames and water and flute's three irrepressible notes, I was alone: except for a huge boar straddling my path. I felt no threat but safe at last, and stretched out to touch the beast, but I was starting to wake up. I tried to will my sleep to stay, but the spell was breaking and I returned to the darkened room, with the ticking clock and two distant cockerels competing for the dawn.

I lay for a long while, trying in vain to prolong the feeling of security the boar had given me, but finally slid out of bed and into the bathroom. The shower was as hot as I could bear it, and, dousing myself with handfuls of rough pungent shower gel, sang at the top of my voice my own improvised profane words to tunes from *The Magic Flute*. The profanities, the scorching heat and the caustic cruelty of the gel finally brought my mind back to the 'real' world, and I emerged a smarting, slightly cooked new man. I felt terrific.

*

The last military invasion of Britain took place in 1797, when two boatloads of poor quality French 'soldiers', led by an American mercenary called Colonel Tate, came ashore in a rocky cove a mile to the west of Fishguard. They had planned to land on the sandy beach of Fishguard Bay, but were frightened off by a salute of blanks fired in their honour by the pensioner and his friend manning the local fort. This incident sums up the farcical nature of the whole episode; within a few days, the invading force had been rounded up and marched into a future more glorious than the actual exploit. Two hundred years later, they had become the lynchpin of the local tourist industry.

The invasion had not been a Normandy or Hastings in scale or historical importance, but it can boast a commemorative tapestry. To celebrate its bicentennial anniversary, the fair ladies of Fishguard produced their homage to Bayeux. For more than two years, before being crated off to a warehouse, it was proudly displayed in a draughty church hall with a door that thundered shut unless closed with a surgeon's hands. It became a mini Mecca for tourists wanting more from their battlefields than graves, concrete bagged trenches and glossy guidebooks.

I arrived five minutes late. Verres was already there, talking in Welsh to a dark-haired young lady with a strong, open face and square shoulders, who was standing behind a counter. The fierce animal concentration on his face with his steady, unthreatening eyes was utterly beautiful in its intensity; I felt that I wanted to stroke him, although I wouldn't have dared. The tapestry was arranged behind glass along three walls of the room, which pleaded for a paintbrush and a duster: half a dozen viewers were respectfully circulating when I arrived.

The door announced my arrival, the young lady winced, and my host turned to me, smiling. 'Refreshed, David?' he asked brightly.

'Sleep works wonders,' I chirped, having all but forgotten the weird dream.

'Have you seen the tapestry before?'

'Yes,' I said, 'two weeks ago.'

'Excellent. And your opinion?'

'I was most impressed.' I noticed the lady with the square shoulders listening to us behind a pretended disinterest. 'The workmanship is excellent, the narrative clear and interesting, it's attractive to look at and displayed with imagination, but

111

most of all I was impressed by the whole concept and design. My main reservation is this hall. The tapestry deserves a better setting.'

'Interesting,' he said slowly. 'This young lady was saying the same thing.' He turned and muttered something to her that sounded like, '*Gwellar chee un deeweather*.' She replied with a huge smile and a few words that were equally indiscernible.

We walked towards the tapestry. 'It seems that this hall is just a temporary home,' he said. 'But no-one knows where it will go from here. The Welsh tend not to look after their treasures.'

A class of well-ordered children, shepherded by two teachers speaking to them in Welsh, came respectfully into the hall. We shuffled back to the wall to make room for them to pass. 'The language, you mean?'

'That of course.' He looked at the children. 'But these young people are heirs to wonderful literature, to legends and a mysterious and magical land, yet when they become adults most of them will turn their backs on it all.' He turned to face to me and chuckled, 'The Welsh are like a governor of the Tower of London who keeps an armed guard on the spoons in the restaurant, and the crown jewels in a cardboard box on top of a filing cabinet.'

The teachers led their charges to a corner by the souvenir shop and seemed to be giving them advice on what to do next.

'Before they release their juvenile energy on the place I want you to look at the tapestry again.'

'Again? I've already seen it.'

'One more time please, David.' He tilted his head a fraction to one side and gently propelled me forward. 'And remember the little talk we had at Ruth's a few nights ago.'

The tapestry was a series of connected panels, each about a yard long, depicting a separate scene in the drama. Halfway around I came to a scene entitled, '*English officers refuse to accept the surrender terms.'* It showed three English officers seated at a table with an English soldier standing behind and a French soldier standing in front of them. The panel was unremarkable, and I had moved on before something I had missed the first time made me stop and return to it. It looked like all the others, but I knew I was missing something. Then I noticed that it was the only one in the hall that hadn't been finished. The seated men were merely yellow outlines; none of their clothing, skin or any detail had been filled in. They were like phantoms, as if they had no physical form; only the French soldier was complete in every detail. I saw too that the man standing behind them was half filled-in and half empty.

'Well?' he asked, after I'd rejoined him.

'Well!' I replied, 'Was that a surprise!'

'I thought it might be. Tell me.'

I told him of the panel with the ghost-like English officers and the half-there soldier behind them.

Pausing for a second he said, 'I'll ask you the same question I asked you two days ago. Who did you identify with in that scene?'

'The soldier standing behind the men seated at the table.'

'Why?'

'Because…' I hesitated, recalling the standing figure who seemed to have no part in the action. 'Because he reminded me of myself.'

'Yourself? In what way, David?'

'It's quite uncanny, he reminded me of myself the other night when we were talking. The man has no role to play and was only half-there, like I was. Half of him is missing like half of me was missing too.'

'Are you aware that you're talking about yourself in the past tense, David. Part of you *was* missing. How about now, the present? Who are you now?'

'Now,' I said cautiously, projecting myself back into the panel, 'I think I'm the French soldier.'

'Because?'

'Because he's complete. Yes, that's right Verres.' My eyes leapt into his. 'There are no voids in him. Surely it can't be that easy. Surely my wolf hasn't escaped so effortlessly.' His silence compelled me to continue. 'What's going on?' I asked, 'You seem to know everything… but to me… I seem to have entered a different world since I met you. Nothing is familiar, nothing has substance, nothing seems the same as it was a few days ago. Nothing… even *I'm* different.'

He smiled kindly before making yet another quantum leap. 'Have you read *Tom Jones*'?

'No, but I've seen the film, with Albert Finney as Tom.'

'So you know the story then?'

'Yes, roughly.'

'Then you remember how the film ends?'

'Yes, he was saved from the gallows at the last minute,' I said.

'And did he get the girl?'

'Yes.'

'Who was the girl?'

I knew he didn't want me to give her name or status, so I tentatively gave him the answer I assumed he wanted.

'His ego?'

'Keep trying.'

Now perhaps I knew the answer. 'Part of himself?' I enquired tentatively. 'Are you saying she was part of his soul that he had lost and now won back?'

A family of holidaymakers came through the thundering door; the two children immediately ran to the souvenir counter and started to covetously finger the keyrings and pencils on display.

'You are ready, David, for us to move on,' he said testily,

ignoring my question. 'I want to tell you something about my recent past and where I've been for the last few years.'

'Ruth told me you lived in Ireland for a long time.' We moved through the filling hall towards the fearsome door.

'That's true.'

'Why did you leave? Why did you come here to Wales?' I asked eagerly.

'You like walking don't you? Let's talk more in the fresh air. This isn't the place for what I have to tell you.'

'Fine,' I muttered, as more and more questions elbowed their way to the surface. 'But why me? I only met you a few days ago. I'm a total stranger.'

'Shall we say Friday?'

'OK, where?' He gave me precise instructions.

'What time?'

'Ten o'clock again.'

'Rain or fine?' I asked.

'Rain or fine,' he asserted, reaching into his pocket and pulling out a sealed aquamarine envelope. 'This is for you. From Ruth.'

'But…'

He walked out, bidding the young lady a warm farewell in Welsh as he passed and closed the door quietly. I stood there full of unanswered questions staring dumbly at the slightly crumpled envelope and read the name written on it: 'David Tanner.'

*

On top of the hill above the harbour I found a footpath, and followed it to the ruined fort where the 'salute' had been fired for the French invasion fleet two hundred years earlier. Alone with the gulls and the wind, I sat on a low wall looking across the harbour towards the Rosslare ferry, pausing against the dock like a giant white torpedo about to be fired at Ireland, and wondered what my new friend could have done over there. A porpoise effortlessly undulating its way outside the harbour entrance reminded me of Ruth, so I pulled her envelope out of my pocket, smoothed it against my thigh and stared at her writing, afraid to break the seal. I feared that the starkness of daylight had destroyed the magic spell we had woven together in the dark hours. The more I thought about her, the more anxious I became, and out of my anxiety emerged a sense of deep loss. I carefully opened the envelope; three red rose petals slipped out onto the ground and lay there like three pools of blood. I picked them up and held them tenderly in my hand as I read her note:

Dearest David,

I think it's best if I went home.
I hope you travel safely and your 'journey' doesn't take too long.
I'll be here for you when you come back.

Yours

Ruth

CHAPTER 13

To Golden Mists

A DENSE, SODDEN swirl of cloud hung over the hills, and I was barely twenty yards from a dark, motionless shape before I recognised Verres. What was I doing here? What compulsion brought me to meet this strange man in these conditions, in such a remote place, high on a mountain road miles from anywhere? A spiteful wind spat from the north, a wind that took its icy dampness straight from the Arctic into my bones. My boots, sweaters and state-of-the-art outer shell clothing must have cost me more than £500, yet I still felt the chill as I approached him. He stood alongside his motorbike, dressed in tweed breeches, thick woollen socks, a thick lumberjack shirt and a large red handkerchief wrapped around his throat. His helmet lay on the ground beside him like a space warrior buried up to his neck in the peat. As I approached he was pointing his face into the wind, eyes closed, nostrils greedily scanning and savouring it like a great bear searching for a scent. He seemed to belong to the wilderness, more beast than man.

He didn't open his eyes until I was a few feet away, then he turned to look at me.

'Good heavens, Verres.' I looked at him and shivered. 'Don't you feel the cold?'

'Of course I do… but only on my skin. Inside I'm like a furnace.' He took a final heave of the wind like a wine connoisseur delving into a rare vintage. 'I like feeling free,' he said. 'Free and uncluttered. Put these in your car, please.' He passed me his helmet and a document wallet containing some papers. 'Let's walk.'

Ignoring my protest about the weather, he turned and loped off into the mist, following the deeply rutted path running parallel to the swaying, steepled outline of a spruce forest to our right. I trotted after him, but soon my expensive gear became a pressure cooker and I started to roast. Piece by piece I undressed, while stumbling and splashing through the puddles after him. We soon left the forest behind and started to cross a peat bog intersected by a network of ditches, each filled with an evil, black liquid; by now I was carrying half my precious clothing under an arm or knotted around my waist, and wondering how long I could keep up with his breakneck pace.

'Hang on, Verres,' I panted. 'Do we need to go quite so fast?'

He stopped and turned to look at my efforts with the disdain of a poker player holding a Royal Straight. His beard was decorated with tiny beads of moisture, his hairy legs splattered with peat and mud, and the breeze tugged at the loose folds of his shirt. 'You'll manage... anyway it's better to run across the bog if you want to keep your feet dry.'

He was right; some of the ditches were too wide to jump without a run-up. 'Come on, there's only a hundred yards or so more of this.'

He thundered off faster than before, leaping each pool and landing on the other side with a small explosion of wet peat. I did my best to keep up but, although the widest rill was little more than five feet across, I twice landed short and sank halfway up to my knees in the clinging black porridge.

He waited for me on the firmer, rising ground, grinning. 'OK now?'

'Where are we going? I asked breathlessly. 'Is this torture really necessary...' He wasn't yet ready to show his hand, but turned and moved on faster than ever.

As we climbed higher the wind grew fiercer and louder. He made no attempt to talk over its banshee wails. Soon he was ten yards ahead of me and pulling away, his outline becoming indistinct in the mist which seemed to get thicker the higher we climbed. I raised a lung curdling gallop and caught him up.

'I don't want to lose you, can't we go slower?' I panted, gasping through the exertion. 'I'll never find my way back alone.'

He seemed more interested in feeling the elements than listening to my whimpering, and didn't respond. A strong gust of wind rippled through his hair, and he pivoted to face it with arms spread wide as if he was trying to stop it like a hilltop Canute. The gust passed and he set off again, at the same relentless pace. I hobbled after him, waiting in vain for a second wind to come to my rescue.

He stopped at a stile and looked back at me. 'Don't fight it, David,' he said. 'You're thinking about how hard and unpleasant this is, aren't you?'

Too right I was. But I had little breath left to unburden the full venom of my thoughts on him.

'Move your mind away David from the fear and from the pain you think you feel.' He stepped up and over the stile without using his hands as if it was twelve inches high, and opened his arms again to embrace the wind.

'Feel the strength of the wind, and let it fill you with energy. Feel the pulse of the land and let it lift you. Run with the wolves.'

He strode off while I clambered over the stile and trotted after him with his words germinating in my head. I joked to myself about even wolves not being able to maintain this pace.

'Look at the grass. See how it harnesses the wind; you do the same.' The coarse brown grass flowed like an irrepressible ocean in the wind, briefly stilled and flattened in a lull before being picked up again in an endless cycle of exertion and ease.

The wolves and the grass helped me to the corner of another wood where the path divided. 'We leave the Golden Road here,' he said, turning abruptly to watch me catch up. 'We're going this way.'

'Golden Road,' I wheezed in disbelief. 'Someone had a sense of humour.'

'Three thousand years ago, David, this was the M1 of the age.' He looked into the mist as if he could see through it and across the shipwrecked hillside. 'It was a very important trading route between Ireland and Britain.'

'Why call it the Golden Road?' I stared along the dismal little track until it dissolved into the mist.

'That's an interesting question,' he said slowly, taking a couple of steps back down the hill to where I stood. I was thankful for an opportunity to recover. 'Most historians say it's because it was a major route for importing Irish gold to Britain.'

'But what do *you* say?' I asked.

'I say it's a Golden Road because kings came this way.'

'Kings? What would kings want to come up here for?' I asked, pulling an energy bar from my pocket and breaking it into two pieces. He shook his head as I offered him one of the halves.

'These old hills, David, may not match the great mountains of the world in scale, but none can match their mystery and power.' He gazed with unfocused eyes into the mist. 'I can see great barbarian processions passing this way; hoards of fierce warriors carrying spears and shields, dressed in plaid and leather and hides, their skin painted and their hair plaited. Leading them on a shaggy mountain pony and closely followed by a guard of the fiercest ruffians, I can see the king. He's wearing a gold torc and has a gold buckle on his belt, and there's a gold pin holding his cloak.' He sighed as though he was remembering a sweet scene from his childhood.

'But you still haven't told me what they came here for,' I said dumbly.

'For the mystery and enchantment in the hills, of course.'

'How do you know all this?' I asked, nibbling a corner of the bar. It was too dry and difficult to swallow so I pocketed the rest.

'I know,' he said simply. 'Ready?'

'Why have you really brought me here, Verres?' I asked again, as we moved up the hill side by side.

'Why have you come?' he replied. I had no answer; however I felt a perverse pride to be invited. Somehow, his interest in me was thrilling.

'I know I'm asking a lot of you, David,' he shouted. 'But you'll soon understand.'

His words helped pile a few more coals on the fire of the growing trust and affection I was feeling for this forbidding old man who was leading me on such a demanding dance. I wanted to impress him more than I wanted to stop and was ready when he moved off again.

His pace didn't slacken, but somehow the next twenty minutes passed in a trice and we were walking side by side, matching stride for stride as the concrete triangulation obelisk of the summit emerged out of the cloud ahead of us. I'd stopped cooking; my breathing was even; I actually felt happy.

'Come this way,' he said, moving to the rim of a shallow crater about ten feet across, a few yards from the top. 'Do you know what this hill is called, David?'

'Preseli Top?' I suggested uncertainly.

'Its correct name is Foel Cwmcerwyn. Does that mean anything to you?'

'Nothing,' I said. 'What does it mean?'

'Roughly it means, the bare hill above the Cerwyn valley.

But think again David, I know Cwmcerwyn is tucked away somewhere in your memory.'

'Cwmcerwyn?' I repeated the name several times to myself. 'I don't think so.'

'Think again,' written on his face was a message I had seen before; it said you'll know when the time is right.

Then I remembered where I had heard the name before. 'What's going on, Verres? Who are you?'

'Tell me what you remember, David.'

'A battle that was fought here between King Arthur and a giant boar called Turk... something.'

'Go on.'

'I've thought a lot about a boar lately, I don't know why, but I wonder...' Unbelievable connections were coming into my head and a sudden chill raced up my spine with such force it almost blew my head off.

'You wonder?' he prompted.

'A boar made me come to live here. It chased me in New Zealand, then again in London, telling me to come home. Could it be Turk?'

His implacability spurred me to continue.

'I first heard the story when I was at school.' I stared hard into the mist to see if I could dredge up anything else from the shards of a lost memory. 'My old headmaster took us to...'

A light dawned. 'Heavens, Verres, he must have brought us here,' I shouted gleefully. 'How about that, I've been here before!' I almost danced in front of him in my excitement.

Fragments of the story, buried for an age in my mind, floated from the cradles of my memory and I blurted them out piece by piece while he stood before me, his arms folded implacably across his chest.

'What was the story really about, David?'

'Greed and power,' I said, remembering how, standing afraid

and alone, I had championed the cause of the boar a quarter of a century earlier.

'Whose greed and power... the boar's?' he asked.

'No,' I said quietly. 'That belonged to what we would today call "the establishment". Turk... no Twrch, I believe his name was, was a symbol of the bountiful earth.'

A sudden giddiness scourged me, and my knees buckled. I may even have blacked out, because I next became aware of Verres' strong hands on my shoulders, supporting me. We were about the same height, yet I seemed to be looking up into the brown, unblinking eyes of a giant.

'You know all this already, don't you?' I said. 'What are you doing to me? Who are you?'

He lowered his hands.

'Who did you say told you the story?' he asked quietly.

'I've just told you, it was my old headmaster. We called him Ticker.'

'What happened to Ticker?'

'That was really weird, Verres. He disappeared.'

'Disappeared?'

'Well, some people believed he went to Ireland.'

Ireland! An electric charge ran through my entire body, and for an instant I seemed to be spiralling and turning over and over as if caught in a vortex. 'You lived in Ireland, didn't you?' I gasped hoarsely. He put his face close to mine, his eyes glowing coals burning through his whiskers.

'Are you Ticker?' The swirling cloud suddenly lifted, and the vast expanse of the cwm opened out below us. My mind plunged deep into it, like a hawk diving after a pigeon, free and certain.

CHAPTER 14

Return

IN THE BUFFETING wind with wolves and grass coursing through my senses, I stood cheek by jowl, eyeball to eyeball with a man who had been dead for twenty-five years. He bore no resemblance in appearance or behaviour to the man who had died. The once civilized and cultured man was now as ferociously free as the wind, and as untamed as the wolves he loved. My relationship with the man who had died was one of a boy to an adult, now it was man to man; before I had only felt awe in his presence, now it was closer to love; yet all the disconnections helped to cement the credibility of this bizarre encounter beyond any doubt.

Once over the first shocking impact of meeting Ticker again, my curiosity went into overdrive. As we slowly returned to my car, a cascade of questions tumbled over each other; most I don't recall, but I do remember asking what happened to him twenty-five years ago, how could he have disappeared so completely, and how was it possible for his appearance to have changed so dramatically, so that no vestige of the man we knew remained?

To all these questions I received the same enigmatic reply.

'All in good time.'

I asked him if I should tell Ruth and Jenkins, but he said that the time wasn't right for them to know yet.

'When will you tell them?' I asked.

'When the time is right for them to know.'

I asked him how he had found us, but he said he hadn't.

'We have been brought together.'

'By what?' I asked. 'The boar?'

'Synchronicity,' he said. 'The boar only "speaks" to you.'

'Why only me?'

'Why does a river flow to the sea? Why does a lion pull down the weakest deer? Why do the roots of a tree break through solid rock?' he answered.

Eventually my questions dried up and he led me back to *his* agenda. 'You need to learn more about what happened to me, and very much more about what you already know.'

'What do you mean, what I already know?' I asked, and immediately regretted it.

'Come on, David,' he grunted fiercely. 'It's time you started looking inwards for answers, not endlessly outside yourself. That's a habit you must break before you can understand anything.'

I resolved to control the 'reflex of asking' and concocted my own 'reflex of knowing' on the spot, making a good start by not asking him how I could break the 'asking' habit.

I found it relaxing to be released from the burbling torrent of thoughtless, unnecessary questions which had endlessly blurted out of me. It was comforting to wait until the answers came to me, as they invariably did, 'in good time'.

I told him about my imaginative encounters with the boar in New Zealand and London, and the insistent instruction to 'come home'. He nodded and said mysteriously, 'I thought it would be something like that.'

Harnessing my 'reflex of knowing' I resisted asking questions like, why me? What do I do now I'm here? How real is the boar? Does he exist anywhere but in my imagination? Is there a parallel world? Because I knew how he would answer; but I did break my rule to ask, 'Am I home now? Is this home?'

He replied by quoting a Greek poet he liked: 'No longer say to yourself where is my home. You must yourself become your home.'

I must myself become my home, I thought; I like that. With my questions temporarily hushed, we walked on in a luxurious silence, in our own thoughts, in companionship, and in ease and each in our own home.

'So I needn't have come here to "make" my home? I could have stayed in NZ and made my home there?'

'Could you?'

I felt like kicking myself. 'Of course… the myth belongs here,' I said. 'As we do, and we need this land of "mystery and enchantment" as a catalyst.' A catalyst for what I knew I would find out, all in good time.

He pointed across the windswept hillside. 'You're right, David, I know you can feel it,' he shouted. 'There's an energy here that once resounded all over Britain.' I listened to his words quietly, not fully understanding, but knowing that he was telling me the truth; I somehow knew that it was this energy, carried to me by the boar, that had brought me here to live.

'But it's not about real estate. It's about people and allowing them to seek their freedom.'

'I'm sorry, Verres.' I shook my head truculently. 'I don't know what you mean by the word "freedom" and I don't care about setting people free. What does that mean anyway?'

'Who said anything about *setting* people free?' he asked. 'People need to find the courage to free themselves. No-one can *set* anyone free except himself or herself.'

I disappeared back into a confluence of concepts and ideas, both grounded and mystical. I had had to take in so much in such a short space of time; so I retreated back into myself and don't remember moving back along the Golden Road, recrossing the stile, leaping the rills of black water in the peat bog or walking alongside the trees. We talked occasionally, but our words were picked up by the wind, carried away in its wild dance and scattered across the hillside where perhaps they still remain in the stones, waiting to be heard by a future passer-by who will understand them.

When my car emerged through the mist I risked being admonished to ask, 'Why have we been brought together again, Verres?' I still thought of him as Verres; Ticker and Dr Lloyd had long departed.

'Twenty-five years ago David, *you* first got me thinking about all this. You were the one who taught me the true meaning of the story of the boar and King Arthur.'

'Me,' I blurted. 'How?'

'You alone in the class sensed the story did an injustice to the boar. You alone perceived how the story had been manipulated by people who wanted to restrict other people's freedom and keep them in perpetual fear. You alone saw that Twrch Trwyth represented the strength and the fecundity of the land that empowered people, and was not the destructive, malignant force he was made out to be by the *Mabinogi*. And you cared enough to creep out of your fortress of silence to say so.'

'What happens now?' I asked.

We walked in silence for a few minutes before he spoke again. 'I'm not going to say any more, David, but I want you to read something.'

'Oh, what?'

'I wrote something a year after my so-called disappearance. At the time I too was confused and uncertain. Writing helped me, and I think reading what I wrote will help you too.'

'A diary?'

'Not really,' he said with a crooked smile. 'I needed a more objective confidant than myself, so I wrote it as a letter to my best friend at school who had died half a lifetime earlier. I've never been closer to any man before or since. It only covers my first year in Ireland, but I think you'll find that it answers most of your questions about me.'

I opened the car door; he reached inside and took his helmet, but left the document wallet on the seat. 'I'll speak to you again.'

He walked towards his motorcycle, squeezing the helmet onto his head. 'Thanks for coming,' he muttered. I wasn't completely sure whether he spoke to me or the wind, and started to reply to his retreating back, but stopped in mid sentence. My platitudes would be absurd after what we had just experienced together.

After priming his machine he straddled it as if it were a child's toy bike, then turned the key. It coughed once and burst into an ear-stunning roar. I looked across at him, almost craving a final nod or wave, but without even a glance he pulled out and hammered off into the fog. I stood without moving, staring trancelike at the spot in the cloud where I had last seen him, until long after the sound of his motorbike had faded into the wind.

I was completely at ease and wanted to stay there forever. The wind seemed to be my friend, and I felt warmth and strength in its buffeting. Grudgingly, I slid into the car and sat for an age, comforted by the gentle rocking of the most violent gusts and the throbbing penetration of Elgar's 'Cello Concerto in E minor' on the CD stereo. Piece by piece, I revived the fantasy experience I had been through, and let it become real for me. The boundary between the incredible and the mundane, the incomprehensible and the blatantly outrageous were broken down, and seemed to exist side by side within me.

As I sat there, too excited to drive away immediately, yet eager to get home to open his package, the mist gently lifted its veil from the hill and the whole mountain became swathed in healing sunshine. Hard-edged shadows formed to highlight scattered rocks; the playful grass gently lay down and rested, while in the distance the eternal river Cleddau serpentined its mystery across the land. I knew I had the courage to be free and wild.

CHAPTER 15

To Reveal

BRILLIANT SUNSHINE SANG over the countryside. My garden shimmered with countless shades of red, yellow and blue flowers, and hordes of happy insects making up for time lost during the earlier dullness. I carried Verres' document wallet inside and lay it on a table unopened so I could savour the anticipation of its contents before reading it, as a child might eat the crust of a tart, leaving the fruit and cream until last. I wouldn't open it until I had freshened up and eaten something; I wanted nothing to distract me once I'd started. Despite my restraint, I broke records for showering, fixing a brie and salad baguette and a cafetière before settling into a comfortable chair with a dog-eared Chaucer's School exercise book filled with his neat, direct handwriting on my lap.

April 10, 1975
Dear Sam,
Twelve brief, interminable months ago my life was ordered, predictable, comfortable and successful. Then I tumbled into a lightless, seemingly bottomless, chasm. If that wasn't bad enough, I didn't fall but chose to jump, and knew that at any time I could reverse my descent and return to the directionless conveyor belt of shallow mundanity, but I had been given a glimpse of my bliss and couldn't turn my back on it. For one brief, glorious moment I saw what my life could be, and in that moment received a mortal wound like the Fisher King. My only hope was – and is – to seek until I find

this glorious vision again, no matter how dire the quest, then to follow it wherever it takes me.

Of course it is the Grail quest!

'She' told me that I will only find it inside myself, and that's where I have to go. But for a year all I've found inside me is a festering wound, unbearable noise and a thousand distorting mirrors making everything seem garish and out of proportion. I need a confidant, a wise and simple friend who will listen to me without judgement. Perhaps as I 'speak' to you, my dear Sam, my head will clear and the storms will subside.

Last Easter I enrolled on a five-day introductory course on Welsh Literature at Swansea University; most Easters I tried to do a short course somewhere on something totally different to anything I had done before. The aim of the course was to introduce English speakers living in Wales to aspects of the Welsh culture. Eight of us were on the course, seven men and Dana. The others were mainly young students but there were also a couple of retired local men making a belated attempt to discover something of the culture of their adopted country.

Dana was a dark, Spanish-looking American, quite tall for a woman, in her mid thirties who had made her home in southern Ireland. She was a commanding, confident woman and in an earthy way, very beautiful – and knew it. The others on the course drooled and flocked around her like lobotomized sheep, which she loved. This is probably why I made a point of disliking her intensely! In class discussion I would amuse myself by taking the opposite view to hers, and whenever she expressed an opinion I would find the words to make it seem ridiculous.

If words were the only criterion I would have won every argument, but I always came away feeling that I'd lost. No matter how devastating my reasoning, she persevered with smiles and shrugs, a hand placed with measured carelessness on my arm, and soft, insistent repetition. This irritated me all the more because I'm never bested in an argument and the harder I tried the more foolish I felt.

On the second evening I found myself sitting next to her during dinner in the refectory. We didn't talk at first but as the meal progressed she seemed to draw me out to talk about my life, my work, my dreams and even my fears. Despite my previous 'reserve', her attention and interest pleased me, and I told her a lot of intimate things I normally keep to myself. In return she told me a little about her childhood in America.

She is quarter Navajo and was brought up by a German grandmother in Arizona but surrounded by her Indian relatives, and claimed to have been influenced by both civilizations in her upbringing. She told me nothing about her present life except that she sang in a fairly successful Irish folk group.

We continued to talk long after we'd finished eating and long after her courtiers, bored at being ignored, had wandered away. We were eventually left alone in the vast room apart from a couple of the kitchen staff. Abruptly she told me that she felt my 'pain'. She said that sitting next to me was like sitting next to a magma chamber under a volcano which was about to explode and she asked me what was troubling me?

I didn't know what she was talking about, but when I opened my mouth to deny any such pain the words stuck in my throat.

Then she told me it was alright to feel pain and called me Thomas. I had last been called Thomas by my late mother when I was a little boy, and a flood of old feelings surfaced gagging any response I wanted to make. Only through silence could I keep control of my emotions, and this was the first time I've even been close to shedding tears since my childhood. I didn't even cry when you – my other self – died, Sam. Then I just felt a profound emptiness.

'Feel, Thomas,' she said but I gritted my teeth to keep control of my feelings in front of her.

She told me that she knew what I was experiencing and that she was 'there' with me; she would never betray me and it was safe for me to surrender to my deepest feelings.

At that moment I hated her. Her compassion was an affront to my masculine confidence and her understanding an intrusion into my private world. I would have told her to 'get lost' if I'd dared to relax the clamp I had put over my tongue.

Then she said an amazing thing that I will never forget. Seeing me the way I was, she said that she could only feel intense tenderness and love for me.

I sat motionless, silently looking down into the Formica clouds of the table but she continued, saying that she wanted to bring me cool water and touch it softly on my burning temples. She wanted to hold it to my lips and ease it gently down my parched throat. I looked up into her face and saw a collage of concern, gentleness and love, but mustered sufficient control to ask her why she was saying this, especially to me when everyone in the room was in some sort of pain.

She told me it was because no-one else was as hungry as me and because I had something important to give her too. She couldn't tell me what that was.

The kitchen staff made us move and soon we were drawn back to the reality of the course and its participants but things had changed between us. After that, we sang voicelessly together in the classroom and became inseparable in-between times although I had to share her with the others for much of the time.

We spoke no more about my 'pain' and I didn't have to fight to keep my self-control again. Very quickly the connection between us grew stronger and stronger and the world seemed to become full of light and play. Soon a strong sexual attraction started to consume us, and I lusted for her with the urgency of a spotty teenager. For the duration of the course we had to content ourselves with mind games, flirting and innuendo, but inevitably arranged to spend a couple of days together after it was over. By the last morning I was eagerly anticipating a refreshing 'dirty weekend' to round off an enjoyable course which would set me up nicely for the hectic summer term ahead.

We stayed at the Imperial Hotel overlooking the Bristol Channel. It had enjoyed its heydays in the Twenties but never succeeded in earning more than three stars by modern standards, and was inhabited by people who, like the hotel itself, seemed to have known better times. It suited me because I assumed the service would be impersonal and we would be able to merge into a multitude of Easter holiday guests and upmarket reps without attracting too much attention.

So it proved to be. After a Friday evening of adolescent adventure, compulsively touching, stroking each other and exploring the world of verbal foreplay, we thankfully locked our bedroom door behind us soon after eight o'clock. I must admit my ardour was complemented with not a little relief. From time to time I remembered my position in life and imagined with grim horror the stories that would get about if one of my pupils had seen me giggling and groping like a fifth former.

For such a dynamic and confident woman, Dana was a remarkably passive lover. For her lovemaking was an utter indulgence. She was like a cat with an insatiable need for endless stroking. She stretched, smiled, made soft purring sounds, whispered endearments and asked for more and more.

I remember you and I once talked about the qualities of the women we would marry. We were walking home after watching a semi-professional opera company 'murder' *La Traviata*. You said that you had fallen in love with Violetta, but I was contemptuous of her unnecessary self-sacrifice and what I called her 'Virgin Mary' complex. However, one thing she said did impress me. I remember deciding then and there that I would never marry a woman who did not enjoy what Violetta called 'the whirlwind of total indulgence'. Well Sam, in Dana I've found her.

This was my first experience of being in love, but it wasn't the uplifting sensation I'd expected. At times I basked in a sleepy, blissful state of 'total indulgence' but the tentacles of other feelings reached out for me. Crushing feelings like a dread of losing her, a will to possess her and a paranoid jealousy of imagined rivals; they all darted in and out of my thoughts and I had no history of dealing with them or skill in controlling them.

We came downstairs on Sunday too late for breakfast, and the Sabbath in west Wales, even in the 1970s, is not the place to find cafés open, so we survived most of the day on a shared packet of crisps and a Mars bar bought from a newsagent. Neither of us was hungry and we didn't even finish the chocolate.

Later in the afternoon we summoned the energy to take a stroll. We drove to Worm's Head on the western tip of the Gower peninsula and with her holding on to my arm with both of hers and snuggling close to me, we meandered slowly along the cliff top overlooking the strange outline of the 'worm' in the water below us. The spit of land surrounded by the high tide looked like the Loch Ness monster and seemed alive in the swirling, restless eddies of the water.

She told me that this was a special place to the ancients and it was a place where they could pass through to reach the 'Otherworld'. I asked her how she knew about the ancients.

'I can see them, Thomas,' she said. 'They are everywhere, passing between the two worlds, tending the land, worshipping the worm... they are all so busy.'

A stinging lick of jealousy swiped me at that moment. Before meeting her I'd never been jealous of anything or anyone. Now I was jealous of every thought and memory she had which excluded me. Was this what love was all about? It was a detestable sensation, so I attempted to push it away. She told me of how the ancient Celts stood on this same spot looking down on the 'worm', watching it move in the water, marvelling at it and honouring it as a blessing to them and to the land.

She was talking so passionately and openly, but I still knew nothing about her or her life. So I asked her who she was and what had brought her to Ireland. Without releasing her caressing hold on my arm she said with brutal simplicity, as if she was telling me her car had a puncture:

'I'm a nun, Thomas.'

CHAPTER 16

A New Horizon

THE TELEPHONE BELL exploded in my head, and my mind was torn out of the compelling depths of Ticker's devastated love life back to my sitting room and an uneaten baguette. I spat a curt 'Yes?' into the mouthpiece.

'David, how are you? Bill Jenkins here.'

'Oh… er… hello Bill.'

'David, I'm coming down next week and I'd like to see you.' His voice sounded tense, and the sharp thrill of guilt sulkily peered out from my conscience.

'That would be nice.' I tried unsuccessfully to sound normal, but was already fretting about possible consequences. 'Give me a call when you get here.'

'I'm coming down on Wednesday morning, will you be free in the afternoon?'

'I suppose so.' I felt fenced-in by his haste and opportunism.

'Shall I come round about three?'

'It sounds important, Bill.' I suspected that the cat had slipped out of the bag in the Midlands and an angry husband was attempting to behave in a civilised way.

'It is,' he replied with a hint of bitterness, 'very important, a lot depends on it.'

'Alright.' Although nothing had 'happened', a lot had gone on between his wife and me so I could foresee an uncomfortable interview.

With a terse 'See you Wednesday' he hung up.

My superficial, one-dimensional, 'thank you ma'am' experience of women was not adequate to help me understand the complexities surrounding either Dana or Ruth. I feverishly started concocting a battlement of lies and excuses to divert the irate husband, then wondered about Dana's bombshell and how Ticker reacted to such a crushing blow. I re-opened the exercise book.

A nun Sam, I was shattered.

In a flash the blissful ache of being in love and believing I had found the life partner I had given up all hope of ever finding, was turned by one three-lettered-word into a bitter sense of loss, deprivation and despair beyond anything I could imagine.

I must have shown my feelings, because immediately she tried to reassure me, but her words made my desolation seem even greater. She told me that she loved me and could still love me and stay with me as well as honouring the commitment to her 'calling'. What I couldn't deal with was that her 'calling' would have to come first and I would have to fit in around it. I had even imagined, in my wildest dream, us getting married and settling down together in Kent. I saw her contributing to school life, entertaining the staff at a garden party once a year and 'living happily ever after'. I couldn't accept what she seemed to be offering me – a life shadowing a veil.

I curled up in a hutch of despair and said very little for the rest of the evening and didn't give a thought to food, so the poor woman must have gone to bed famished. Only as we lay side by side without touching in bed that night did she finally ask me to tell her what was troubling me. In the darkness I opened my heart. I spoke of how, despite our brief time together, I had entertained wild dreams I'd waited a lifetime for, only to have them swept away in a mini-second. I told her I felt my insides seemed as if they had suddenly been entered by an Arctic winter.

Suddenly she sat up in bed, flicked on a bedside light and gave me a good 'telling-off'. She told me that I was behaving like a spoilt child, that it was time to stop thinking of myself in such a pathetic way and wallowing in helplessness. I was a man, a great man, and seeing someone with all my gifts behaving in such an infantile way was repellent. The vehemence of her outburst stunned me, but she hadn't finished. She went on to tell me that I was the man she loved and wanted. She said that I hadn't lost her 'YET' but I would if I couldn't behave more like an adult and make adult decisions.

I was stunned. Not by her words, but by how humiliated I felt. Until that moment it hadn't occurred to me that I had pride, or that my ego had become so pathetically weak and dependent on admiration. She had stripped me of my massive self-delusions; I felt naked and exposed.

Her eyes were still on fire. 'Forget all that sentimental crap,' she said, 'Forget that precious doctorate of yours, that's crap too, and doesn't impress me. I want your essence, not your poxy certificates.'

'You confuse me,' I said after a few moments. 'You sound like no nun I've heard of.'

She calmed down and told me about her 'Order'. It demanded no vows of chastity and obedience, but allowed its 'sisters' complete freedom of choice on the best way to serve the Universe. She had a gift of healing, and this was the path she was being taken down and nothing could divert her from it. If I wanted her as much as I said, I would have to go with her, live with her and leave behind the life I had led up until then. She told me that I had to make a choice, a choice between going forward into an uncertain future with her or going back to the ordered, predictable death-life I had been living.

'You can't mean give up everything,' I said.

'Everything,' she replied simply.

'What, my job, the people who depend on me…?'

'Everything.'

I asked how I could make such a momentous decision. It was too big for me to make, because whatever I decided would mean losing an integral part of my life. It was like having to decide whether to have my legs or my arms cut off.

'Pray,' she said.

I told her that I didn't believe in the concept of a God. She said neither did she, but we could still 'pray'. I could pray to whatever or whoever was important to me – to my pupils, to her or even to myself.

She turned over and went to sleep. I had little choice but to pray.

I lay the book down, went into the kitchen, turned on the kettle and thought about Ticker's dilemma. The choices given to him seemed unreasonable, and I felt angry with Dana for forcing them on him. 'Why couldn't she give up *her* life?' I asked myself indignantly. 'Who's she to say that her healing work was more important than his teaching vocation?'

My thoughts raced along like wild horses, and inevitably my concern for Ticker lying in the darkness with his desperate predicament gradually turned to my dilemma with Ruth and Jenkins. Why did he want to see me so urgently? What had she told him? What was the worst thing that could happen? Perhaps a messy divorce; but we'd only 'larked about', and that was no grounds for disrupting three lives. I hadn't given living with her a single thought, and believed I was too old a dog to have to start, even with her; yet as I leant against the kitchen sink, waiting for the kettle to boil, I wished like hell that she would telephone me. I made a fresh cafetière and returned to Ticker's less troublesome quandary.

I may have slept, but at about three o'clock became wide awake and peered around the darkened room. There was not a glimmer of light, but as my eyes became accustomed to the darkness, the murky features of the room started to emerge. I looked towards the sound of gentle breathing and saw the rounded outline of the woman sleeping beside me. I reached across and shook her shoulder gently. She murmured and rolled over to face me. 'Well?' she asked sleepily, 'What have you decided?'

I told her I had no real choice but to jump into the abyss. She shunted towards me with her arms open and wrapped them around me. Drawing my head into her soft warmth she murmured, 'Come, my love'.

My eyes smarted as tears welled up and the moist trickle of a single tear slipped across my cheek and onto her shoulder. She kissed my eyes and that opened the sluice holding back the flood. I wept for the life I was rejecting and leaving behind. I wept for all the hopes and aspirations of my youth that now seemed lost forever. I wept for the realization that these long cherished hopes were not worth hanging on to anyway. I felt my tears on her soft flesh. Then we laughed. We laughed and chatted and cried together. Then as the first light of a new day came to awaken the room we united our bodies.

For a day and a half we continued chatting, laughing, crying and making love on every conceivable opportunity until, exhausted but far from depleted, we found ourselves looking through the morning mist across the estuary to Little Island as the ferry carefully entered Cork harbour. Then she told me a little more about her Order.

It was a pagan sect, loosely structured and unattached to any organisation. Its members were spread throughout Ireland crossing all social, class and religious boundaries. All the women were called 'nuns' for historical reasons, vows were not taken because they acknowledged that people changed with passing time and therefore making a vow or promise was not natural. 'How can I be expected to make a promise on behalf of the stranger I will become next year, or in twenty years' time?' she asked, 'It's a crazy thing to do.'

This logic seemed too convenient to me but I kept quiet because it suited me. Morality seems contingent on circumstances, doesn't it, Sam!

I asked her about training, how she had joined, meetings and rules, but she simply said they were 'flexible' as I'd soon see for myself.

We collected her car from a garage then drove north through the vivid green countryside of central Ireland passing through towns with magical names like Cahir, Birr and Roscrea, which seemed to be symbols of the strange new world I was entering.

She lived in the valley of the Boyne in the county of Meath and it was raining when we arrived a few hours' later. The light was still good enough for me to see she had a fairly large cottage, set on its own in a few acres of land left largely to nature with wild flowers everywhere, plenty of nettles and a small copse of sessile oaks. She kept a small kitchen garden for herbs, a couple of shrubs and more wild flowers. The river meandered down the valley a few miles away.

The unreality of the life I had entered became submerged beneath waves of passion and love as she gently led me deeper and deeper into their wonders. For two weeks we lived like honeymooners, totally engrossed with each other. Everything we did together manifested our love, and everywhere we went seemed to become a secret place, which only we could enter. A short walk from her cottage is Tara, the ancient capital of Ireland where the old kings lived and administered the entire country. All that remains of this 'Athens of Ireland' is a complex series of grassy mounds and dykes surrounding a hilltop. It is difficult to imagine today that this place was once the gaudy, bustling, probably corrupt centre of a flourishing kingdom – especially with an incongruous statue of St Patrick staring with stony disapproval at the unholy place where pagans had worshipped before he came to 'save' them.

She took me there for the first time about dusk on the second day after our arrival. The sky was heavy and dark, a chilly northerly breeze slapped the light rain against our faces and down our necks. 'Are you sure you want to go up there in this?'

This silly question was a relic of my previous life with weather forecasts and umbrellas.

We reached the top after half an hour but there was little to see other than sullen mounds of damp grass. We came to a small hollow. Without warning she slipped her coat off and, laying it on the grass, told me to do the same with mine. Then kicking off her wellies she slipped her dress over her head and lay down on our coats completely naked; without a word she reached out her arms to me.

I still had all my old inhibitions but grudgingly lowered my trousers to my knees and feeling utterly stupid and very cold knelt down beside her, but she giggled and said simply, 'Everything off.'

Completely naked but for my socks, I lay on top of her feeling abjectly miserable, ridiculous and as sexually dynamic as a lettuce. 'What now?' I asked.

'Wait and see,' she said.

I told her that I wasn't capable of doing anything other than shiver, but she replied that it didn't matter. She said she hadn't brought me there for us to make love. We had come to offer our bodies to the male and female spirits of the hill.

'Give yourself to them,' she said. 'Relax and let go.'

I wasn't convinced but eventually managed to give myself to the situation. I don't know how long we lay there, a few minutes or an hour, but after a while I no longer felt cold, wet and self-conscious, but unbelievably strong, complete and centred. I felt as if I was covered in hair and was appalled to hear myself grunting like a pig yet, inside her, making love sweetly and profoundly.

We climaxed together and the whole land seemed to glow with an inner radiance so powerful that I felt dizzy and couldn't discern where she and I ended and the land began. For a timeless moment we basked in the glow and I knew I belonged here.

It is impossible to pull wringing wet cotton clothing over soaked bodies in the rain, so clad only in raincoats and with a soggy bundle of clothing under our arms, we scurried back towards the house, giggling like lunatics.

The black night had silently crept up on us, it was raining quite heavily and soon we were picking our way gingerly through the bushes in the general direction of a distant light. Close by, an owl seemed to be celebrating our idiocy, in the shrouds covering the trees. I shook my head as if to clear my thoughts and asked her what had happened. She told me that our bodies and our seed had been used to fertilize and re-empower the land. An hour earlier I would have thought this to be fanciful nonsense, but now I believed her without a querulous thought.

So much more has happened since then that it's impossible for me to put things in any sequence. A couple of times I've felt guilty at having left everything behind me without trace, and suggested to her that I should contact the school and friends to tell them what had happened. She asked me why I needed to do this and what difference it would make if I didn't.

She has visitors from time to time; two in particular came quite frequently. One is a strange young man calling himself Mongan. He is stockily built, well above medium height with thick wrists and receding black hair. He looks furtive, as if he's being hunted, and talks in short unfinished sentences, but has an intensity bordering on brooding that suggests a lot going on under the surface. He didn't seem to like me from the start, which I don't understand; but when I told Dana that I should have it out with him she said it wouldn't help because his 'problem' had nothing to do with me. I asked her what the problem was and all she would say was it wasn't my concern so, against my better judgement, I've kept quiet so far. I suspect that he and Dana were once lovers. They have been singing together in the same folk group for five years. He has a strong voice and I must admit that he's a gifted musician; he can make a tin whistle sound like a Stradivarius.

No-one enquires or talks about anyone else's past here but I suspect Bran was a professional man – solicitor or civil servant are my best guesses. He told me that he had a serious car accident, which left him with one leg a little shorter than the other and the loss of grip in his left hand, so he retired and moved to Ireland where he eventually built up a flourishing alternative healing practice treating exclusively with water. Dousing, drinking and the use of cold compresses are his main methods. Dana says he's the only person she trusts when she is ill, which seems to be never. He is about my age, tall, lithe and utterly engaging; we became close friends from the start. He swims in the river most days, winter and summer.

I was soon able to get my finances in order so I couldn't be traced through accounts, so inexorably the bridges connecting my past and present life are being burned. Soon all possible connections with my former life will be severed forever. This seems to be what I want, Sam, but it's also threatening and there are still moments when I wonder if I'm doing the right thing. These moments are getting fewer – I don't think I'll be going back now.

Well that's about everything my friend. The weeks have flown and I've met lots of other people, many who speak to each other in Gaelic; also a so-called Shaman. This is a sort of Irish witch doctor who says he makes journeys into other worlds where he claims to meet creatures from the subconscious. I've been to gigs, drunk Guinness and met unhappy, hopeful people who Dana is attempting to heal with touch and prayer. From what people tell me she is very effective. Generally I like what I've seen and everyone I've met – except Mongan. I wonder what's really troubling him!

I closed the book and reached for my coffee. It had gone cold, so I slumped back into the chair, staring at the predicament confronting Ticker. Abruptly the phone jolted me back into the present.

Ruth. It must be her. I hurled the receiver to my ear.

'Hi.'

'David, I can't wait till Wednesday. I'm coming down tonight. Can I see you tomorrow morning?'

'Alright Bill,' I said gloomily.

CHAPTER 17

Deceit Destroys

JENKINS SLOUCHED CROUCH-BACKED against the Welsh monsoon, a stylish but probably semi-porous designer raincoat draped over his head with the arms hanging empty and limp, his face hidden in the shadow beneath the collar and his trousers sodden. I quickly ushered the dripping shape into the hall, alert to any clue I could glean about his mood. He paused for a moment inside the open door and thunderously shook the coat dry before looking around for somewhere to hang it. I took it from him and he mumbled a half-hearted apology for arriving early. He seemed preoccupied but I detected no hostility towards me, so I offered him breakfast and a change of trousers.

While I made poached eggs, toast and coffee he poured out his lament. Ruth had been behaving strangely recently. He had eventually forced her to admit that she had a lover who lived in Wales. If he believed it was me, he seemed to be very casual about it, and my anxiety was soon allayed when he said he suspected some 'jock' at the gym club and even asked me to find out who it was for him. I suggested employing a private detective but he wanted total discretion, with no whisper of scandal or divorce to jeopardize his chances of a bishopric.

'What about other places, like the golf club or even the cathedral?' I asked.

'I don't think so,' he said thoughtfully. 'The gym is the only place I don't go with her.'

'I can't get too involved.' I was trying to wriggle off his hook.

145

'I don't want to get dragged into a domestic between you and Ruth.'

'Just a few discreet enquiries,' he pleaded. 'It's not asking a lot. I know you can do it.'

'OK, I'll ask around,' I promised grudgingly, although I'd never been to the gym club and hadn't lived here long enough to go around asking 'discrete' questions of such a sensitive nature.

'Today?'

'If you insist.' I had already started thinking up a 'cold collation' of lies for him and even saw the funny side of the situation.

'I'll owe you,' he said, with almost pathetic exaggerated sincerity.

The telephone started to ring and I reached for the kitchen wall phone.

'Hallo, David Tanner.'

'David, my dear, thank heavens I've found you.' It was Ruth.

'Oh, h-hallo Mary.' I was flummoxed. 'Fancy hearing from you!' Jenkins appeared to be concentrating on his eggs but from the angle of his head I knew he was listening intently to my call.

'Who's Mary? This is Ruth,' she said sharply. 'I've got to see you.'

'OK that will be fine,' I said with a metal edge to my voice. 'But I'm a bit busy at the moment, can I call you back?'

'Don't you even want to know what it's about?' she demanded reproachfully.

'I think I already know, but it's difficult to talk at the moment.'

Jenkins was now making no pretence at disinterest, and was watching me with quizzical eyes over the coffee cup.

'Just give me a minute please David, I think the cat may be out of the bag.'

'Oh. What cat?'

'I think Bill knows about us.'

Jenkins smiled at me, drained the cup and hiccoughed.

'I don't think so,' I said.

'Well I do,' she replied indignantly. 'And I think he may be on his way to have it out with you at this very moment.'

'I'm sure you're wrong Ru... er... m'dear.'

Jenkins smiled at me and gave me a thumbs-up whispering, 'Your life's even more complicated than mine, old friend.'

'You sound strange, David. Is something wrong?' she asked.

'No, everything's fine, it's just that there's an old friend here who's come to see me on an important matter and...'

'Is it as important as this, David?'

'Equally, I believe.'

'Well all I can say is that you've got problems, mister. I'll leave you to her,' she snapped. 'I'm sorry to have bothered you.'

'Don't hang up,' I pleaded. 'It's not another woman but an old school friend. He has something very important to talk to me about and I really can't speak to you now. Please understand.'

'Oh my God.' Ruth's limp voice was barely audible. 'Bill's there already, isn't he?'

'Yes, that's right, Mary.'

Jenkins, now unashamedly enjoying my discomfort, put two thumbs up this time.

'Is everything alright?' she whispered anxiously.

'Perfectly. You don't have to worry about anything, everything will be fine. I'll call you back after he leaves.'

Jenkins handed me a memo pad and I wrote down his own telephone number as dictated by his wife, taking great care to ensure that he didn't see it.

'I hope I'm not putting a damper on your love life, young man.'

'Not at all,' I smiled. 'You spice it up, if anything.'

He left burping, and emotionally calmer. He refused to tell me what he would do when I'd discovered the phantom lover, but he had something I was sure I wouldn't like in mind. He scurried back through the downpour to his car in his sodden raincoat, awkwardly climbed favouring his bad hip and quickly drove off throwing me a brief wave as he passed. I studied his car disappearing over every inch of the drive to the gate to make certain he'd gone, then called Ruth back.

I called a dozen times during the next four hours, without a reply. Then Jenkins called me. I recited my pre-prepared make-believe story which I hoped would divert his suspicions away from Wales. I told him I'd made some phone calls and was convinced of the impossibility of his wife having an affair with anyone at the gym. I lied my soul into darkness, telling him that she went on women-only nights; that I knew a woman who went on the same night and saw her in and out, and that the only 'jock' was a caretaker in his sixties, arthritic and kept on a four-inch leash by his dragon-slayer wife. I told him it couldn't possibly be anyone down here but he remained unconvinced, although he agreed to speak to Ruth again. I was desperate to know where she was, but he finished the call with thanks and without mentioning her again.

I looked into the dead phone, wondering where to go from here. Wary I most certainly was, rather ashamed of my blatant lying but also exhilarated by the prospect of swimming out of my depth once again. It was an irresistible, awful situation.

*

After Ruth had spoken to me, her mind had been in turmoil. She had to get away from the house and incessant callers, so she spent most of the day walking and ruminating alone in the Malvern Hills. By early afternoon she had calmed, and her usual confidence had returned, so she did some shopping and returned home.

Her husband met her as she came in, greeting her with, 'Who is he Ruth? Where does he live? You must tell me.'

'Why such a fuss, Bill? Nothing has happened. You've never made such a to-do before.'

'The other times you just blatantly played around. This time you're secretive and serious.'

'How can you say that, Bill?'

'Aren't I right?' She remained silent.

'Would you leave me and go to live with him?'

'We haven't spoken about it. For heaven's sake Bill believe me, I've met a guy I like, like a lot but nothing has happened and we've given not a thought to any future between us or even meeting again.'

'But this could change as you have changed.'

'Bill, this is all hypothetical. Nothing has happened, we've made no plans and are unlikely to. Why can't you get it into your overheated head.'

'That's what you say.'

'Tch,' she growled, stomping past him. 'Enough. Do I get you some food?'

Jenkins sighed heavily. 'What a mess. Just assure me it is not anyone from around here.'

'It's no-one from around here for the bishop to find out about, if that's what worrying you.'

The interrogation drifted on in circles with mixed recrimination and acceptance, bullying and pleading until she became so confused and angry that she confirmed in desperation she had met the guy on one of their visits to Wales. 'We went out once together. We said goodnight...'

She was stopped in mid lie when Bill seemed to see a light. He abruptly slapped his forehead as if a holy vision had appeared to him. 'Hallelujah, I've been so stupid. How could I have been so blind?'

He stomped upstairs to his study, slamming the door behind him and locking it. He immediately picked up the telephone. Ruth ran out of the door into the fading light to find some breathable air.

She returned half an hour later; Bill was still in his study. Curiosity overcame scruples so she, as lightly as a bird alighting on a reed, lifted the kitchen extension, praying the soft click wouldn't be noticed, covered the mouthpiece and listened.

'So there's absolutely no doubt about it?' Jenkins was talking.

'None,' came a terse reply.

'Can you get me copies of the Garda photographs and fingerprints?'

'It'll take a few days.'

'And newspaper cuttings?'

'No problem. I can send those off to you tomorrow.'

'Do I need to wait for the Garda records before going to our police?'

'Not necessary. The cuttings will be enough. They'll hold him on them.'

'So, all I need to do is present the cuttings to our police and that will be enough for them to hold him until the Garda come to collect him?'

'That's what I said. He *is* a wanted man and will be on their lists.'

'I want the cuttings tonight. Can you get them to me?'

'It's late, but possible.'

'Do it then, Mr Roberts. Will you be bringing them?'

'No. I know a man in Birmingham. I could fax the stuff to him and if he's in, he could bring it straight over.'

'OK, Mr Roberts, do that then.'

'It would be less complicated if you paid him cash, and I'll bill you separately for the other work I've done over the last couple of months.'

'How much?'

'£250.'

'Heavens, that's a lot.'

'Not if you want it tonight.'

Jenkins paused for a moment, 'No, get it here before ten o'clock and I'll have the money ready.'

'That's tight. Can't promise, so I'll get on with it now.'

'I won't keep you any longer… thank you Mr Roberts… very much.'

The three receivers were replaced, and their handlers confronted their own thoughts and problems. Ruth immediately concluded that her husband had been looking into my past, discovered something shady I had been involved with in Ireland, and the Garda were after me. It seemed obvious to her that he was going to get me out of his way because he'd worked out I was her lover. Mr Roberts had mentioned 'other work' and she wondered what that could be, could he even have been watching her, too? She shuddered at the thought, but had no time for such indulgences; she had to warn me, but how? She couldn't call from home with her husband there, and he'd borrowed her mobile phone, so she decided to slip out again and call me from a public call box.

*

Her first attempt got the engaged tone, with the same result from another call box, before she turned onto the motorway leading to Wales. Soon her little Golf was pushing up to 100mph. She stopped three more times; at a service station near Ross, in Abergavenny, and finally at the Pont Abraham services. Each time there was no reply and between each attempt she was drawn deeper and deeper into the glowering twilight of the menacing western land, with her foot holding the accelerator flat down.

On hearing the door tones I thought Bill had returned but his wife, anxious and frantic, stood before me. She fell into my arms, while I glanced furtively through the open door for her irate husband.

'Is Bill with you?' She shook her head. Relieved, I took her face tenderly in my hands and looked deeply into her dear troubled eyes. All the confusion and uncertainty that had flirted in and out of my mind during the day dissolved on seeing and holding her. Rapture replaced worry. 'Darling,' I said.

'David, we don't have much time, you're in terrible danger.' She tore herself out of my enthusiastic embrace. Her eyes were wide and wild with anxiety and adrenaline but I was too full of feeling and delight to see the threat. To me they merely demanded to be kissed.

'No,' she said. 'Be serious, the danger is real.'

'In danger? Yes, I know I am, and it's where I want to be,' I said, pulling her back towards me.

'Shhh, listen to me.'

'Alright, my love, but come in first.'

She walked briskly past me into the house and went straight into the kitchen where she turned to face me. She pushed me away as I attempted to hold her again.

'Listen to me. This is bad, David.'

She told me of the telephone conversation she had overheard, and that the police would probably be coming for me at any minute. She looked at her watch. It was 11.15. 'They could be on their way now. You've got to get away at once. Hurry.'

I tried to fit the contradictory pieces into place. 'Bill called me an hour ago,' I said slowly. 'He told me he knew who the guy is. It isn't me.'

'Not you?' She looked amazed. 'Who, then?'

'Verres.'

CHAPTER 18

Even Where
Love Persists

FOR THREE HOURS and a hundred and fifty breakneck miles, Ruth had been sustained by her crusade to save me from her husband's machinations. This physical and emotional outpouring, plus the breathtaking absurdity of discovering she had rushed all this way to rescue someone who didn't need rescuing, reduced the flimsy spine of her reserves to rubble. She slumped into my arms and we stood as one body while she wrestled with the enormity of her mistake. My thoughts were on a different course. What had started as yet another game of 'sex and ladders', as one lady in the past had described my relationship with her, had changed. The lust was still there but accompanied now by a growing sense of caring for the woman, caring quite deeply.

'Are you sure?' she asked, looking up at me with wide, earnest eyes.

'Completely.' I led her inside to a chair and knelt before her, cradling her thighs in my arms and telling her about her husband's visit and subsequent phone call.

'David,' she said when I'd finished, 'It's a travesty of how things are… his insatiable ambition is driving him crazy. As for Verres and me, it beggars belief.'

'Where does it leave us?' I asked, perhaps a little selfishly.

'Darling,' she said, 'What's more important at the moment is where does it leave Verres.'

A net seemed to be closing in around the man I had come to respect above all others. I wanted to tell Ruth who he was, and believed circumstances had changed sufficiently to justify breaking my promise to him, but resisted the temptation.

'Do you have any idea what he's done and why the police want him?' I asked.

'Not a clue,' she replied. 'But I do know it must have been something serious.'

'Are we sure he's really guilty of a crime?'

'Does it matter?' She jerked to her feet. 'Come on, we have to go and warn him.'

With a renewed surge of adrenaline she drove fast and well along the narrow twisting lanes. At first I watched the road in the headlights, then half-turned to study the woman I seemed to be falling in love with. I loved the passion of her concentration, the frugality of her hand movements, the shushing of her thighs brushing against each other as she changed gear and the decisiveness of her decisions. Above all I loved her intensity when, like now, she was on a mission and focused. Loving someone like this was a novel experience; I didn't feel in control of the situation but didn't care. I wanted her with an intensity that made me feel vulnerable and insecure, and the near certainty that I wasn't her first post-marital 'adventure' made no difference. It would be much later that I came to see that desiring was not the same as loving.

'Bill was quick off the mark.'

'What do you mean?' she asked, not taking her eyes from the road.

'The private detective,' I said. 'If he only decided Verres was your boyfriend this afternoon, this Roberts character must be a cross between Sherlock Holmes and Flash Gordon.'

'Two months ago,' she said calmly, 'Bill told me that he was concerned about allowing someone to rent the flat without knowing anything about him.' She briefly touched my knee as if to make sure I was still there. 'He said he felt that someone in his position should know who was living on his property. The letting agent's checks had been too superficial to satisfy him so he got this Roberts to check up on him.'

'And Roberts, you say, says he's found out that he's wanted by the Garda?'

'That's how it seems.'

'And you thought they were talking about me?' I laughed.

'What else could I think?'

We turned through the familiar gate and stopped outside Verres' door. A lighted window was wide open in the loft above the glowty. I slid out of my seat, leaving the door open, and ran around the car in the spitting rain.

'Why the rush, David?' I almost leapt out of my socks as Verres emerged from the shadow. 'I heard the urgency in your driving miles away. Good evening Ruth,' he said as she quietly left the car. 'This is a pleasant surprise.'

'Good evening, Mr Verres,' she said formally.

'I take it you've come to see me.' His voice seemed to laugh at us. 'Do I sense a crisis?'

'We haven't got much time, my friend,' I said importantly, putting a hand on his elbow. 'I think you're in danger...'

'Danger? You'd better come inside and tell me all about it,' he said calmly. 'A crisis is much more manageable in the light.' We followed him up the stairs to the flat, me with the impatient eagerness of a squirrel, Ruth with the quiet deliberation of a cat.

His calm made my sense of urgency more compelling but he

wouldn't be rushed. Finally after sitting us down, he said, 'Now tell me what's brought you here in such haste at this time of night.'

'The police have been told about something you did in Ireland,' I blurted. 'And they could be here at any time.'

He showed not a glimmer of a reaction. 'What was it I did in Ireland?' he asked, gliding away from the window.

'I don't know and it's not important right now. What is important is that you grab some of your things and get out of here immediately.' I don't know how it happened, but Ruth and I were now holding hands. 'You can come to my place, you should be safe there until things quieten down a bit.'

Ruth, who had been studying his face intently, inhaled sharply and I felt her hand and arm stiffen. 'What did you do in Ireland, Mr Verres? Did you do something illegal?' she asked.

He turned to look at her; his face was relaxed, and his arms hung loosely by his side. 'Some questions, Ruth, can be answered with a simple yes or no, but most need more complex answers. Could you answer yes or no if I asked you if you'd been a good mother?'

She didn't answer him but I felt her hand tighten, then relax in mine.

'Yes, I am wanted by the Garda,' he said simply. 'It's a long story.'

'Tell us later,' I interrupted. 'We've got to get you out of here before the authorities arrive.'

'How do you two know all this?' he asked with intimidating casualness.

'I told him,' interrupted Ruth, releasing my hand and stepping up to him. She was a head shorter than him but their eyes seemed to be on the same level as she told him, half apologetically, about Bill checking-up on him and of her listening to his telephone conversation with a private detective earlier in the evening.

'Roberts?' he asked.

'That's right. Do you know him?'

'I know of him.' He returned to the window, leant out and appeared to be listening to the wind again. Rain was blowing into the room and wetting the curtains and chilling the air, but he left it open.

'Anyway,' Ruth continued, 'Mr Roberts is sending someone to Bill tonight with newspaper cuttings of something you are supposed to have done in Ireland. Bill must have had them by now and has probably passed them on to the police. So you see Mr Verres, you have very little time.'

'The coffee's percolating,' said Verres, sniffing the aroma seeping in from the kitchen. 'Let's go and enjoy our final minutes here.' Dumbfounded or not, we meekly followed him out of the room and left it and the flapping curtains to the mercy of the wind and rain.

'I think we have plenty of time,' he said, drinking from a glass of French spring water while Ruth sipped from her mug, and I warmed my hands on mine. 'I've been expecting something like this to happen and am prepared, although it has come a little sooner than I would have liked.'

'What are you planning to do, Mr Verres?' Ruth asked.

'Later, Ruth,' I grunted. 'Can we get him to a safe place first?' I leant over the steaming mug and deeply inhaled the exotic aroma.

He ignored me and turned to Ruth, 'I can see you're torn, my dear. You're torn between the respectable clergyman's wife, the stalwart of countless diocesan committees, upholder of law and order and a free-willed, passionate, feeling woman. Which is the real Ruth?'

She replied instantly without giving the question a moment's thought, 'They're both me?'

'I'm not talking about roles, Ruth. I'm talking about your soul.

It's important to me that you decide which one is in command of your soul, Ruth. One of them knows who I am and trusts me instinctively, the other doesn't care.' He drained his glass and refilled it without taking his earnest gaze away from her eyes.

Ruth sipped her drink before answering.

'I care for you and I believe in you,' she said simply, without flinching from his invasive scrutiny. 'Although I have no idea who you are or what you've done, I care because David cares.' She raised the mug and drank without breaking eye contact. 'I trust David's judgement although I don't understand it.' Verres remained as impassive as a marble statue; only his eyes betrayed his concentration, more on her than her words.

'I think David is right,' she continued. 'You shouldn't loiter here. Bill seems to have the bit between his teeth and I don't know what he may do.'

'You subject yourself to David's judgement, Ruth,' he replied. 'But what is your judgement?'

'I'm totally for you,' she replied again without hesitation.

Verres nodded, then asked, 'Are you going to tell me the real reason Bill is doing this?' We looked at each other; Ruth blushed and looked past him into the wall.

'Can't it wait?' I asked.

'Of course,' he said evenly, still studying Ruth's averted face. 'What's important to me, my dear,' he said, touching her arm, 'is that you came out to help me. Will you please indulge me for a few more minutes?'

A tiny nod helped him to continue.

'Ruth?' his voice was hushed but insistent. 'Look at me. My appearance has changed but some things haven't changed. Look beneath my skin and my beard, do you see someone you once knew?' She looked perplexed. 'Feel with your instinct, my dear, don't think.'

She looked at him for a few moments then looked away,

confused. 'I'm sorry, I don't understand what you're asking me to do.'

'Ruth,' he said sternly. She looked up at him again. She seemed uncomfortable and had to do something so she climbed onto a high stool where she sat facing him. Their faces were now on the same level and he stood before her with a gentle expression on his well-worn face. 'I knew you when you lived in the house of Beautiful Maidens, Piety was your name,' he said.

'I'm sorry, Mr Verres, I don't know what you're talking about.' His expression changed to quizzical; I had to let him tell her in his own way, so remained silent.

'Who am I, Ruth?'

'Please Mr Verres, I don't like this game.'

'It's no game to me my dear; it's a matter of crucial importance. Go back to the house of Beautiful Maidens; don't think, remember.'

'Remember what?'

'Your intuition will help you.'

'I'm a clergyman's wife and obey rules and protocols. There's no place for intuition in my world.' She abruptly stopped and pursed her lips. 'Isn't the house of Beautiful Maidens in *Pilgrim's Progress*?'

'And Piety?' he asked.

'I think I remember that she lived in that house.' Ruth was getting more and more agitated, with her eyes darting about from wall, to Verres, to floor and back inevitably to Verres like frightened mice, but I dared not come to her rescue.

'Who called you Piety?' he demanded without pity.

She started to sob, then put her head in her hands while we stood by, but for less than a minute. She abruptly stopped, dried her face with a clean tea towel, blew her nose in it, looked directly at Verres and said with a smile, 'You could have made it easier for me, Dr Lloyd.'

'Welcome home,' he said, taking her like a soft doe into his arms. 'Now I suppose you want an explanation,' he said, releasing her.

'I do, but it will have to wait. We need to whisk you away from here and you will need time to get your things together,' she said, sniffing vigorously.

'I'll need ten seconds,' he laughed.

'Isn't it strange,' she said, 'I don't feel surprised or shocked or… it's like I've always known who you are.' She turned to face me, 'And you knew.' I shrugged guiltily. We shyly smiled at each other before walking back to Verres.

Verres simply softened his eyes, while I remained quietly in the background as they immersed themselves in their newfound intimacy.

CHAPTER 19

Rebirth of Hopes

V ERRES WAS TOO agonizingly casual for Ruth, so she took charge.

'Now then,' she asserted, 'What about your books and your clothes and things? Perhaps we should start being practical.'

'Nothing is irreplaceable,' he said. 'I've been a fugitive for a long time and know the routine.' He lumbered over to the window and scented the wind again, tilting his head with small subtle movements to catch the meanest elusive sound or smell. 'There's no immediate threat,' he announced, rejoining them by the door.

'We've time therefore to pack some of your stuff...'

'Everything I need is already packed Ruth, thank you. All I need to do is pick it up and go.'

'Go where?' she asked.

'Hunted animals always have bolt holes they can run to. I really have no problems and no urgency.'

He opened his arms like great enfolding wings and draped them around us, but she struggled free. 'Doct... can I still call you Verres?'

He placed his massive hands on her shoulders, kissed her gently on the forehead, then produced a square envelope from a pocket and handed it to her.

'All you want to know is on this disk... it accounts for my years in Ireland. David will tell you how I arrived there.'

He picked up his helmet. 'May I make one request?'

'Of course,' she said.

'Keep my identity to yourselves. I don't want anyone else to know who I am, especially Bill, for the time being.'

Picking up his bags, he left the room without another word. Neither of us spoke or moved but simply stood on the spot wondering what to do next. Even when his bike roared into life and moved away we listened mesmerized by the unreality of the situation until it had faded into the night and the spell was broken. I softly put both hands on her shoulders and gently stroked the outside of her arms, as much to reassure myself as her. 'Are you alright?' I asked quietly.

'I do believe I am, David,' she said carefully. 'When the dust settles I think I may be better than I've been for a long, long time.' She meditated for a few seconds, then added, with a puzzled look on her face, 'You know David, it's so strange, but I believe I knew all the time.'

I wanted to go across to Bill's study immediately to print Verres' disk, but Ruth suddenly became transformed from the shell-shocked woman who'd crawled into my house on a wave of emotion earlier that evening, to someone utterly at peace with herself and thinking with icy clarity. 'Once the police arrive, they'll trample over his remains with their muddy boots. I couldn't bear that.'

So we set to and removed everything that reminded us of him. Some books, odd items of clothing, including a colourful sweater I'd coveted although it was miles too big for me, and two wall posters; one showed a wolf standing in a blizzard looking directly at the camera with deadly, steady, stone-grey eyes. Beneath it were the words, 'In Wildness is the Preservation of the World'. The other was a painting of a Red Indian standing in front of a mountain and the words, 'Man and the Land give strength to each other.'

Eventually she looked around, satisfied. 'Now we can look at this disk.'

As we crossed the drive to the house I felt a chill in the night air and pulled on his voluminous sweater, much to Ruth's amusement. 'You look like a pantomime horse in that thing,' she laughed. 'Which way is front?'

We put Verres' other things into a cupboard, which she locked; then went upstairs to the study where she set up the computer to print the disk's contents. Then she confronted me.

'Now, my lad, come and tell me all you know.'

As the printer began to expose the last twenty-five years of Verres' life, I sank into a well-worn, calf-leather-covered swivel chair. She sat behind the desk like a company director, gave me a look which I read as 'I want to know everything' and said, 'Shoot.'

I told her every detail of Ticker's letter to Sam. Every word was indelibly printed in my brain so they flowed accurately and fluently in quick time. Not once did she interrupt, and, or strangely for her, ask a single question although I had to run through it all a second time for her. When I'd finally finished, her face was thoughtful, with a little smile twitching at her lips; I asked her what she was thinking.

She took a few moments to gather her thoughts before answering, 'I'm glad he decided to go with Dana. It would have been terrible for him if he hadn't and returned to us.'

'So you approve?' I asked, mightily relieved.

'It's not a matter of approving or disapproving, my dear dumb man. It was simply *right*.' She rose from her chair, came over and pecked me on the cheek. 'Now, are you ready to find out what happened next?'

'OK.'

'I need a hug first if you can crawl out from under that woollen haystack.'

We sat on the floor face to face with our legs stretched out on either side and our arms wrapped around each other. We didn't sleep or speak or watch the time but simply sat in each other's auras, basking in nurturing energy. Gradually the balance between us was restored.

'Are you ready to read this?' she asked, getting up and collecting the printouts.

Ruth and David,
When you read this you will already know what happened to me after I left you in Wales and of my first months in Ireland. This is an account of the next 24 years.

During the first six months I had been like a baby, trying to make sense of the strange world I had entered. There were times when I had doubts and wanted to return to my old life, but most of the time I was filled with a spirit of adventure, discovery and a blind, all-consuming love for Dana.

'Healing' was the core of her life, but she also sang in a popular folk group. She had a pleasant, light soprano voice, which combined beautifully with a rasping bass, an enthusiastic tenor who had more gusto than polish, and an assortment of ethnic whistles and flutes. It sounded to my non-musical ear that they all sang half a note out of tune, however the end result was a compelling cocktail of harmonies and melodies.

Mongan was the bass. He liked to remain inconspicuous and never sought the limelight, but without his background growl the lighter voices would have sounded thin, their melodies vague, and they would not have had a springboard to make their wild flights. The tenor was a whimsical Irish dreamer called Sean who lived in the clouds alongside his voice, and seemed untouched by any of the practical stresses of life on earth, such as musicianship. The two men played a variety of unlikely looking country instruments, ranging from a one-string fiddle to a hollowed out stick with holes in it, which seemed perfect for their voices and their barbaric Celtic music.

Shortly after I wrote my letter to Sam, they started rehearsing daily in Sean's home for a new season, so I saw little of Dana during the day. A month later they were on the road and I saw even less of her.

I went to a couple of their shows but felt out of place in the near hysterical atmosphere they generated, and wondered how she could keep so detached from the hyperactivity that surrounded her. She came home whenever she could, to see me and a few patients, but was never able to stay for more than three or four days. Each time she was smiling and calm and said that she didn't even notice the mayhem because she lived in the music where nothing could touch her.

During her early absences I started to become increasingly listless and entertained deep doubts about the direction my life was taking. The bliss I thought I had been following seemed to have been replaced by monotony, dark moods, lack of direction and worst of all, guilt! One day I expressed these concerns to Bran, a good friend of Dana who became a dear friend of mine. He told me that he had gone through a similar crisis after moving to Ireland following his car accident, but had been turned-around when someone introduced him to 'water'. 'Water helped me to recover and gave me a reason for being here,' he said, adding 'I may have stumbled on an answer to your problems. No, not water, but something that flows just the same: words.'

Next day he rang and asked me to drive into Dublin and meet a writer friend of his. The writer, Frank, was an ex-teacher who made a living writing magazine articles, children's books and sub-editing an Irish 'glossy' magazine. His abiding passion was to write the definitive book of Irish myths and legends, but wasn't making much progress as he didn't have the time or the academic background to carry out the considerable research needed for such a tome. To cut a long story short, I agreed to do the research for him. He couldn't afford to pay me, but that wasn't important because I had found a direction. The following week we started a ten-year liaison that never produced the book but which brought us both great pleasure, and to me a justification for being brought to Ireland.

When I look back it is now obvious that this was the 'bliss' I was meant to follow and not a cozy idyll with Dana – that was merely the carrot.

In my letter to Sam I mentioned that for the first time in my life I had experienced feelings of jealousy and possessiveness concerning Dana. These wretched feelings became even more powerful during her absences during the first years; in addition to their painful and destructive natures, I was very disappointed with myself for entertaining such petty emotions at all. Dana was quite open about the way she related to people who needed healing. She believed she had the gift of 'opening people to their possibilities' and had to use this gift. Sexual contact, with both men and women, was the way she occasionally did it. She told me that she used sex merely as a 'tool', as a short cut to the souls of wounded people and it shouldn't affect what *we* had. I believed her and understood her reasoning, yet it still brought me pain and dark broodings. It was a long time and a lot of dark brooked before the incoming tide of negativity turned and ebbed out of my heart for ever.

As the year moved on, I saw more and more of Bran and Frank, and started hunting the libraries and colleges around Dublin in search of the Irish myths. I enjoyed Bran's company and we often sought each other out simply to 'be' with each other, often in silence. Despite slowness resulting from his accident, we often went for country walks together and even played badminton occasionally. I never got as close to Frank, who was vague, disorganized and utterly impracticable, but his enthusiasm for the book was contagious and before very long I too had caught the 'bug'.

I became mesmerized by the shimmering 'Otherworlds' of Celtic myth, and of travellers like Finn MacCool who could slip effortlessly through the veiled portal from the visible to the unseen. I wanted to know who these people were and the relevance of their stories to the present. I wanted to know more about the seers and the Shamans, like Merlin, who travelled in a different way to Finn, but the magic of their journeys was just as monumental. They could travel in time, across the dimensions of reality and into the dark depths of their own unconscious, yet physically remain in the same place in their 'real' world. They often learnt sorcery and shape shifting, where they could change their physical forms to plants and animals at will.

As I sank deeper and deeper into the exploits of the enchanted, dream-like Celtic world, it became evermore real to me. I had but to close my eyes to experience what it was like to sail with Brendan (a Celtic Sinbad) in search of the 'land of promise', and see the miraculous creatures he met on his fabulous voyages.

The deities from which Bran and Dana had taken their names appeared in many of the stories. They were prominent powers for bringing fertility and healing to the world and I could see how my two friends absorbed their qualities by using the same name. It seemed that, in many ways, they had become them.

From time to time they would ask me if I had thought of changing my name. Almost everyone who moved in their circle had done so. It helped to cut them away from their past and to fit the new personalities they had become. I always said I hadn't because I liked Tommy, the name everyone called me; anyway, I hadn't come across a character in the myths I truly identified with.

As seasons slipped by, I travelled around Ireland, visiting places where some of these wondrous events of Celtic mythology had taken place. My first stop was at a pair of hills in County Kerry called Dá Chich Anann which means the Breasts of Anu. Anu was one of the mother Goddess' names. I sat there one bright autumn evening just before sunset, trying in my imagination to make the years roll back to the time when the myth was born. I was singularly unsuccessful and felt disappointed not to be able to enter the magic world as the others appeared to. As I walked back to my car, it dawned on me that for two hours I had been thinking only of Dana and for the first time since I'd met her, my thoughts were sweet, not accompanied by the bitter sting of jealousy.

That was my first experience of the mysterious way magical places work on people in the modern world; the dark thoughts never returned. This was only the start, and many times since, the power of magic places has redirected my self-concept.

After visiting eight or ten different locations, I noticed that they had something in common; they all pointed directly or indirectly back to Tara. Dana's cottage seemed to be at the hub of pre-historic Ireland. Its significance went back thousands of years, to times before records were written down, to the times when the myths we hear about today actually took place.

After a year, I had exhausted everything available in English but knew there was more to find. Much of what I had been reading was in translation and therefore polluted. I redirected my energies to learning these ancient Celtic languages.

Languages come easily to me, but it took me two years of single-minded study before I become a fluent enough speaker and reader to be able to read the stories and discuss them in the original language; but I was only halfway down the road. I had learnt contemporary Gaelic and Welsh; next I needed to learn the older forms that were used when the stories of the oral tradition had been first written down. I settled down to learn the ancient forms. Irish Gaelic proved to be impossible, but Middle Ages Welsh, which the earliest bards used, had Latin constructions and was relatively easy to master.

I'm telling you all this in detail because it was the path I trod to find a book that brought about yet another monumental change in my life. The book is called *Llyfr Coch Hergest*, The Red Book of Hergest.

I had read an English translation at university, but reading it the way it was written down over six hundred years ago, in the language it had been handed down in for a thousand years or more before that, revealed the stories in an entirely new light. The characters lived and breathed, their deeds were more vivid and their emotions more personal. They became real characters who I got to know as well as I knew Dana, Bran and Frank. Of all the characters, I rediscovered the way one stood out above the others in his zest for life, his raw animal energy and power and in the way he affected friend and foe alike. He was an old 'friend' from my schoolmastering days, the boar, Twrch Trwyth.

'Do you remember Twrch Trwyth?' I asked, noticing for the first time that Ruth was wearing reading glasses. 'Should I?' She put the papers down, slipped off the spectacles and stretched. 'Let's have a break, there's a lot to take in.'

'Yes, you should,' I said, moving to the divan. 'Come over here.'

She came over to me and nestled into the *cwtch* I created for her.

'Comfy?'

'Mmmm,' she hummed, 'Now tell me, Mr Clever Clogs, who is Turk Truith? Have I said it right?'

I reminded her about the first time the boar had entered our lives on the cliffs with the sea gulls and small boats and Ticker, but her memory of that distant day had faded; so I told her all I could remember of our journey across Pembrokeshire with

Ticker and the story he told us of the boar. I don't know when she fell asleep, but soon after my eyelids grew heavy and closed too. We must have looked like the babes in the wood, sleeping contentedly in each other's arms without a care in the world, blissfully unaware of the gingerbread house and the witch who was stealthily creeping towards us through the shadowy trees with a cage in her hands.

CHAPTER 20

Unchain the Hawk and Lion

T YRES SQUEALED, A car door slammed and headlights swept across the ceiling. We leapt out of our skins, our bodies aware of danger before our stumbling minds. We heard many feet running on the gravel drive, someone was banging on a door, and strained voices shouted a confusion of commands and directions.

Ruth reacted first and seemed to hurdle the desk, gather up the scattered pages of Verres' narrative, switch off the computer and printer and glance out of the window in one coordinated sequence. I was slower, but managed to slip the precious disk into my pocket, straighten the cushions, fight my way into my recently acquired jumper, pick up Ruth's shoes and hand them to her as we tumbled onto the landing, giggling with a release of near hysterical nervous energy.

Downstairs the front door opened. 'Ruth!' Jenkins was going from room to room, calling her name.

'Quick, into the bathroom.' I didn't need to be told twice. 'Lock the door,' she hissed from the top of the stairs.

'Ruth.' I heard the bottom stair creak beneath his tread.

'What's all this, Bill?' Ruth's voice sounded cold and imperious. I imagined her descending the stairs like a queen, icy, disdainful and armed with indignation.

I looked out of the bathroom window. The drainpipe was out of reach and I wasn't going to risk a fifteen-foot drop onto uneven ground. Clearly there was no escape that way so, with satisfying presence of mind, I flushed the lavatory, counted up to twenty slowly, then ambled out onto the landing crooning 'Strangers in the night, exchanging glances' as my modest tribute to Sinatra. The couple stood facing each other at the bottom of the stairs in the middle of icy hostility which my timely entrance melted it into incredulity.

'So it was you making all the racket,' I joked, descending the stairs with as much nonchalance as I could compel my trembling body to show. 'I thought the last invasion was being re-enacted.'

Two surprised faces followed my magisterial progress all the way to the bottom of the stairs.

'Good God! What are you doing here, David?' he asked with more disbelief than welcome in his voice.

'I'm the house detective,' I said, giving him a knowing look. He immediately understood my intended meaning and allowed himself a full smile. 'But seriously,' I said, keeping his eyes wedged on mine, 'I had an invitation to Verres' farewell do. For a reason best known to himself he suddenly decided to leave, and wanted to say goodbye to Ruth and me. My car is laid-up so she came round for me.' Jenkins nodded his understanding, held out his hand which I grabbed and shook heartily.

'Who are those men?' Ruth asked indignantly, walking to the open door. I whispered to Jenkins, 'He's gone for good and there was *nothing* going on between him and Ruth. That's gospel!'

'Speak to you later,' he whispered; then in a louder voice, 'Well it's good to see you again. Thank you for coming over and looking after Ruth. I was worried about her.' Ruth looked around at his back and tossed her head contemptuously.

'What's that policeman doing there?' she exclaimed

indignantly from the door. 'And who are those men coming out of the flat?'

We went to the door and saw a police car with a uniformed constable standing beside it and Jenkins' BMW next to Ruth's Golf. The door to the flat's stairs was open, and four grim-faced men stood talking by it.

Jenkins, now more relaxed, led us outside. A second, uniformed constable and two others, who I assumed were plain-clothes policemen, meandered slowly across the drive talking intently while a tall, academic-looking man with grey hair stood thoughtfully in the flat doorway, one hand in his jacket pocket, studying a deep depression in the gravel that Verres' motorcycle tyres must have made.

Ruth and Jenkins marched across towards them, while I ambled along in their slipstream trying to look like a tourist.

'Chief inspector,' Jenkins called in the 'keep your distance – men at prayer' voice cultivated by clergymen, 'I'd like you to meet my wife. Darling, this is Chief Inspector Williams.'

'Pleased to meet you, Mrs Jenkins,' said the policeman pleasantly.

He was barely an inch taller than Ruth, needed a haircut, and wore a crumpled suit, dirty raincoat and the remains of an ancient meal on his tie.

'And my friend, Mr Tanner.' We shook hands.

'Are you local, sir?' he asked, looking at me as if I was a Martian.

'I live nearby, chief inspector,' I said, adding with guilty lack of necessity, 'We were all at school together.'

'At school together,' repeated Williams, as if it were the crime of the century. 'And this is Detective Sergeant Blower.' Jenkins nodded towards the other plain-clothes policeman.

'Morning all.' Blower casually raised a muscular hand. He didn't join our circle but seemed to maintain a languid interest in our conversation. I was more impressed with him than his superior, despite the stud in his ear. He was tall and strongly built, perhaps getting a bit podgy, but he looked intelligent and altogether too relaxed. The designer pigskin coat over a tan polo-neck shirt, well-cut Levis and trainers didn't fit my image of a policeman, nor did his cheery grin and disarming body language.

'And this is Commissioner Stoker from Ireland.' Williams turned respectfully towards the distinguished grey-haired man who stepped forward confidently and shook our hands in turn. He walked with a slight limp, but his grip was firm and his misty eyes warm, humorous and reassuring. It was difficult not to trust him instinctively, but instinct warned me not to.

'Good morning to you Mrs Jenkins. Please excuse us for descending on you so unexpectedly.' He spoke with a watered-down Irish lilt. 'It's a pleasure to meet you both.'

'What on earth are you all doing here at this ungodly hour?' Ruth asked, turning to Williams using the 'speaking to imbeciles' voice she had developed to keep overeager parishioners at bay. 'It all seems so terribly... zealous.'

Williams looked puzzled and scratched his head. 'We would like to speak to Mr Verres,' he said.

Ruth told him that he had left hours ago and she didn't know where he had gone.

'You have a lovely place here,' Stoker said to Ruth. 'This looks great walking country. Is that what brought you to live down here?'

'Mr Stoker, sir,' Williams called, 'Can I pick your brains?' Stoker excused himself before walking over, leaving the three of us standing in limbo. Jenkins cleared his throat, shuffled his feet and cleared his throat again. Ruth glared at the huddle of policemen while I studied the roof architecture.

After a brief powwow Williams came back to us. 'I think we'll need to be here most of the morning, sir,' he said deferentially to Jenkins. 'I hope that will be alright.'

Jenkins looked uncomfortable. 'Is that really necessary? The bird's flown and I'm sure he won't be coming back.'

'Flown?' Ruth seemed needlessly defensive and I knew it was not unnoticed by the policemen despite the amiable, laid-back front they presented.

Williams ignored the question. 'Possibly, sir.' He ransacked his raincoat pockets looking for something urgently. 'But procedures have to be followed.' Turning to me, sniffing, he said, 'You won't be leaving just yet will you, sir?'

'I have things to do, Mr Williams. Why?'

'We'll need a statement before you go, sir.'

'What about?'

'Why, Mr Verres, sir.'

'But… is it really necessary…' I was trying to bluster my way out of the action like a man who wanted to know nothing but really knew everything.

'It's just a formality. Ah… Ah…' He pulled a filthy handkerchief out of his sleeve, 'atishoo!'

*

The morning sun climbed higher in the clear sky, warming the land and raising ghostly veils of evaporating water from the trees in the valley while we waited for the tediously methodical policemen to interview us. There was no food in the house to make breakfast, but Ruth supplied the garrulously grateful constables with milk-less tea and stale biscuits.

Williams and Blower flitted about with aimless inconsequence, going through whatever procedures they felt necessary without any evident urgency or direction, while the Irishman spent the whole morning in the flat reading some of the books Verres had left behind. He read standing up, leaning against a window frame with one hand in his jacket pocket, the languid posture of an academic trying to look relaxed. Every so often Blower would go up to speak with him, then come trotting down the stairs to report back to Williams.

It was difficult to gauge Jenkins' reaction to events. He excused himself and retired to his study after asking me to pop in and see him before I left. Everyone seemed to be relaxed and the atmosphere was anticlimactic, almost holiday-like, although Ruth and I were still as anxious as rabbits. At the first opportunity to be alone, we slunk into the kitchen on the pretext of making another drink for the invaders.

Ruth shook her head slowly. 'It's not natural. Nothing seems to be happening. They're up to something, I'm sure.'

'I don't think they know anything,' I said, looking around conspiratorially. 'So let's keep them in ignorance.'

We hastily concocted a whispered story, keeping as close to the truth as possible. It seemed prudent not to admit knowing anything of Verres' past, either in Britain or Ireland. The explanation I had given Jenkins for my presence in the house wasn't watertight, but we were stuck with it and hopefully no-one would think to delve into it, as their quarry was Verres, not us.

Suddenly I noticed Blower standing in the door. I didn't know how long he'd been there.

'Hi, can I come in?' he asked cheerily.

If he had overheard anything he didn't show it and brightly asked us if we were ready to make our statements.

*

'Well, that wasn't so bad.' I peered around the door to reassure myself that Blower had really left us. Our statements had been brief and empty; he showed no curiosity about glaring omissions, and the business was over in half an hour.

'What's he doing now?' asked Ruth, looking out into the yard.

Instinctively, like a pair of nosey neighbours behind lace curtains, we watched Blower cross the yard and speak briefly to Williams who nodded in the direction of the flat. He went in and a few moments later was talking to Stoker who appeared to think something was very funny. Still laughing, they glanced in our direction and we guiltily sidestepped out of sight.

Two forensic officers arrived mid morning and, after heaving themselves into white boiler suits, carried their bags into the flat with Williams in attendance. Fifteen minutes later one of them came over to take our fingerprints.

'For "elimination" purposes,' he reassured us. 'Because you were in the flat last night.'

We assumed that keeping us largely uninformed and throwing a tidbit of information occasionally was a deliberate tactic to make us edgy. If so, the tactic didn't work on me. With passing time I became more confident that they were not interested in us and had probably not even noticed our caution and reticence. Ruth suspected they were holding back on us and we should be on our guard, so she followed all their movements like an owl with instinctual suspicion.

With our statements made, she proposed that I should go home. 'I'm OK now. It might be diplomatic to ask Bill to drive you.'

'No, I need a good walk,' I replied. 'I haven't had enough exercise lately.'

I offered to smuggle the computer printout home with me, but she said it was hidden where no-one would find it and that it would be best if I left without it. 'I won't read any more without you. I promise.' She seemed more at ease and asked with a sweet smile, 'When will you get home?'

'In a couple of hours, I guess. Just one more thing,' I said, taking hold of her arm. 'Be careful of Stoker. I think he may have been connected in some way with Verres in Ireland.' She nodded. 'And,' I continued, 'a police commissioner is a pretty big fish. He's doing more than standing in a window reading. He's attempting to put two and two together and I'd bet he's good at maths.'

She looked serious again and turned to glance up at the flat where the Irishman stood in the window gazing at us. He waved and smiled. 'Yes, I think you're right,' she said, 'and he's altogether far too friendly.'

I went to bid the briefest of farewells to Jenkins, but he kept me for half an hour while I emphasised again that his wife had no lover in Wales. His gratitude was embarrassing. My intention to slip away inconspicuously was thwarted by Williams and Blower, who were loitering near their car.

'Are you going?' Blower asked.

'That's right,' I chirruped brightly without stopping. 'Goodbye, it's been a pleasure.'

'Just one thing, sir,' crackled Williams, coughing. I stopped and turned to look at him. 'Mr Stoker asks if you could please pop up and see him before you leave.'

'I'd like to get away, chief inspector,' I said. 'What does he want to see *me* for?'

'He didn't say, sir.' He smiled slyly and shrugged his untidy shoulders. 'I'm sure he won't keep you long.'

CHAPTER 21

Beguiling Words

BEFORE GOING UP to see Stoker, I paused at the outside door to pull my thoughts together. Williams turned away but I noticed he was watching my reflection in a car window. I was almost certain I knew who Stoker was, but my suspicion was largely speculative and based on a great deal of supposition, so I wasn't completely sure. He seemed to be a canny man who liked to play mind games but, if I was right, I believed I had a clear advantage over him and may have even been able to trick him into giving himself away. So with a pointed glance at Williams who was still studying the car window, smugly composed and comfortably confident I pushed the outside door open and trotted up the stairs.

'Lovely morning, Mr Tanner.' He was sitting in a chair that he had moved to the window, and had a book open in his lap.

'Yes. Yes it is, Mr Stoker,' I said breezily. 'You wanted to see me?'

'I do?' he asked, apparently surprised.

'Mr Williams said so.'

'Oh I see,' he said laughing. He put his open book on a table, spine up, but remained seated. 'No, he misunderstood me. Anyway, now you're here, sit down. An Irishman never needs an excuse for a chat – we need to talk as other people need to breathe. That Blarney stone has a lot to answer for.'

'So you *are* Irish then?' I had every intention of enjoying this game. 'You don't have a strong accent.'

'I'm what I call an adopted Irishman, Mr Tanner. I wasn't born in Ireland but have lived there for most of my life and have come to feel Irish. And where are you from?'

For a few moments we talked about our backgrounds and upbringing. Although he told me very little, I found him to be engaging and disarming; I couldn't help liking him, especially after I'd managed to read, upside down, the title of the book he had been reading, *The Zen of Pooh*. My confidence was high, and I baited a hook for him by taking the initiative. 'I'm intrigued to know why a police commissioner would come all the way from Ireland to see one man arrested.'

'Are you indeed?' he enquired. Evidently I used the wrong bait.

'Did you get what you came for?' I asked with a smile, trying a different fly.

'And what would that be?' he smiled back.

'You tell me,' I riposted, thinking I would let him run a little.

'Well, Mr Tanner, I find if I have no expectations I'm never disappointed, and always go away with more than I could have hoped for.'

'Only a true Irishman could give me an answer like that,' I said, laughing, 'But seriously, what brought you here this morning?'

'Simple. I was over here on another matter and got called in. They needed someone who could identify your friend.'

'So you know him then?' He was elusive yet I felt I still could be able to trap him.

'Know him? I wouldn't claim to know him, but I would be able to identify him.'

'You met him in Ireland?' I came back at him instantly.

'I did indeed.'

'And what terrible thing did he do in Ireland to get our constabulary up so early?'

He studied me for a moment with a lost smile, trying to get out of his deep, misty eyes. 'At last, Mr Tanner, you've asked *the question*.'

'Excuse me?'

'I've been trying to puzzle out all the morning why neither you nor Mrs Jenkins has asked what he's done to merit such attention.' His unquenchable smile grew brighter but the villain behind it peeped out and moved towards my jugular. I fumbled with a flimsy excuse about being preoccupied with other, unspecified, things in an attempt to slip his barbed hook embedded so deftly in my hard palate, but I felt like a fly that had been squished.

'Well, what *did* he do?' I asked belatedly.

'Oh dear me, Mr Tanner, that's a very long story, and if you don't already know I can't tell you because the information is what they call "sensitive". Although to civil servants even an indent for toilet paper seems to be "sensitive".' Tasteless jokes didn't fit him, perhaps I imagined it.

'So you're a civil servant now, not a policeman?' I said spitefully.

He laughed. He laughed, as he smiled, too easily for my comfort. They were masks concealing trouble for Mr Tanner if I wasn't more careful.

'In one way I am, in another way I'm not. I'm semi-retired but occasionally the government raid the old people's home and drag me back, usually to take the blame for their mistakes.' Getting a clear statement out of him was like picking up water with tweezers.

'You don't look old enough for an old people's home,' I said, trying to sound kinder.

'Ah, you flatter me, Mr Tanner.' He stroked his fingers around the edge of the book on the table besides him. 'You seem to have gotten very friendly with Mr Verres in a remarkably short time.'

He looked up at me with a benign tolerance, as a maiden aunt would at a favourite nephew.

'Not too close, and I would hardly call him my friend,' I said defensively. 'Despite what you think, I only met him once or twice when I came to see the Jenkins.'

A lightness came into his eyes which I assumed to be his lie detector. 'So you never met him anywhere else?'

I felt a guilty flush sweep across my face and brushed away an imaginary fly to conceal it. 'Well, perhaps we did go for a couple of walks together...'

'You did, now? I didn't know that... very interesting. So you must have had some long talks with him, then.' I'd stupidly opened a door an inch and he'd jammed his foot in it. 'What did you talk about?'

'Gosh,' I said, pretending to appear to be thinking but really feeling naked and exposed before him while my brain cells went into hiding, 'I don't remember... Nothing in particular, perhaps nature, religion, philosophy...'

'Philosophy?' He leapt at the word like a cat onto a mouse. 'What would you say his philosophy is, Mr Tanner?'

'I'll mind my business and you mind yours sums it up, Mr Stoker.'

Stoker roared with laughter. 'I like it,' he spluttered through his laughter. 'What a sport you are, Mr Tanner. I must remember that. What did you make of him?'

'A bit strange,' I said, relieved to have an opportunity to give a straightforward, honest reply. 'But underneath I think he is a kind man. Sometimes his directness was disconcerting, but I always found him caring and interesting.'

'Caring and interesting. Yes, I found him caring and interesting too,' he said wistfully. 'Did he ever talk about his time in Ireland?'

'Never,' I said, possibly too emphatically.

'Never?'

'Not that I recall.'

'Not that you recall? So he may have talked about Ireland…'

'No, he didn't.'

'And you say you wouldn't call him a friend?'

'Not really.'

'Not really? You seem uncertain.'

He seemed to be squeezing the innocence out of everything I said, and the confidence I had entered the room with was long gone. I desperately wanted out.

'He was more like a casual acquaintance I met along the way.'

'And do you think he was the sort of man who made casual acquaintances along the way?' Coming out of his mouth, my words sounded evasive and devious.

'I don't know.' He looked at me quizzically. 'Perhaps not,' I added.

'Perhaps not, hmm. What, then, was his interest in you?'

I felt giddy and had to sit before I fell. He didn't move but seemed like a spider in the centre of its web luring a fly closer and closer. My thoughts were jumping over each other in confusion. 'I can't say,' I said weakly. 'He never told me.'

'Don't you have any idea?' he asked in his mountain-pasture-sweet, always-smiling voice, which concealed serpents in the long grass.

'I've never thought about it.'

'You see Mr Tanner, what mystifies me is the way I'm adding up even numbers and always getting an odd-number answer.'

'Oh?'

'Indulge me for a moment.' I wanted to close my eyes, but was afraid diverting them would make me seem even more vulnerable that I already felt. 'Here we have a reclusive, insular man, whose freedom depends on secrecy suddenly befriending an alert and perceptive stranger for no apparent reason. He even goes to the great trouble and risk of meeting this stranger to say "goodbye" while the authorities are closing in around him. Don't you think it strange?'

'Well, put like that perhaps, but…'

'Another "perhaps" Mr Tanner,' he mocked. 'Don't you ever say "maybe"?'

He flung his arms wide. 'Please excuse my levity, it's kindly meant.'

I was in the centre of the web and didn't have a response left in me.

'Then there's another thing, which seems even odder. This intelligent and perceptive stranger never once asks him any questions about who he is and where he comes from. What's more, he drops everything and comes dashing over at his behest to say "goodbye" to him in the middle of the night.'

His merry eyes burnt into my thoughts and he spread his hands wide to show perplexity; for an instant I imagined one of his hands didn't belong to him, but he put them back into his pocket before I could look again. 'It's a real mystery to this simple old adopted Irishman, Mr Tanner.'

'Are you accusing me of something, Mr Stoker?' Bluster was my last refuge, and I shunted to my feet indignantly.

'Heaven forbid. Please forgive me, Mr Tanner,' he said imitating genuine contrition in the same effortless way as he could imitate warmth and charm. 'I'm so clumsy with words sometimes. Of course I'm not accusing you of anything, and I apologise if I've offended you.' He gestured me back to my chair. I obediently sat down again.

'Why are you asking all these questions? Where are they leading?' I blurted, although I should have been hiding behind silence by now.

'Sometimes when I get confused Mr Tanner, I've got this

terrible habit of thinking out loud. It gets me into all sorts of trouble, but occasionally I find it is the best way to get things straight in my head.'

'Well I'm sorry I haven't been able to help you.'

'Oh quite the contrary, Mr Tanner, you've been an enormous help already. You can help me a little more if you would be so kind.'

'If I can,' I muttered suspiciously.

'It's such a lovely day, and I've been stuck indoors all morning. I wonder if you can recommend a little walk I can take, nothing too taxing, about five miles or so and somewhere I can enjoy some of this wonderful scenery?'

I suggested a couple of walks along the coastal footpath, but he said he would prefer an upland walk where he could look over the land.

'The Preseli is the highest part of the county,' I told him. 'You might enjoy it because on a clear day you can see the Antrim Hills from the top.'

He questioned me about the hills as if he was a genuine walker wanting to know about access, walking conditions, places to shelter, views, geology and birds. I knew almost nothing about any of these, but my ignorance didn't dampen his enthusiasm. 'It sounds just the sort of place I need to blow away the cobwebs.'

He stretched and looked straight into my eyes like a seducer. Not a single movement seemed superfluous; everything he did seemed to be full of meaning, suggestion and enticement.

'I've really enjoyed our little talk, Mr Tanner. I don't suppose you'd like to join me in a walk this afternoon would you? I'd consider it a real privilege.' Such was the power of the man's encircling charm that I almost agreed. However, I feared him too much, so clumsily made excuses about having work to catch up on.

'Of course, you are a busy man I know. We'll have another opportunity to meet again.' He rose and held out his hand.

'That would be very nice,' I replied graciously, returning his warm handshake. As I turned towards the door he said, 'Oh there is one other small thing David, excuse me, Mr Tanner.'

'Yes, what's that?'

'I'm so forgetful, you must excuse me, but last night?'

'What about last night?'

'How long were you and Mrs Jenkins here at the "farewell party"?'

'About half an hour,' I mumbled cautiously.

'Half an hour!' he repeated. I was getting irritated at the way he stressed some of my throwaway remarks. 'What did you do?'

'He made us a coffee, told us he was leaving and wanted to say goodbye. That was all.'

'And that took half an hour?' He looked puzzled. 'What did you talk about?'

'I don't remember. Just pleasantries and good wishes and that sort of thing.'

'Small talk!'

'Sort of.'

'Did he *sort of* say why he was leaving?'

'No, he didn't.'

'Or what he was *sort of* going to do?'

'No.'

'Didn't you *sort of* think of asking him?'

'It didn't occur to me. Sorry.' My lies were so embarrassingly transparent I wore my humiliation like a rainbow-coloured coat.

'Or where he was going?'

'I'm afraid not.'

'Didn't you think it curious that he was leaving in the middle of the night?'

'I'm afraid I didn't, Mr Stoker.'

'And I assume that Mrs Jenkins was equally uncurious?'

'You'll have to ask her, but everything happened so quickly,' I said with a little more spirit. 'It may seem strange to you, but Verres was running the show and we were little more than observers. If you knew him you'd know what a powerful personality his is. He sort of mesmerizes you.'

'Mesmerizes, yes. I understand perfectly Mr Tanner, he does have a very… shall we say, compelling manner. And I take it he didn't arrange to get back in touch with you at all?'

'Why should he?'

'Interesting question. Had he any reason to?'

'None that I know of,' I replied miserably.

'Just one final question, before I let you go back to all the important things you have to do.'

'OK,' I said, feeling one more question couldn't possibly drag me down any lower. I couldn't imagine how I had inveigled myself into this sorry position, or why I felt it was necessary to lie for Verres. Would it have been so terrible if I'd told Stoker all I'd known? What harm could that possibly have done to him? Yet it was too late. I had burnt the last bridge long ago and was now committed to the mendacious path I'd chosen. 'Last night. Did you spend all your time in this room?'

'Here and the kitchen.'

'But none of the other rooms?'

The rat smelled too strong even for me not to notice. 'Well after he'd gone, I had a look around to see if he'd left anything.'

'And had he?'

'Only what you've seen for yourself.'

'So you took nothing away and left everything as it was?'

'That's right.'

'And he carried all his things on his motorcycle… interesting. Thank you Mr Tanner, I believe that explains why your fingerprints were found everywhere. I look forward very much to our next merry meeting.' He picked up *The Zen of Pooh* and held it in both hands momentarily before sliding his left hand back into his coat pocket. Its fingers hadn't moved or gripped the book.

I tottered towards the stairs, needing to lean on the walls to steady myself. 'I love the sweater, by the way,' he said, as his *coup de grâce*.

CHAPTER 22

Hidden Beneath
the Leaves

F EELING LIKE A hunted stag with barbed arrows hanging from its flanks, I almost bolted down the drive, vainly hoping to outrun a festering sense of shame. Even worse than my pathetic and humiliating lies was my contamination by the sweet deceit of Stoker's smiling, seductive incredulity.

I found a public footpath, short-cutting a big loop in the road, which led me downhill around the edge of two fields and into a dense copse of mixed deciduous trees. I plunged into the wood, but after taking no more than a dozen paces felt I was not alone. I stopped and looked around, almost flinching in my state of agitation, fearful of a confrontation. I saw only trees, stationary in the still air like silent giants, waiting. Not even a bird flew between their branches, but the presence remained; it was all around me. I could even smell its earthy scent, more animal than vegetable, hanging heavily on the air. After proceeding a few more yards, I heard something moving close behind me in the undergrowth and spun around quickly. The path was empty and still nothing moved in the trees, but the smell was stronger than ever. I started to feel the prickly sensation one gets entering a dark room when someone is already there, unseen and unheard.

I continued through the wood and the 'presence' kept

pace with me. It neither threatened me nor played with me, mocked me nor harassed me; it was like the trees, neutral and everywhere. Occasionally I heard a grunt or snort, but each time I looked around the wood appeared empty and silent. Very soon I even felt reassured by its presence. When I finally cleared the trees and entered the field beyond, it was no longer with me and the Stoker-induced unease returned, although with diminished intensity.

I turned to look back at the trees, then slowly and deliberately retraced my steps the way I had come, to the waiting giants, willing the 'presence' to reappear. Once in the trees it again surrounded me. I moved deeper into the shadows, stopping at times, trying to alert my senses to every nuance of its being. When I reached the heart of the forest, I stopped to concentrate on the sensations coming to me from all around. Their gentle insistent rhythm reverberated through my body, a sense of deep peace crept over me, and I felt a healing power purging the stains of my recent encounter with Stoker. Gently, ever so gently, without looking left or right, I edged my way back along the path, luxuriating in the new-found joy I was experiencing. Before reaching the field the wood had become silent and I was alone, but that was alright; it had served me and I was able to let it go. Feeling an almost mesmeric calm, I let the contours lead me down into the valley.

The humiliation and sense of defilement from Stoker and the policemen was completely gone, replaced by a feeling of relief, even detachment from the world and my surroundings. Technically I became completely lost, and had no idea how long I walked or what directions I took. I remember seeing nothing and nobody until a squeaky hinge on my gate welcomed me home, and the key to my front door appeared in my hand as if of its own volition. My immediate thoughts were of Verres, and uppermost was that I had remained loyal to him; I had protected him and stayed steadfast, despite being made to look an idiot and trampled on by Stoker's charming and humbling innuendo. I had left feeling deeply ashamed and dirty; now I felt proud and clean.

I thought too that I knew what had been with me in the trees. A thought I would have considered absurd a year earlier and believed worthy of having me committed.

*

Ruth rang in the late afternoon to announce she was on her way to see me; twenty minutes later her car stormed down my drive, and slithered to a stop outside my door. Her mind was buzzing with excitement and impetuosity; she wanted straight away to continue reading Verres' letter. I wanted to talk about the morning and my walk home, but she was irrepressible and carried a package wrapped in newspaper past me into my sitting room, gaily chattering about her afternoon like a happy schoolgirl reliving her first flirtation. Apparently, the police had left soon after me, followed by her husband who seemed to have pressing local business. She had spent much of the day with Stoker, who had waylaid her in the garden. They walked around the house, admired everything they saw and passed a jovial hour in each other's company. He invited her to lunch in Newport if she would drive; she agreed, so they spent the next two hours chatting, laughing and lingering like old friends over a delicious meal in one of the little town's excellent restaurants. He didn't ask her a single question that had any bearing on his investigation, and neither of them even mentioned Verres. A car came for him later in the afternoon.

Soon afterwards, Jenkins returned, looking self-righteously pleased with himself and announced he would be staying the night. Ruth promptly told him that she would be returning to the

Midlands. She quickly packed a small valise and couldn't remove herself quickly enough from his smug, scheming presence.

'What about you, darling?' she asked finally. 'You looked so unhappy when you left but you seem alright now.'

'I'm terrific,' I whispered, stroking her arm. 'Will you be staying here tonight?'

'I wish I could, but I told Bill I was going home and he's sure to ring me later.'

I wondered if we were fated to remain celibate forever, while she removed the interrupted printout from the newspaper parcel. She pushed the neatly arranged bundle of papers into my hands. 'Will you read please?'

We settled down comfortably in separate chairs and I looked at the top sheet.

'Where did we leave off? Ah yes, Ticker had learned a couple of Celtic languages, became an authority on Celtic mythology and had just become re-acquainted with our old friend Twrch Trwyth…'

By now I had been living in Ireland for over seven years. These years had been so full of vivid, larger-than-life experiences, so that my previous existence as a teacher had become like a faraway childhood memory. My new life and my new acquaintances had become my present and my past.

Only Dana knew my history, and the only other link with the man I had been was my name. Everyone now called me 'Tommy', except Dana who stuck to Thomas. It seemed as if I had never had a surname.

The early problems I experienced over Dana's lifestyle and with our frequent enforced separations had long changed from fretful apprehension to comfortable acceptance. We seldom saw Bran now. He abruptly stopped practising his water healing, saying he'd found a new direction for his life. I was disappointed both in him and in his apparent rejection of us without an explanation, but he and I remained friends of opportunity. From time to time he'd visit the cottage to stay for a few days, but he'd pull down the blinds whenever I asked him about his new life, so I stopped asking.

By chance I ran into him outside Trinity College library on one occasion. He appeared to be giving instructions to a group of five men. When he saw me approaching he said something quickly to them, they immediately hurried away and he came towards me arms open and beaming. 'Don't ask me,' he said, 'I can't tell you.'

The folk group flourished, but I was still unable to warm to Mongan. His voice had deepened, become richer and was by far the most interesting sound in the group, but we rarely spoke although I often caught him studying me and wondered what was going on in his dark, animal mind.

One day I was browsing through an antiquarian bookshop in Dublin when I came across Twrch Trwyth again, and stood in the semi-darkness re-reading the story. This was the first time I'd read his story in the Old Welsh, and it triggered the most dramatic recall. A memory leapt out of the shadows. Your class of ghostly sixth formers appeared before me, gazing up with enquiring, inquisitive eyes on those far-off cliffs circled by swooping seagulls and the sun sparkling off the sea. I hadn't given any of you much more than a passing thought for years, but the recall was vivid. Of course Bill dominated as usual, with his wild red hair, impish smile and intelligent perceptions. Ruth was there too, a prim and serious young lady but, even in those days, signs of a strong personality were emerging. And there was David – hesitant, sensitive, insecure David, who that morning stood up before the world and told it that he was right and the world had better get out of his way.

Everything you had said, about the boar being the source

of power for the land and the popular interpretation of the boar being evil was a distortion of the truth, now rang true for me like a peal of church bells on a frosty spring morn. I couldn't believe how I could have been so dense, or how long it had taken the clouds of ignorance to clear.

I used to tell you to read between the lines, but had not done so myself. I felt refreshingly humble as, at last, I followed my own advice. I became increasingly angry at the way the boar had been maligned down the centuries, but I reserved my greatest anger for the forces that had done this terrible thing. Initially I blamed the Christian Church, then my spleen spread to governments, then to teachers, and even parents. Finally I realised everyone is playing a power game over someone else and there are no winners. There is always someone scheming to take his neighbour's power. Most people give it up willingly, and inevitably they gaily come under the control of the greatest schemers.

We are all still killing the boar and I grimly acknowledged the part I played in this debilitating dance. This insight was all very well but now I was confronted with the dilemma of what was I going to do about it. I decided that before I could do anything I had to know more about Twrch Trwyth himself. I needed to know about the source of his power, who he really was, what was his real story and, most importantly of all, find out if the harm done to him was irreversible or not. From that time onwards, my obsession with the dynamic personality, the devious mind and the immense vision of this incredible creature grew and grew.

Soon he had stepped out of myth to become a real creature that had once lived, and for all I knew still lived. I travelled throughout Ireland, scouring obscure documents, books and records in libraries, book shops, university archives, even private collections and town halls. Often I came away empty-handed after painstaking hours in a dusty storeroom; occasionally I found a promising trail; but quickly I was running out of paths to follow.

So intensely had I absorbed myself in the research that after a year I felt as if I had become half a real man and half a mythical character from a Celtic version of the *Arabian Nights*. I stood alongside magical packs of hounds, menageries of wild beasts, each possessing otherworldly qualities like an owl with second sight, a stag able to carry the rider through different dimensions and a salmon able to shapeshift. I met great princes and knights mounted on talking horses able to leap oceans and mountains, magicians able to devour themselves, and came to mighty castles that would appear and disappear according to the wisdom of the traveller. The 'Celtic Nights', however, differed from the Arabian in that the stories all had a beginning but very few had a middle or an ending. I had entered the enchanting world of 'magic' and discovered that magic is everywhere, all around us, all the time. But man doesn't see or understand this, so he simply chooses not to believe it. He turns his back on this wondrous force because ignorance is easier to believe in.

Out of this teasing mess I managed to isolate a few consistencies which more or less confirmed the story I told you from the *Mabinogi*, but I was no closer to understanding the boar himself or finding answers to the questions I had set out to uncover a year earlier.

As the sources dried up I was left with only one way to go. I had to somehow enter the mind of the beast so that I could experience the world and his identity as he had known it. I started taking long walks in the hills acting 'as if' I was him, and soon found that the gloaming hours before dawn and after dusk were the times when it was natural for 'him' to walk abroad. My walks became longer and through the night, until my eyes and senses became sharp enough to know where I was and what was going on around me even on the blackest nights or in the densest forests. Fleeting insights started to dart in and out of my head, and gradually I was able to harness them like I would a half-broken stallion.

One morning before dawn, I was returning home when I sensed danger. In the distance I heard the belligerent baying of hounds and the insistent rally of a horn. I ran into the wood and lay down in some thick cover to listen. Not only could I identify the individual dogs, I could also smell decaying flesh on their breath and the woody sweat of the horses. The hunt was getting closer, and something warned me that I was the quarry. I needed to reach the river, so cautiously made my way through the cover until I had to make a dash across open ground. The hounds immediately picked up my scent and urgent barking warned me that the chase was on. The leading hounds were at my heels when I turned on them, snarling, and with my bare hands tore open the belly of the leader, seeing its intestines slither over the wet grass like a bucket of snakes. Then I sliced through the throat of another. In its death throes frothy, creamy blood gushed like a fountain out of its neck. Another clamped its jaws on my haunch but I flicked it off with a kick, sending it thundering into a tree. I heard a murmur of air escaping from its throat as it crumpled into a twisted heap amid the gnarled roots of the tree, its back broken. I turned on the other dogs in a rage and they fled, wounded and howling in fear and pain.

They fled past the laughing, screaming, blood-crazed huntsmen who descended on me with spears held high above their heads. I was too quick for them. The missiles glanced off my hide as I scythed them down, tore at their terrified mounts and devoured their spilled guts. None escaped as I hunted down the last man. He fell to his knees before me in prayer and supplication. I hurled myself at him, hitting him like an avalanche. I felt his bones crunch beneath my weight and heard a scream dying in his chest.

I awoke amidst the leaves and sounds of the forest,

and slowly walked back up the hill with the incongruous statue of St Patrick beckoning me on.

Later that day I told Dana that at last I was ready to change my name. From then on I was Verres – the Latin word for boar.

Bang! Bang! Bang! We were jolted back into the present by a demanding thundering on the outside door. We looked at each other and didn't have to say anything.

Whoever it was banged the door again, evermore insistently.

'Coming!' I called. 'Who the hell can it be?' I muttered anxiously to no-one in particular.

'Bill? No, he would never bang like that.' Ruth had shot to her feet with a 'time for quick decisions and action' look on her face.

I went into the hall. 'Who is it?' I called through the door.

'Police. Open the door please.'

'Just a minute,' I called, looking back to catch Ruth's attention, but she had vanished. Opening the door, I was confronted by a cold-eyed Sergeant Blower standing squarely before me, looking very serious. Chief Inspector Williams pushed passed him with a piece of printed paper in his hand which he held in front of my face, too close to read. 'I'm very sorry sir, but I have a magistrate's warrant to search your house. Will you please step aside.'

Behind him stood four officers wearing black berets and bulky bulletproof waistcoats, automatic weapons were held diagonally across their chests with fingers along the trigger guard.

CHAPTER 23

Save the Hunted

W HILE I ACTED out the role of an outraged householder on the doorstep, the policeman pushed past me and under Blower's directions searched the house. Clearly they were looking for Verres. Williams brought up the rear like an anxious mother looking for a lost child; he came up to me scratching his head in apparent bewilderment.

'We have compelling reasons to believe that Mr Verres is hiding here, sir.'

'Reason, what reason?' I knew the cupboard was bare, so felt secure on firm ground playing the innocent without having to walk on the shifting sands of lies; my earlier performances on the sandbanks had disgusted me and I was determined to avoid a repetition.

'I can't tell you that, sir,' he said, leading me into the conservatory.

'Why all the drama then, Mr Williams? And why the guns? You're never going to convince me that he is an IRA terrorist on the run.'

'No sir, I'm not, but he's a dangerous and violent man and we can't take any chances with him.'

'What nonsense,' I guffawed, to the back of his dirty raincoat disappearing into my house. 'You've been watching too much after the threshold TV, chief inspector.' He rightly ignored my cheap jibe, for which I was grateful.

I followed him into the main living room. Everything had

happened so quickly; I had overlooked the letter we had been reading. The pages had been untidily scattered over the table and floor when I'd left the room but now they were nowhere to be seen. Ruth was fighting a doughty holding action against the predictable but insistent forces of British law enforcement, flitting from room to room like an all-seeing avenging angel, instructing the unfortunate men how she would like the search conducted. She warned them not to scratch the paint on the skirting board or kick the furniture with their big boots. She reprimanded one for not wiping his feet after coming in from the garden, and gave him a dustpan and brush to clear up a trace of barely discernable dirt. The policeman dutifully brushed up and thanked her.

'Be careful with the ornaments gentlemen; some of the china is two hundred years old and priceless.' That was a 'slight' overstatement, but the exaggeration was justified by the response; the two younger policemen seemed to be more frightened of her than their 'dangerous' quarry. She even found time to fill a kettle and turn it on and arrange mugs on the kitchen table; she seemed totally at her ease, the skills learnt keeping Jenkins' parishioners and colleagues in order were being put to good use.

'Good evening Mrs Jenkins,' said Williams meekly. 'I apologise for this intrusion. I hope…'

'You have your job to do chief inspector,' she said sweetly. 'When your men have finished doing what they're doing you will have time for a cup of tea I hope. What *are* they doing by the way?'

'That's very kind of you, but I don't think we can stay,' he replied, hopping from foot to foot.

'And are all those big guns to protect you from us?' she asked mockingly. 'I can assure you we won't harm you.'

'They're looking for Verres,' I said. 'The chief inspector

says he's dangerous and what was the other word?' I turned to Williams, who was rummaging through his pockets again. I handed him a box of tissues but he waved them away. 'No, it's alright sir, thank you.'

'Violent?' I pointedly answered my own question.

'Oh, chief inspector,' she mocked. 'That would be funny if this whole situation wasn't so bizarre. What's he done and why do you think he's here anyway?'

I told her he was acting on information 'received'. 'But how did you know where I live, chief inspector? Only Ruth knew that.'

Blower came into the room. 'He's not here guv.'

'Back outside then,' said Williams, playing the bumbling fool role to the end. His men shuffled out, a couple remembering to thank Ruth on the way. Williams was last but she stood in his way.

'You're not leaving here without an explanation,' she said icily. 'I was followed here chief inspector, wasn't I?'

'I don't know madam. I'm sorry for any embarrassment you've been caused, but I only follow orders…'

'That won't wash chief inspector,' she said defiantly, standing in the doorway like a rock so he couldn't escape without physically removing her. 'You know what's going on. Now tell me who ordered you.'

'I'm sorry, Mrs Jenkins, you have to take this matter up with my superiors…'

'It was my husband, wasn't it?' she blurted. He studied his dirty shoes.

'Thank you Mr Williams,' she purred. 'You need say no more. There's nothing quite so eloquent as silence.'

'Goodnight,' he said, looking hopefully towards the door behind her. 'Thank you for your cooperation… I trust we haven't damaged anything.'

She stepped aside and the policeman shambled out, briskly by his standards.

I followed him to the outside door and watched him shuffle across to his car. 'Good night sir,' he said with a diffident wave. I waited until the headlights had moved down the lane and out of sight before returning to Ruth. She stood by the door where I had left her, dumbly staring at the floor.

'Well, well, well,' I said brightly. 'That was an experience.'

'Bill has been spying on me; he's done it before,' she said, looking up. 'He must have told them I would lead them to Verres. He still believes that he's my lover.' She straightened her shoulders and a tight smile broke across her clouded face. 'God, what a mess.'

'Come here,' I said.

We slipped into each other's arms like hands into well-worn gloves which fitted perfectly wherever they found contact. The tension of the last few minutes very slowly dissolved into the night. It was too good to last, like stroking a scorpion, with a jerk she stung me. 'The letter.'

She disengaged, scurried into the kitchen and opened the refrigerator. The incriminating evidence was in the freezer compartment, peeping out from between a packet of frozen peas and a pizza.

'Phew. Thank God.' She looked at me and smiled wanly. 'I must leave soon, Bill is devious and can play dirty when he's unsure of himself, but we must finish this first!'

This time she read:

I had discovered myself at last and knew the boar's cause was my cause, his passion my passion and if it had to be, his destiny my destiny. However, although I identified with his essence I didn't share his innate violence; after all, he was a wild animal and I a civilised Homo sapiens.

I soon realised that I could move in and out of what I called 'Twrch consciousness' at will. I understood him better each day and began to experience his driving forces, his responses and his reactions as my own. I could see what an enormous challenge he posed to people who cherished power, and why he had been hunted, persecuted and maligned down the centuries. Similarly, I could see how other individuals were drawn to him as a way to release their own power.

Sometimes I felt his energy, like a dynamo resonating throughout my whole being until it became unbearable. I learnt to release it by going on long, furious runs through the woods and over the hills until calm returned, but wondered if there was a way to use the energy positively; pouring it away like this seemed to be a terrible waste. The energy belonged to the world, not one individual, and his duty was to make sure it moved through him into the earth where everyone could benefit from it if they so chose.

I was getting to know Twrch Trwyth well, but didn't assume at this stage that I was destined to take over his burden and become the new channel for this energy. Many more years of learning lay ahead of me before I would get any sense of that mantle being placed over my shoulders.

I continued to travel around Ireland. Although my direction was neither planned nor aimless, I seemed to be taken on a journey by an unseen guide. Very often I failed to see the point of going to a particular place, but was past the stage of questioning what I did. I trusted the impulses and simply followed them.

As the years passed, Dana and I lived our lives separately and together in equanimity and harmony. We cherished times spent alone together and bought a thirty-five-foot six-berth sloop, which we moored at Dingle, and often spent days alone sailing wherever the winds and tides allowed.

One glorious Indian summer, several years after I

had become Verres, we anchored in a tiny, lonely inlet on the West coast after a three-day voyage into the Atlantic vastness. We sat on deck watching the hazy autumnal sunset and sharing a silence when Dana became reflective.

She talked about our life together as a journey through uncharted seas and of all the challenges we had faced. She thanked me for loving her and for giving her so much, but as she plundered through her box of old, much-loved but half-forgotten memories and unspoken thoughts, she seemed to be holding something back.

As the ruddiness subtly faded in the western sky and the comforting misty light of approaching night transformed the world, she started to talk about the ways I had changed. In many ways I was the same man with the fevered brow she had brought cool water to in Swansea, but I had acquired another dimension. She said that she had always admired me and respected me but now, she said, she was looking at me more and more in awe and asked if I was aware of the changes.

I was; but they had been deeply internal, so I hadn't thought I'd changed much on the outside.

She asked me if I had noticed that sometimes people were frightened of me and that I could be an intimidating figure. I was appalled. I perceived myself as full of kindness and reason and gentle persuasion. She reminded me of occasions when I had challenged people, sometimes complete strangers, who had been behaving badly, especially when they appeared to be harming others less powerful than themselves. These had been trivial events to me but significant to her. She mentioned times when I'd 'spoken' to people who were being 'careless' with animals or children. Always I had been polite, but no-one dared to ignore me. On one occasion I chastised a man who had been ridiculing his wife in front of friends – he aimed a punch at my head, but I caught his fist in flight and squeezed it, gently I thought, but it was enough to break three fingers and a metacarpus. Brittle bones, I'd thought.

She said that my appearance had changed, too. I was heavier, and seemed to have developed a greater awareness of my body. I asked her what she meant. She said that the 'strain' had left me, now I did things effortlessly. She said that our lovemaking was different, too. She now felt a calm intensity that hadn't been there in the earlier days. Her words surprised me, yet they didn't – she was telling me things I knew but had never brought up to the surface.

Weeks and months passed, and I found myself becoming more and more the defender of 'creatures' who were 'put-down' by others. I attended public meetings and challenged the pompous and self-important on the platform. I became a minor media celebrity, writing regular pieces in several journals and appearing on Irish TV. When an anti-establishment voice was needed in a discussion programme, I became an embarrassment to the power brokers in education, the church and politics. Naturally they struck back at me with ineffectual jibes and put-down names like the 'Irish Zapata' and the 'Rabid Voice of Chaos' but I was impervious to the taunts and didn't take them seriously; to my cost as it turned out.

This brief summary leads us to the time when the irresistible, elemental forces of change once again took a hold of my life and shook it so violently that everything that had gone on before seemed inconsequential.

A rednecked American senator from a southern state, whose views I found particularly repulsive, had been invited to speak at an important political rally in Dublin. The media coverage was immense, with television companies from both Ireland and US and reporters from the main newspapers. It was an occasion made for me to tilt against my favourite windmills of institutionalized humbug and political double-dealing.

I rarely made speeches, but relied on pointed

questions, pithy responses, quick thinking and the persistence to probe evasive replies into extinction, so when the opportunity came I rose to my feet and asked my question. Of course I was rewarded with a statement that had nothing whatsoever to do with the question, so I started twisting the knife. The senator blustered and prevaricated and played beautifully into my hands, to the delight of the media and the neutrals in the audience.

However, my reputation as an irritant was greater than I had believed, so my intervention had been anticipated. The senator was losing control and becoming incoherent when the chairman nodded to stewards at the side of the hall. Two heavyweight boxer types started moving towards me from either side of the row. With a few Neanderthal grunts, they took an arm each in an attempt to remove me. I grabbed their shirt fronts and held them at arm's length while continuing my harangue of the speaker to the apparent amusement and approval of the majority of people in the hall, and I'm sure the TV producer. Some of the audience were now on their feet and shouting in my defence but I was in control of my micro situation, or so I believed!

The 'bouncers', unable to impress me with their fists, produced a truncheon each and started flailing away with them at my head and arms, so I tightened my grip on their necks, raised them both off the ground and shook them. When they dropped their truncheons I gently lowered them. Both promptly collapsed to the ground with their necks broken and windpipes torn out of their lungs.

CHAPTER 24

Amandlas Unleashed

THE PAPER SLIPPED out of Ruth's hand and floated to the floor. I leapt after it and read the shocking words over and over again, as if I expected them to change before my eyes.

'I can't take it in,' she said

'Neither can I,' I said dumbly. 'But we have to. At least we now know.'

'Yes,' she whispered. 'And he chose this way to tell us, not very kind of him.'

'What's a kind way?' I asked. 'The real question is, where do *we* go from here?'

We sat in a pitiless silence for a few moments before she said, 'Let's sit down and have a boring cup of crisis tea, then finish his letter. I hope that's the last shock he's got in store for us.'

With the tea cooling at my elbow and the papers arranged neatly on the dining room table in front of me, I restarted reading from where Ruth had finished.

```
I assume this will come as a shock to you. I can
assure you it was a thousand times more of a shock
to me. I had no idea that I possessed such physical
strength and what I had done horrified me. You can
imagine the turmoil that followed in the hall and the
sensation it made on TV.
I won't go into all the details of the arrest and
trial. My solicitor insisted that it had been 'self-
defence' and he could get me off with a guilty plea of
```

manslaughter, but I had different ideas. If I could do such a terrible thing so casually and unintentionally, I believed the public should be protected from me, and I should be locked up. I dispensed with the solicitor's services and pleaded guilty to murder.

This wasn't a futile, atonement-seeking gesture or even because I considered myself a murderer, which I didn't. I pleaded guilty because I was frightened of the monster I had become. I no longer knew myself or what I might do next. The only place for the monster was behind bars.

I took little notice of the trial or early months of prison life. My thoughts we focused intensely on planning my future. I looked forward to the time when all the formalities would be over and I could settle down into the next phase of my life.

My two closest friends showed their true worth. Dana was distraught and a constant visitor, especially during the first few months. We spent many hours talking about the new way of life that was unfolding for us. She quickly came to accept that this wasn't the end, but simply the next step. It was a time for us to be physically apart but also a time for us to grow and prepare ourselves for what was to come next.

I didn't see Bran until the trial was over and I had been shuffled away to an allocation centre for 'assessment'. He was his usual intelligent, whimsical and practical self. I told him what my plans were and he said he'd use what little influence he had to help me. His 'little' influence proved to be considerable. Within a year I was comfortably installed in my own cell with a computer and direct computer access to libraries and other resources all over the world. I enjoyed contact with the other inmates at mealtimes and took advantage of the multigym for a daily workout, but otherwise I spent my time in the monastic confines of my cell studying, meditating and treating myself with the finest medicine man can give himself – silence. It was a prolific time and I became truly contented and at peace with myself.

Mongan, to my surprise, also emerged out of his den of reticence. He was a man who had to struggle to find words and whose heart had been closed to the outside world from his childhood. His life had become a windowless room of music, with Dana his only door to the outside. My incarceration had brought him out of this room and he opened his heart to me for the first time. In short sentences he told me of his love and devotion to Dana, and of his initial fear but later respect for me.

During that time he did countless small things to make my transition smoother and showed kindnesses I would never have expected from him, yet he always seemed to be holding something back. Much as I wanted to believe in his new-found regard for me, I still felt uneasy about him.

Never in my life had I had such an uninterrupted opportunity for study and research. It wasn't long before I had an article on the Celtic legacy published in *Life* magazine. This stimulated an interest in academic circles on both sides of the Atlantic, and brought me more commissions. I specialised in Celtic studies and my work targeted academia, so after a few years I had become a worldwide authority in the field. A regular correspondence developed with several large universities, mainly in the US, and more and more postgraduates were using me as a resource in their research. I was even invited to contribute to the *Encyclopaedia Britannica*.

After five years I had become utterly absorbed in my work, and didn't for a single moment look upon my freedom as being restricted. I was doing everything I wanted to do and there was nowhere my mind and imagination couldn't go. Even my life with Dana was richer, and we became closer and more in love as the years ticked by.

She had the amazing knack of anticipating my readiness for change and for providing the perfect trigger for me to squeeze at the appropriate time. One birthday she brought me a copy of the life and writings of Nelson Mandela. Of course I had been impressed by his story, but had not looked closely at the man before.

As I read the book, it gradually dawned on me that he was one of the few men alive who seemed to be truly empowered. That set me off along a trail of books and articles that eventually brought me to the point of writing to him. I wanted to 'touch the hem of his cloak', so to speak. I also wanted to see how he would answer questions I had about his concept of 'amandla' – power. In one of his speeches he said:

'OUR DEEPEST FEARS ARE NOT THAT WE ARE INADEQUATE, OUR DEEPEST FEAR IS THAT WE ARE POWERFUL BEYOND MEASURE.'

I wrote the letter but never sent it. I didn't send it because it wasn't necessary. I 'knew' what his answers would be.

V: Why are we afraid of becoming powerful?

NM: Power means responsibility. That is, responsibility for who we are, our actions and the consequences of our actions. Also, at a deeper level, we are responsible for the actions of others. To take on these responsibilities is truly awesome and intimidating and it's little wonder we fear it.

V: What can we do about this fear?

NM: Look at it in a different light. Fear is not a tyrant to run away from but a friend and counsellor to welcome into our lives. It cautions us, protects us, defends us, guides us and strengthens us. What is there to be scared of?

V what does empowerment mean?

NM: I call empowerment AMANDLA and it is different for every individual. We all have to find our way towards it and help others to find their own way. It means knowing and doing what is the right action without illusion, expectation, hope, advantage, reward and accepting that the consequences may even be disadvantageous to us in worldly terms.

V: What about moral action?

NM: There are no morals in nature. Morals are merely concepts devised by man for his own devious ends – usually to impose on others.

V: You have met many powerful people. Have you met anyone who you believe is empowered?

NM: Muhammad Ali.

V: What is the difference between an empowered person and a powerful person?

NM: A powerful person who is not empowered can rule a continent yet still live inside himself in chains. An empowered person can live in chains yet rule himself.

V: Would you say that you are an empowered person?

NM: Anyone who believes himself to be empowered, isn't!

Meeting Mandela in this way unsettled me. For the first time in many years I wondered if I was doing the right thing by sheltering myself from the challenges of the world. I saw parallels between Mandela and myself and between Mandela and Twrch Trwyth. The three of us had challenged the established power structures. The three of us had been persecuted and 'put away'. Mandela had re-emerged to enchant, enrich and possibly re-empower people everywhere. Twrch hadn't, and disappeared into disillusion and ignominy. Now I had to decide what I was going to do.

Again a timely gift from Dana helped me; a book of Welsh poems from the Middle Ages.

One evening I read a poem by Dafydd Nanmor. Dafydd was a fifteenth-century bard who made a comfortable living writing poems in praise of the landed gentry. He wrote this poem when living in the house of a Rhys ap Rhydderch near the mouth of the river Teifi. Rhys had a son who we would describe today as a spoilt brat. The young man appeared to lack motivation, drive and any sense of his responsibilities and duties – so Dafydd wrote him a poem.

The poem describes the '*Chain of life*' of which we

are all a link. Some of us are small insignificant links, others large important links. Dafydd told the young nobleman that he was a large link, which the other smaller links needed and depended on to sustain the strength of their 'chain of life'.

In beautiful, lyrical language he called him the 'Rose of Tywyn' and described him as the stag that leads the race uphill, the eagle who flies to the topmost branch of the oak, the power in the lion's roar. He tells him not to be afraid of all this power and strength, but to take his rightful place in the chain for which he had been forged. This was, said Dafydd, the whole point of him being put on the earth.

I read and re-read these wonderful thoughts and imagined how wonderful it must have been for the boy to read these words and feel the inspiration, and what a difference it must have made to his life. I tried to put myself in the boy's position believing that the poem had been written for me. Its message pierced my soul like an eagle's claw as I became aware that *it had been written for me*. My days of preparation had come to an end, and it was now time for me to get back into 'the chain of life' and play my rightful part as a vital and huge link.

Planning and arranging my escape was easy. For eight years I had been a model prisoner, refusing countless opportunities to go on escorted visits, so was not considered to be a security risk. Consequently, I was allowed considerable freedom, like a canary that always returns to its cage at night. One night the canary didn't return. I had re-entered the 'chain of life' with my mission to help bring amandla to the world.

How? I don't know yet. I know only that I can't do it alone. I will need your help. It seems to be part of your destinies too and, like me, my dear young friends, you have no choice.

CHAPTER 25

The Chain of Life

T O ALLOW MYSELF time to think, I slowly tidied the separate sheets of paper and straightened the edges with deliberate care.

'Will this mean us living outside the law and being on the run?' she asked, then answered her own question. 'What rubbish! He wouldn't allow that.'

'I think this letter is his way of giving advanced warning of what's coming,' I said.

'And without him having to make lengthy explanations,' she added.

Looking back on those moments I believe we responded well. We were flabbergasted and clueless, but not dismayed or doubtful. We seemed to accept without question that if and when we were called to help him we would be ready. We read through the last few pages again and a third time. Each reading brought us to a greater state of readiness, and by the time we went outside for some mind-clearing night air, we were actually looking forward to the next step.

We walked to the end of the garden and looked out over the bay. The glittering constellations spread over us like a protective cloak of light; Orion the hunter was overhead to the east with his dog, Sirius, glittering at his feet as if waiting for a command or a rub behind the ear. A shooting star briefly appeared, then disappeared like a fox into the darkness. Ruth walked over to the gate, her face like ivory in the light of the rising moon, and rested her hands on the catch.

'Do you love me, David?' she asked, in mock seriousness. 'I don't know what that means,' I said, picking up her tone and putting my hands softly on her shoulders. 'If it means wanting you, preserving you, honouring you and…'

'David, come on.' She turned to face me, her eyes in shadow. She grabbed the front of Verres' voluminous sweater I seemed to live in these days. I wasn't sure now how serious she was.

'What would you give up for me?'

'My life,' I said smugly, but that wasn't enough, and she punched my chest. It stung.

'What more can I give up?' I pleaded, unable to find the elusive 'right' answer she expected.

'You twit. You flaming twit.' Two flaming eyes flickered in the shadows on her face. 'Haven't you learnt anything from Verres?'

'I want us to live together,' I said weakly. She strengthened her grip on the sweater, put a foot behind my ankle and made a futile attempt at a judo throw. Belatedly I allowed myself to fall into the dew-moistened grass, and she followed me down and started pummelling my chest with soft fists and spontaneous grunts from the exertion.

'OK, OK, I'll do the washing-up for you.' She was now astride my middle, bouncing up and down and laughing.

'I'll have your baby, I'll wash your car, I'll let you use my toothpaste.'

I gasped my pleas as she continued to persecute my diaphragm and dunk me in the dewy grass.

'It's your money I want, you dumb man,' she laughed, diverting her attack to my ribs. I grabbed her, held her close and growled into her ear, 'I draw the line at tickling.'

She stopped struggling, the tension left our bodies and we

lay quietly in each other's arms, listening to our unsynchronised breathing. Then I knew the answer to her question. I knew too, for the first time in my life, what it meant to really love someone. I knew with certainty and comfort, the abrupt understanding didn't even surprise me.

'I would give *you* up if I knew it was the best thing for you,' I whispered softly. 'But I pray I won't have to do that.'

'Now I know you love me.' We rolled over. 'Uurgh, it's all wet.'

Pushing off my chest she rose onto her feet. I followed her back into the house, leaving romance to the moon, the sea and the stars, musing to myself, yes, that's the only way I could let her go. If it was best for her if I did so. Then I would do it without hesitation.

'Will you leave Bill and come here to live with me?' I asked, after we'd discarded our sodden clothing and settled together onto the sofa.

'Yes,' she said immediately.

'When?'

'As soon as I can. The time has to be right. I have responsibilities, I don't want to walk away from them. That would start us off on the wrong foot.'

I knew she was right.

We lay together for a while, then I walked over to the window to close the curtains.

'I hope this business doesn't get too complicated.' The curtains wouldn't run and I gave the pull cord a series of short jerks; eventually it broke, and I stood like a prize monkey looking, bemused, at the remains of the curtain draped over my hands.

'What if we get into trouble with the police?' she asked, smoothing her dress and pulling the belt buckle into the middle, ignoring my plight.

'We have to support him,' I said, dropping the remains of

the curtain behind the sofa and turning back to face her. 'I'll do whatever he asks.'

'Would you kill someone for him?'

'He wouldn't ask me.'

She looked up at me earnestly. 'I know he wouldn't ask you, but the time may come when you may have to make a decision for yourself. Would you kill to save him?'

'I'm not a killer. I wouldn't know how,' I said evasively.

'Are you sure of that?'

'Absolutely.'

She looked doubtful. 'That's what he would have said, until…'

'Let's drop it, Ruth,' I grunted peevishly.

She rose and came over to me. 'Can't you see why I need to ask you?'

'Are you testing me, Ruth? Don't you think I'm able to commit myself to him?' I asked.

'Oh I know you can, my dear. I want to make sure that *you* know it too.' She put her arms around me. 'You're a big man, David. He knows it, I know it, but most importantly, do you?'

We stood silently without moving for a time, while her words travelled to my heart like salmon returning to their home river. Gradually my arms encircled her, and I knew she was right and that the knowledge gave me awesome responsibilities.

'David.'

'Mm,' I said dreamily.

'Tell me one thing.'

'What's that?'

'What's a girl got to do to get kissed in this house?'

Our lips didn't come together on tip-toe as I had rehearsed mentally many times but like rutting stags fighting for a harem. I grabbed her shoulders, roughly pulled her onto me and we unleashed the hounds of frustration and tension upon each other as we slid to the floor. Still entwined like two wrestlers unable to release their holds for fear of leaving an opening, I pulled my face away from her neck. 'Come to bed,' I said.

She touched my face with gossamer fingers, then like a crocodile holding my head as tight as she could, shook it with tender roughness. 'Is that how you want it then? On the mats in the gym store?'

My body winced as if someone had screamed from a closed grave. 'How do you know about that?'

She squirmed and laughed. 'Half the sixth form knew before the start of the first lesson next morning.'

'I never knew that. How?' I eased my grip on her, but she tightened hers on me. 'Did someone see us?'

'God David, don't tell me you think you've been keeping a secret for twenty-five years.'

'Did Kelly tell you?' I puffed.

'Tell *me!* She rounded up most of the girls in the year and gave us a blow by blow account.'

'Each time?' I asked.

'Just the once,' she said aghast. 'Don't tell me you did it twice?' I grinned in secret triumph.

We lay entwined and slightly uncomfortable on the floor, swimming in our separate pools of thought for several minutes.

'Do you still want to go on the gym mats?' she asked.

I picked her up and carried her to the bottom of the stairs where I tripped and almost dropped her. She grabbed my arm with her left hand and I noticed she had somehow removed her wedding ring since we had come in from the garden. Without another word we walked upstairs, in step in every way.

*

She left for home much later than she had originally intended. 'Don't get up, darling,' she said, while dressing.

I lay in our bed listening to her busy movements in the bathroom. She came back to kiss me goodbye before going downstairs and letting herself out. As the sound of her car edged into the night I slipped out of bed, dressed and charged downstairs. My mind was putting on a fireworks display, but first of all I had to read Verres' treatise again.

When I'd finished I went to a bookshelf in search of Mary Benson's book on Nelson Mandela. I had bought it in a charity bookshop for 40p a few months earlier but not previously opened it.

The first chapter was headed, 'A Reasonable Man, not a Violent Man'. That could also be Verres, I thought. Both were reasonable men who had committed violent acts. Then I wondered about myself and tried to explore a scenario in which I could reasonably do a violent act. I must have gone to sleep at this juncture.

*

About midday I was up, perky and breezing about the house with a duster, a tin of polish and a ménage of joyous thoughts that all revolved around Ruth, when the doorbell rang. I answered it and came face to face with the smiling and confident Commissioner Stoker. To my surprise I was genuinely delighted to see him. Without hesitation I told him so, and invited him in.

'Sit down,' I said. 'Can I get you something to drink?'

He took his shoes off inside the door like a Buddhist, then conducted himself on a leisurely tour of my sitting room looking at book spines, ornaments and pictures. He poked his nose into the conservatory, then took a quick look out to sea through the nautical telescope on a tripod, before leading me back to the sitting room.

'You've got some lovely things here, Mr Tanner.'

'Thank you.'

'It shows another side of you,' he added thoughtfully. 'Very male but sensitive and thoughtful. If I may say so I think your taste is eclectic but immaculate.' He stopped in front of an abstract dominating one wall. 'Mark Rothko if I'm not mistaken.'

'Well done.' I moved alongside him. 'I'm impressed, Mr Stoker. It's one of a limited edition and signed by the artist on the back.'

'I remember seeing a lot of Rothkos in Paris,' he said, tilting his head a little to one side. 'He was very popular in certain circles but I was never able to work out which way up his stuff is supposed to be.'

'That's easy,' I said lightly. 'Look for the signature, that's a dead giveaway.'

'Look for the signature,' he repeated, moving away from the picture. 'That's very profound Mr Tanner. Yes, I'd like a coffee, thank you.' He glanced at the slim parcel wrapped in *The Guardian* on the floor beside a chair. 'I see Mrs Jenkins has left her parcel,' he said, bending to pick it up. I was too quick for him, and snatched the bundle from under his nose and slipped it into a drawer.

'Excuse the mess Mr Stoker; I'm such an untidy devil.'

He merely smiled tolerantly, glanced once at the drawer, making sure I saw him, and followed me into the kitchen.

'I assume this isn't a social call, Mr Stoker. What brings you here again? Sit where you like. Has it anything to do with last night's police raid?'

'I hope it wasn't too big a shock for you,' he said, inspecting the kitchen before gazing out of the window. 'Especially as it was pointless anyway. It was obvious that our man wouldn't be here. That's why you didn't see me. You like birds I presume, from your books and telescope.'

'I certainly do, especially birds of prey.' We looked at each other with perfect understanding and laughed.

He watched me make a cafetière and empty half a packet of chocolate and ginger biscuits onto a plate.

He helped himself to a biscuit before I offered them. 'Mmm, my favourite. I'm here for two reasons. First to apologise for yesterday and mend a few fences. Secondly, to assure you that the idea that Verres and Mrs Jenkins are having a… sexual liaison… is utterly absurd. He wouldn't allow a thing like that to happen.'

We moved into the conservatory. He picked up Verres' still damp sweater which I'd carelessly discarded the previous night. 'Weren't you wearing this yesterday?'

'Yes, Verres left it behind and I borrowed it. But let's get to the point Mr Stoker.'

He laughed lightly and his soft eyes twinkled. 'I like the new David Tanner. Yesterday I looked at the picture you showed me of yourself, but the signature was upside down. Perhaps I'd like to look at the picture the right way up.'

'You're still talking in riddles, Mr Stoker.' I arranged the coffee cups on a low table. No mugs for this gentleman, I thought.

'Talking in riddles is a failing of mine, Mr Tanner. These are good.' He reached for another biscuit. 'I felt that I got off on the wrong foot with you yesterday, and thought with twenty-four hours to think about things you may be able to tell me more about your relationship with Verres.'

'Milk? Sugar?'

'As it is, thanks.' He looked into the steaming dark depths of the cup as if it were the cauldron of wisdom, then asked directly, 'Has he contacted to you since he left?'

I was done with the cagey game we had previously played.

He was too good at it anyway. My game now was straighter and more direct. 'Yes, Mr Stoker, he has.'

His eyes widened in surprise. 'Oh, when?'

'Last night.'

'Was he here?'

'No.'

'Did he telephone?'

'No. Ruth brought a letter from him.'

He looked thoughtful for a moment. 'Wrapped in the newspaper?'

'That's right.'

'May I see it?'

'No! It's a personal letter to us.'

'It looks as if it was a long letter.'

'He had a lot to say about a lot of things… and a lot of people.' Our eyes met knowingly and I knew he understood my insinuation.

He was clearly surprised by my new-found frankness, but seemed to approve. I expected him to become a heavy-handed policeman ready to bully me into handing over the letter and was ready for that, but again I had underestimated him. 'Of course, I understand completely.' He sipped his coffee. 'Interesting blend,' he said dividing his attention between me, the coffee and a magpie clumsily floundering for the nuts in the bird feeder.

'I suppose, therefore, that there's a little more to your relationship than you were prepared to admit yesterday?'

'Yes there is,' I said. 'We have become good friends. I'm sure you know all about the bonds of friendship, Mr Stoker.' He looked at me with his clear light blue eyes. Perhaps I imagined seeing in their depths a cloud of sadness briefly come and go.

'Do you know what he did?' he asked quietly.

'Yes, I do.'

'That he killed two men with his bare hands?'

'Yes, and escaped from prison.'

I couldn't help liking Stoker even more now we were playing the game with our cards face up. He had no need to lay traps for me or give double meanings to his words and a natural, easy trust was growing between us.

He looked at me earnestly. 'Whatever he wrote in his letter, Mr Tanner, it has had a remarkable effect on you.'

'I'll tell you another thing, Mr Stoker.' He sipped his coffee, but he raised his eyebrows to tell me he was listening. 'He may have been responsible for the death of two men, but he's not a killer. He's a man of reason, not violence. If you know him as well as I believe you do, you'll know this is true.'

'Mr Tanner.' He put a hand on my arm and the gentle expression on his face melted my heart. 'I wish I had a friend like you.'

'Mr Stoker,' I said putting a hand on *his* arm. 'You did once, didn't you?'

We didn't move our hands but he looked at me curiously without replying. 'Do you remember your friend's name, Mr Stoker?'

'It was a long time ago.' He took his hand and his gaze away from me and returned to studying activity around the bird feeder. 'It was in another lifetime.'

'It was yesterday, Mr Stoker. Tell me his name.'

'I think you know it,' he said, quietly turning back to face me.

'Say the name, Bran.'

He looked at me, brimming with relief as if my saying the name had released a burden he had been carrying. Then his eyes moistened with feeling and he whispered, 'Tommy'.

CHAPTER 26

Forged in a Web that Weaves

EARLY-RISING WORKERS WERE already on the streets before Ruth arrived home. Endlessly reliving the hours we had shared earlier in the night, she had driven most of the way on a wave of energy and excitement that had overridden her body's need for rest and sustenance. However the dark, tired streets of Midlands suburbia changed her mood and utter weariness rapidly came over her, so that by the time she pulled up outside her front door, she could barely find the will to stay awake long enough to get out of the car and drag herself into the house.

Once inside she dropped her bag, and with a groan leant heavily back against the door. She felt the catch click, then kicking off her shoes and allowing her coat to slip off her shoulders to the floor, lurched towards the darkened stairs. Suddenly the lights swarmed on and her heart jumped like a cricket.

'Where've you been?' Jenkins was standing on top of the stairs, looking down at her like a skulking carrion crow.

'Oh Bill, you almost gave me a heart attack,' she gasped wearily.

'Where have you been?' he asked again.

'What do you mean? You know where I've been.'

Slowly she climbed the stairs towards him using the banister rail for support. He didn't move.

'It doesn't take twelve hours to get home from Wales,' he glowered. 'Where have you been?'

'What is this Bill? What are you doing here anyway?'

'You've been with your precious lover. Admit it.'

Physically exhausted from lack of sleep and emotionally exhausted by the endless trawl of surprises, she dragged herself to the top of the stairs.

'Yes Bill, I have.' She was too weary to lie any more. 'Why should it suddenly concern you? It hasn't bothered you before.'

'You disgust me,' he grunted, recoiling from her. 'He's old enough to be your father.'

He stepped backwards into the landing still facing her. 'At least in the past you've shown some… some… discretion.'

She shouldered past him looking straight ahead, trusting her lifeless legs to take her as far as her bedroom.

'Don't you have anything to say?' he taunted, following her. 'Don't tell me you've run out of lies.'

She swung around towards him and he stopped. 'Bill, I'm tired. I'm tired of your endless obsession with yourself.' She took a step towards him and he took a half-step back. 'I'm tired of your stupidity. For an intelligent man I can't believe how stupid you are.'

'Stupid?' Jenkins held his ground and they stood defying each other, not twelve inches apart.

'Yes, your inane fixation about Verres and me is plain stupid.'

'Well if it isn't him, who else could it possibly be?'

'David, of course,' she said in a low voice turning her back to him to open her bedroom door. She was too weary to hold the lid down on our secret any longer. His eyes widened and he studied her for a moment before a savage smirk slowly curled across his eyes and upper lip.

'Ruth,' he said without following her. 'I've known you for over thirty years and in that time you've never stooped as low as now, trying to drag poor David into your sordid scheming like this.'

She felt nothing, and with dry eyes watched him go into his study with an air of righteous dignity, and lock the door.

'Poor man,' she muttered to the empty landing. 'What happened to him?'

Without another thought she retreated into her bedroom, flopped onto the bed and fell instantly into a restless and dream-cursing sleep.

*

Alone in his study, her husband sat behind his desk with a satisfied smile on his lips and hands in a praying position, but with only fingers and thumbs touching. He was not praying; he only ever did that before an audience. Now he was contemplating his next move.

'Alright, my lady,' he said aloud. 'If that's the way you want to play your game let's see how you like the way *I* play it.'

He reached for the phone and pressed out a number.

'Yes?'

'Mr Roberts?'

'Who's that?'

'Good morning, this is Dr Jenkins.' No reply. 'Are you there?'

'Do you know the time?'

'Sorry, but the police bungled and our bird got away.'

'I told you, didn't I!' The voice sounded stronger.

'Yes, you were right,' Jenkins agreed. 'I don't think they even got close to him.'

'I knew they wouldn't. What now?'

'It's imperative for us to bring our bird down. It seems that it will have to be your way after all.'

'Alright.'

'My name has to be kept out…'

'Don't say any more. We'll have to meet.' Roberts sounded wide awake now.

'When? Where?'

'Call me tonight.'

The line went dead. Jenkins replaced the receiver, grimly pleased with himself. He then unscrewed the top of his fountain pen and started preparing a talk he was due to give the dioceses' young clergy which was advertised as: 'Living with the Truth – It's not so difficult.'

*

Ruth woke about midday. She got up immediately, showered and went downstairs prepared for a 'scene'. The door of Jenkins' study was open and he looked up and beamed as she passed.

'Come in, dear,' he said. 'And before you say a word, I apologise for last night… I was anxious because I thought you may have had an accident and in the darkness my mind started playing tricks…'

'It's no good, Bill,' she interrupted. 'I'm leaving you.'

'Oh.' He looked crestfallen. 'Where are you going to go? To him? What will you do when he's caught and taken back to prison? Have you thought about that?'

She sat down on the sofa by the window and looked vacantly at her husband.

'I don't know where I'm going to go, Bill. We've lived for years without love, but chugged along well enough with mutual respect. Now even that has gone, and there's nothing left. I have to get away.'

Jenkins left his desk and came over to sit near her.

'Look, dear.' He twisted around to face her, while maintaining a non-threatening distance between them. 'I can't blame you, I know I've behaved badly, but I've thought of nothing else all the morning and can promise you that I still have profound respect for you.' He took a deep breath. 'I don't want to lose you, my dear, and will do anything to get your respect back.'

For an hour or more they bartered for their futures. He appeared full of remorse and reasonableness and argued for a fresh start based on independence and acceptance. She was unconvinced by his contrition and wanted to end the marriage immediately. However, the practicalities of an instant break were insurmountable, so they agreed on a trial separation as soon as was practically possible for both of them. In the meantime, they would continue to live under the same roof and maintain a public semblance of normality, although privately they would live separate lives and continue to sleep in different bedrooms.

'If you still feel this way in six months' time,' he said, 'I promise I won't stand in your way.'

'I'm thinking more in terms of weeks, not months, Bill,' she said from behind her rigidly folded arms. 'Four at the most.'

He fiddled silently with a large wooden crucifix for a few moments, and she prepared herself to resist whatever new idea he came up with. He took her by surprise.

'OK, if that's what you want,' he said, looking up. 'I've been a bastard and this is what I deserve.' He held his hand up in benediction to arrest any response. 'You have every right to leave me, and if that's what you really want to do, I'll do all I can to make it easy for you when the time comes.'

She was momentarily dumbfounded.

'I know I've got no right to ask anything in return and will understand if you say no, but can I ask you just one small favour? Not in return, but out of the goodness of your heart.'

He smiled sheepishly, which reminded her of the audacious young man she had fallen in love with when they were at university. Her heart didn't exactly melt, but it warmed a bit.

'What is it, Bill?'

'Well,' he said slowly, 'I've got a few crazy months coming up, and I hate to impose on you, but I can't see how I can get through them and the turmoil of us breaking up.'

'Do you mean the lectures you've been preparing?'

'They are only a part of it. There's also my other book. It's coming out next week and, as part of the contract, I have to do the unavoidable round of promotional signings and interviews and...' He lowered his head like a sinner at confession. 'Perhaps it isn't as important to me as it was twenty-four hours ago, but I've been told that I'm favourite to chair an important committee Canterbury is setting up.'

'Oh, that's news to me.' She looked accusingly at him but he kept his head bowed.

'I was sworn not to let it out, not even to you.'

'What's it about?'

'Getting bums on seats, basically.'

'Pews!' she corrected perversely. 'The days of bums on pews are gone forever, Bill. People don't want to put on their best clothes to be preached at once a week. It's at best meaningless and, to most people, an interference in their ever more and more complicated lives.'

'You're right. I need to hear your sanity when I get all muddled. I need you to help me through the opening weeks of this committee but...' He lowered his head. 'At last I'm able to put your needs before mine so if you can't...' He let silence complete his sentence.

'For how long Bill?'

'That's the problem.' He leaned back and spread his hands. 'I can't honestly tell you exactly, you know how one thing tends to lead to another, but it shouldn't be much more than a couple of months.'

She'd set her heart on leaving immediately, and the thought of a day longer than necessary was stultifying; yet she wanted to be fair to the man she had once loved. Also, she saw the need of time to get the children used to the idea.

'Let's give it two months, Bill. That should be long enough to get yourself sorted out.' She felt the concession was fair, and it would be mean-spirited not to give him the extra time if it was really important to him.

He slowly rose to his feet, trying not to look triumphant.

'Dear Ruth,' he said. 'Thank you. You won't regret it.'

I already do, she thought.

*

Six hours later, Jenkins came home feeling very pleased with himself after having had a profitable telephone call from Canterbury. Ruth dressed in jeans, trainers and a replica rugby top was potting plants in the kitchen. He put his head around the door.

'Just got to make a quick call, see you in a minute.'

He went directly into his study and listened furtively for a moment in the doorway to sounds of Ruth working in the kitchen before going in. He locked the door and prodded out a number from memory.

'Yes!'

'Dr Jenkins here,' he whispered.

'Why are you whispering?'

'My wife is home.'

'Do you have an extension?'

'Of course…'

'Don't say any more. Meet me in Fishguard next Wednesday?'

Jenkins opened his desk diary.

'Next Wednesday is out of the question. Friday is the earliest…'

'Meet me off the midday ferry on Friday. Have your mobile phone turned on.'

'How will I recognise you?'

'Just be there; I'll recognise you.'

'Have you got my number?'

The disengaged tone sounded. Jenkins held the receiver to his ear for a minute, listening for the click of the extension phone being replaced, but heard nothing. He lounged back in his chair with his hands behind his head, looking out of the window into the distance with a self-satisfied smile on his face, which brightened to a broad grin as he rose and left the room.

He met Ruth in the hall. She had put on a light coat over her gardening clothes and was carrying her handbag.

'I'm popping out for some peat and a few more seedlings,' she said. 'If you can wait I'll get something to eat about eight o'clock.'

'Are you going out like that?' He looked down at the grubby jeans and trainers showing under the coat, and her peat-black fingernails.

'I want to get over to the garden centre before it closes.'

'See you later then,' he said, wisely keeping for another time a little lecture about having to maintain an appearance in keeping with their status.

During the afternoon, she too had had an important phone call to make; but after four attempts had still not got through. She drove to a late opening garden centre near Kenilworth, which was almost deserted with only three other cars in the car park.

She parked in a corner farthest from the entrance and pressed out a number on her mobile phone.

*

I was leaning on the gate at the far end of the garden, looking at the sea, 'lovely daying' the occasional walker and admiring the beautiful display of dandelions in the lawn when the telephone's outside bell rang. I sprinted back to the house and picked up the kitchen extension.

'Hello,' I said breathlessly.

'Guess who this is.'

'Oh your majesty,' I said, trying to put the sound of bending knees and knuckled forelocks in my voice. 'I'd know your voice anywhere. How are the corgis? Has my knighthood come through at last?'

'Oh you fool,' she laughed. 'What are you doing?'

'Something so degenerate I don't dare tell you. Will you kindly ask me an easier question.'

'Perhaps I should call you back once whatever it is you've taken has worn off. I was hoping to have a serious discussion.'

'So "guess who this is?" and "what are you doing?" is your idea of having a serious discussion is it?'

'Look David, there have been developments here and I have to talk to you. Is now alright?'

I listened to her relate her conversations with Jenkins without interrupting. 'He's conned you, darling,' I said after she'd finished. 'If you're not careful, two months will become three, then half a year. You'll find yourself sucked into the old routine and will never get away.'

'No, that won't happen,' she said. 'But you may be right about him conning me. I simply don't know, but I've decided to give him the benefit of any doubt because… because, well, a lot of things are happening in his life all at once, and perhaps he really does need me behind him until the worst is over.'

I wasn't convinced; but she'd clearly made her mind up, so I let her continue without interrupting. 'I wish him no ill, and hope he gets all the success he wants from his life.'

'When you finally leave Bill, will you come here to live with me?'

She was silent for a few seconds. 'The thought has never entered my head... you stupid man.'

'There's nothing I've ever wanted more in my life,' I said, tiring of flippancy.

'That's how I feel too darling, eight short weeks...'

'Say "darling" again,' I interrupted. 'The way you say it almost gives me an orgasm.'

'Oh you ass... those weeks will fly by. I will need all that time anyway, to get my little life redirected. What do you mean *almost*?'

'Will we see each other before then?' I was thinking clearly now and juggling with ways of making the next few weeks tolerable without having to cover our feelings with throwaway one-liners.

'We must,' she said passionately. 'I need to wake up in your arms, then go back to sleep and wake up again with your arms still around me. I can't wait two whole months for that. Last night was exciting, thrilling and sweetly illicit, but I hated having to get up and leave you while it was still dark.'

We talked on as lovers do, as if time had stopped, and led each other on a fairyland journey full of fantasies, dreams, impracticalities, sensuality and downright smut. She said she would come down as soon as she could. The conversation ended in anticlimax, as she announced that she had to go home to prepare supper for her husband.

I walked back to the dandelions as if I was walking on air,

and in my favourite position, leaning on the gate, basked in our plans and promises. Then a freshening wind from the sea chilled me; a cat's paw of troubled water puckered across the bay, and I wondered what game Bill was playing. He was up to something.

CHAPTER 27

On Crossing Waves

A DOZEN CARS and two buses were parked around the harbour exit as the Rosslare ferry disgorged its passengers into a Welsh monsoon. Leaning into the wind, huddled under rain hoods and wrestling with aerobatic umbrellas, they scurried off to the dejected vehicles. A lone BMW waited apart from the others; a man standing alone scrutinized it from a distance. He wore a brown ankle-length stockman's coat, done up to the throat with its tails blowing behind him like wings on his legs, and a broad-brimmed hat which he held in place with one hand. Suddenly he hurried across to the BMW. As he approached, Jenkins leant across and opened the passenger door.

'Dr Jenkins?'

'A dirty day Mr Roberts, get in.'

After a curt exchange of pleasantries they drove off to a more secluded place to conduct their business. Roberts needed to return within an hour to catch the ferry's turnaround, and already passengers were dribbling towards it.

Up the hill overlooking the harbour, a long a series of narrow, puddled lanes led them to a mean little church that the French invaders had ransacked two hundred years earlier leaving it empty and desolate, which is how it remained.

'We won't be interrupted here, Mr Roberts,' Jenkins said, staring fixedly ahead.

'Down to business,' the passenger said gruffly. 'What do you want?'

'I want Verres out of the way.' Neither man had yet looked at the other. 'And no foul-ups by blundering policemen this time.'

'Permanently?'

'Permanently.'

'You sure?'

'Absolutely.'

'And you'll give me a completely free hand to do it my way?' Roberts still stared ahead.

'Are you sure you can do it? He's very resourceful, and seems to be a jump ahead of everyone.'

'He won't be a jump ahead of me, Dr Jenkins. It's me who's a jump ahead of him.'

'So you know where he is?' Jenkins half-turned so he could see Roberts' bullet-like profile.

'No, but I will soon.'

'Then what?'

'Do you really want to know?' Roberts pivoted and returned the gaze, quizzically raising the stubbly skin of shaven eyebrows.

Jenkins looked away. 'No. Not really, but understand, after we part today I've never heard of you, nor you me.'

'That's understood.'

'And we won't speak to each other again?'

'If that's what you want.'

'And one payment of £2,000 in cash is all you want?'

'That's correct.'

'It doesn't seem very much for what…'

'It's all I want,' he uttered icily. 'It'll cover expenses. I'd do it for nothing if I had to.'

Oh Jesus, what am I doing? Jenkins thought, as he slid a sealed manila envelope across to him. Roberts opened it, thumbing through its contents before back-handing it into an inside pocket.

Jenkins noted Roberts' hands; they were square and muscular with blunt, almost brutal, fingers. He could see such a hand nailing another hand onto a wooden cross. He shivered. 'When?' he asked.

'He's gone to ground for the time being, but I'll know as soon as he shows himself... then I'll do the business.'

The man frightened Jenkins, but his career needed Ruth and he would break a lot of rules to keep her. His conscience made a weak last-minute appearance. 'We are talking about getting him back in police custody aren't we, Mr Roberts? Nothing more serious!'

'That's no longer your concern, Dr Jenkins.'

Jenkins stared into the rain beating on the windscreen. He felt uneasy and disliked Roberts in the flesh more than he had done on the telephone. For a second he flirted with second thoughts but finally said, 'I'll take you back to the ferry.'

Not a word was spoken during the return journey. Roberts got out of the car at the harbour entrance and turned to look at the driver. Although only an inch or two over medium height, he was solidly built, and standing there with his legs apart against the wind he looked, to Jenkins, immovable. A giant defying a tidal wave of honour and decency. He had a cold, emotionless resolution that chilled innocence.

'I don't suppose we'll meet again, Mr Roberts.' Out of habit he started a flowery farewell speech.

'Let's hope not.' Roberts turned and walked away towards the gate, pushing the wind aside as he went.

'Amen to that,' Jenkins intoned fervently.

*

Before I saw Ruth again the swallows were already gathering for their long journey south, and the ferocious garden growth was slowing down to a walking pace. I'd found someone to look after it, so left everything to him with a clear conscience and simply enjoyed watching living things grow around me.

She'd telephoned me when she could, but was gradually becoming more distressed about her situation.

'I feel trapped, darling,' she told me once. 'It seems that I'm getting sucked deeper and deeper into Bill's world. Every time I think I can get out, something comes up. If I don't have to be hostess to his precious committee or sit alongside him dumb and smiling for a TV interview, I have to stand in for him with the Woman's Union while he's away signing books in Edinburgh. That bloody book has taken over my life and now they're talking about a reprint, translations, a paperback and a book club edition. God, it's a nightmare.'

'Be patient sweetheart,' I said. 'Just let events take their course.'

'How can you be so complacent?' she retorted indignantly. 'Don't you care any more?'

'What has caring to do with accepting the way things are?' I asked, laughing.

The truth, which I didn't admit to Ruth, was that I had spent a fascinating summer with a Landranger map in my hand exploring places where prehistoric man had lived and left his mark around my home: standing stones like guardians of permanence waiting to be awakened; the outlines of roundhouses half-concealed beneath mounds and brambles; burial chambers of ancient warrior chiefs; and rangy hill forts rimmed with the remains of stone defences, all still claiming their place in the land after thousands of years. Soon I started to feel more and more empathy with the ancient people who had lived and died in these places, and would sit for hours letting my imagination take me back to those times. I came to understand them, and believed they must have lived completely in the moment, without either the hopes or fears that grip the lives of modern man like a vice.

One day I returned from a walk, carrying an armful of wild flowers. I arranged them in various containers around the house, tidied the kitchen and lounge, stocked the larder, changed the bedding and was emerging from the shower when her car came down the drive.

'Thank heavens you got my message,' she said, immediately noticing my preparations. 'I hate arriving anywhere unannounced.'

Only then did I notice the message light blinking on my telephone answering machine. I killed it, thinking, weird, how did I know?

The long separation had changed nothing. We came together with comfortable, easy intimacy with no embarrassment or timidity or even a timetable to keep. It wasn't until we were having a late breakfast in the conservatory next morning that we came round to talking about practical matters.

I dared to ask, 'Is this it? Have you come to stay for good?'

She shook her head sadly. 'Not yet, but I'm sure it won't be long now. The success of his book seems to have given Bill a new sense of direction, and he's even talking of resigning from his wretched committee which he says is going "nowhere". Soon he'll get what he wants, then he won't need it, or me.'

'But do you think he'll ever let you go?' I didn't share her faith in his 'new dawn'.

'He promised.'

'And you still believe him?'

'I've no reason not to.'

'Even though you've already overshot your original time limit by almost two months?'

'That's not his fault.' She abruptly got up and clattered the breakfast dishes in the sink. I skated away from the thin ice.

'How is it that you've managed to get away now?'

She had told me in the message I hadn't heard that he had suddenly been called to the States for the launch of his book over there. I asked how long she would be able to stay.

'Can you put up with me for a week?' she asked roguishly.

'Have I any choice?'

'None.'

Our eyes met and the silent message was understood; our clothes were off again before we reached the bedroom, the dishes unwashed and, with no credit to us, unbroken in the sink.

*

Late one afternoon three days' later we were in the conservatory absorbed in separate activities; she was writing a letter and I was studying a map on my lap when I stood up so suddenly the map plopped onto the floor a yard in front of me. She started. 'What is it?' She looked up anxiously.

'She's coming.'

'Who?'

'This is absurd, I can't believe it,' I said, walking to the front door. 'This is happening more and more frequently.'

We reached the hall when the doorbell rang.

I opened the door and we came face to face with a woman who must have been sixty, but had the relaxed athletic bearing and eyes of a girl. She was tall, with sweptback dark hair starting to show wisps of grey held in place with a coloured ribbon. She wore old jeans and a creased green anorak over a designer blue jumper; red-and-yellow deck shoes peeped cheerfully out from under the jeans.

She smiled and said, 'Hello. David?'

'Come in, Dana,' I said. She floated up to me, scrutinized my face like an antique dealer looking for signs of a fake, then smiled approval, kissed me and turned to Ruth. They hugged each other like long-lost prodigal daughters.

'At last,' she said, turning towards us after looking into the garden. 'I've heard so much about you both; I feel you are old friends.'

'I hope now that we've finally met, you'll stay? Do you have a bag?' I asked.

'Not this time.' She shook her head. 'I've only come to deliver a message from Thomas, then I must go. We sailed over and have to catch the tide.'

'Is he in the boat?' Ruth asked. 'Can we see him?'

'No, I came with Mongan. We're moored in Newport harbour and have to get to Aberporth before dark, if possible.'

'To meet him?' I asked.

'I don't know, I'm just following his instructions.'

'Just a drink of something, then?' said Ruth.

'Nothing, thank you.' She unzipped the map pocket of her anorak, took out a crumpled envelope and held it out for me to take.

Inside was a piece of white card with a brief message in Verres' handwriting:

'Cofio' – Thursday – Midday.
V.

Ruth looked over my shoulder. 'Is that it? What does it mean?'

I showed it to Dana.

She shrugged. 'I can't help you,' she smiled. 'You know what he's like. Now I have to go. Mongan will be fretting.'

'It's only a few minutes in the car, I'll drive you. Coming, Ruth?'

'Try to stop me.' She was already skipping towards the door.

As we drove down the lane I asked Dana about something that was starting to nag me.

'Why didn't Mongan come here with you?'

'He's very shy,' she said. 'It takes him a long time to relax with people he doesn't know.'

'Hmm.' I still felt uneasy. 'I'd like to meet him one day.'

'I'm sure you will, David,' she said, sensing my unease. 'I've known him for many years; he's one of my best and most loyal friends but... but he doesn't mix well with other people.'

The testimonial sounded sincere and I had no doubts about Dana, yet I was still not comfortable about the man.

'He couldn't have been kinder or more supportive to Thomas when he was in prison. He loves and trusts him like a brother.'

'I'm sure you're right...' I turned the car into the road leading to the yacht club without finishing the sentence which would have started with a lie.

'But?' asked Dana.

'Well, I've a vivid imagination and lately I've been able to see all sorts of things in my head as clearly as if I'm watching a film, but always when I try to picture him, his face is an empty space. I can't see who he is.'

Dana laughed. 'That's typical of him. Very few people manage to get to know him... you're not alone in finding him inscrutable.' We didn't talk any more about Mongan and soon we were laughing and chatting as if we had known each other for years.

I parked alongside the ugly concrete wall of the yacht club and, as we were getting out, Dana said, 'I can see now why Thomas loves you two and has such hopes for you. I know you are already my friends too.'

'Yes,' Ruth agreed. 'Friendship doesn't have to serve a long apprenticeship for the right people.' I held my tongue.

The yacht was anchored alongside the main buoyed channel about a hundred yards from the wall. I got my feet wet helping Dana launch her rubber dinghy, which was secured on the pebbles under the wall. She sculled away smoothly with barely a splash, smiling her farewells and occasionally turning to check her direction. Halfway to the yacht the diesel motor started. Soon after, a shadowy figure wearing a coat with the hood up went forward and raised the bow anchor, leaving the craft secured at the stern and impatiently tugging in the fast ebbing tide. The moment Dana climbed aboard, he tied the dinghy's painter to the stern and raised the other anchor before disappearing below. Dana took the wheel and steered the craft through the winding channel, waving a final farewell before giving her full attention to the passage ahead of her.

We watched it disappear around a sand spit, then Ruth jumped down onto the damp sand. 'Come on, let's walk back, you can collect the car later.'

We crossed a wet beach and reached firmer ground before she asked, 'Do you know what 'cofio' means?'

'Huh, fat chance, but I've got a Welsh dictionary at home.'

'Race you,' I called, running off. She chased me shouting, 'Cheat'.

I let her touch the gate first and she rewarded me with 'Sexist'.

'It's difficult to win against you,' I said, closing the gate behind us.

'Impossible,' she shouted, running up the garden. I caught her up at the door and we both won.

'Cofio means "to remember",' I said. 'What does he mean? Remember what?'

Ruth looked thoughtful. 'Cofio is familiar; I've heard it, rather, I've seen it somewhere.'

'Where?'

'I remember!' she clapped her hands. 'Verres had a poster called "Cofio". You took it away, where is it?'

'All his stuff is upstairs, come on.'

We ran upstairs, dived into a cupboard in the third bedroom and emerged with a cylinder of posters held together by a polka-dotted handkerchief. We unrolled them on the floor. 'Cofio' was the second. It was a poem in Welsh, printed over a painting of a cromlech with a low, craggy hill in the background.

'That's Pentre Ifan,' I chirped. 'I went to see it last week.'

'That must be where he wants us to meet him,' she said. 'God, I feel so excited. I don't know how I can wait until Thursday.'

*

The cromlech consisted of three upright stones about eight feet high supporting a capstone about sixteen feet long. It was probably a burial chamber many thousands of years ago and later used by the druids for their ceremonies. It was then forgotten and ignored until it was rediscovered by archaeologists in Victorian times.

'What a lovely spot.' Ruth looked around. 'And there's the mountain on the poster.' She pointed to the rocky outcrop.

'Carn Ingli,' I said. 'You can see it from my garden.'

We read the plaque in front of the stones, admired the view again, spotted the squat Norman tower of Nevern church in the valley below us and watched a buzzard gracefully thermaling above the valley.

'Gosh, it's past twelve. Do you think we're in the wrong place?' Ruth grumbled.

'No,' I said. 'He's waiting.'

'What for?'

'Those people to go.' A couple with an overactive camera, who had arrived after us, were now leaving. They came over to me and I dutifully took their photograph. Soon we had the place to ourselves and the lone buzzard.

'Have you washed that sweater in hot water?'

I looked down at the sweater I was wearing; the one I'd taken from Verres' bedroom. 'No, I haven't, why? Do you think it needs it?'

'It seems tighter than it did. It used to hang on you like an old blanket. Perhaps you've been eating too many cream cakes, young man.'

'Thank you for coming.' Verres and Dana appeared from the cromlech and were walking towards us hand in hand.

'Oh!' Ruth jumped. 'Where did you come from? Out of the ground?'

CHAPTER 28

The One at Last Released

VERRES HAD CHANGED considerably during the months following his dramatic midnight departure. More grey streaks lined his beard and his gnarled face seemed even more so. He still moved with elegance and balance, but with a slower and more measured rhythm. His eyes, however, were still a window to his shining soul; they flashed with the old inquisitive energy, sparkled with life and understanding and exposed his compassion and humanity. I longed to know where he had been since he had left us so dramatically, but knew better than to ask.

'Verres, one day I will not be amazed by your appearances. I won't ask you where you come from. Hi Dana.' My delight at seeing him again came close to being passionate as I compulsively hugged him. The women exchanged gentle glances; from their first meeting an understanding had existed between them that made words unnecessary. Strangely Dana and I needed words.

'What have you been doing since we last saw you?' I asked. It had been a long time and I'd heard nothing from or about him; the world seemed to have swallowed him up. 'A lot of things have happened to us.'

'What have I been doing?' He put a hand on my shoulder and

his expressive eyes sparkled. 'What I've been doing is receiving a neat little lesson in humility from the universe. As for the other things that have happened to you...' He shrugged his great shoulders, 'they are just the start. From today you may find things getting even warmer.'

Dana released his arm and joined Ruth. *Now* they talked! Verres slipped an arm around my shoulder and shunted me around slowly until we were facing the cromlech, with the irregular outline of Carn Ingli showing behind it in the distance.

'I don't have much time left, David,' he said confidentially. 'And we have a lot to do.'

'Please explain.'

He told me that he had started his life since leaving prison with a grand vision of a 'task' he had to perform, but had now discovered that it wasn't *his* task; it was someone else's, and his role was merely to prepare the 'someone else'. That was his 'little lesson in humility'.

'Task? Are you going to tell me what this task is?' I asked.

'I had such monstrous delusions,' he said with a stunted laugh. 'I actually believed that I had been chosen to redeem the world and change lives. Ha, what arrogance. What vanity. What absurdity.' He looked at me, smiling merrily. 'Don't let anyone tell you the cosmos doesn't have a sense of humour. It's such a neat joke.'

'Where is this leading, my friend?' I asked. 'Don't tell me that *I* have a task to perform as well.'

He didn't reply directly. 'You've come on, David, faster than even Dana said you would.'

Come on? I stifled the question, as the women rejoined us. He spread his arms like all-embracing wings and we merged into a huddle with arms curled around each other's waists and shoulders, like children playing a secret game.

'Dana has told me that David has a task to perform and I'm part of it,' said Ruth. 'Please tell me more.'

'Thomas feels that it's almost time for him to move on, that his part of the task is nearly completed,' Dana said, stroking his back gently. 'Soon you'll be able to rest, my love.'

He nodded, then explained. 'In my vanity I believed that I was the one chosen to bring the power of the Boar back to the people living on this little island.'

'And it's David?' Ruth asked quietly.

He tilted his head. 'I'm not yet certain but it looks like it.'

I wanted to ask a torrent of questions: What is the task? Why can't *you* complete it? Who is the Boar? What is the Boar? How will he appear? Why me? But they remained unasked because I had learned from him that answers come from asking questions not answering them.

'I believe you may be the "One", David,' Verres said, very quietly. 'The chosen one. I'm more convinced because you are not asking any of the confusion of questions that must be chasing around in your mind.'

At that moment it didn't occur to either of us that there could be more than one 'One'.

He started to walk slowly towards the cromlech. 'I'm a little weary, and have a long journey to make.'

Dana came over to us. 'He loves you both very much and is very, very proud of you.'

'We feel the same about him,' said Ruth. 'But I still don't understand what he's trying to tell us and why he wanted to see us. He's really told us nothing.'

'He's said what he came to say. Now it's up to you. I must go.' She spun on her heels and scurried after her man. She gently took his arm and they melted into each other.

I took Ruth's hand. 'It's alright my dear, everything will soon be clear to us.'

I called after Verres. 'We will see you again?' I was almost too afraid to ask because I needed to say a proper 'goodbye' to this man who had become the guiding star of my life. 'Surely this isn't the end?'

He looked over his shoulder with a familiar grin. 'You haven't got rid of me yet my friends.' He draped his arm over Dana, who looked up into his face and spoke to him earnestly. He tilted his head towards her, listening intently, then with a loud laugh but without turning around raised his free arm and gave us a cheery wave. We walked towards the car, leaving them alone with each other as we knew they wished. We didn't look back.

*

The time was close for Ruth to return home; we didn't know when we would see each other next, so spent our remaining days and nights entwined in a Gordian knot of love and released desire. Yet there were times when we needed to go into separate spaces. There was no regular pattern for this, but when either of us felt the need to be alone we would simply say something like, 'I'd like a little time on my own' or 'I'm going for a walk' and the other would understand.

Two days after meeting Dana and Verres at Pentre Ifan, I felt in need of space. It was after ten o'clock, so Ruth went to bed with a book while I drifted out into the benighted garden. Although there was enough ambient light to see and recognise shapes, it was too dark to pick out colours or details. Across the bay, house lights and an occasional car headlight pricked the gloom. As my eyes got used to the dark, I was able to find my way around the garden, even in the shadows, without difficulty. 'Order in wildness' seemed to be the philosophy of Ffred, my gardener. Behind the trim lawns and measured shrubs and hedges he left lots of places where he 'let nature do the gardening'. In these places wild flowers grew, insects found a happy habitat, small mammals and birds felt secure and, according to Ffred, the spirit of the garden held court.

I saw something dark and motionless in the 'wild' part, and went closer to investigate; it was a molehill. I knelt down and pushed the earth away with my fingers to find the hole and exposed a small black circle, just discernable in the darkness from the soil around it. I put my ear over it and listened, but heard nothing except the restless fussiness of the sea breeze in the trees. I pushed my index finger into the hole; it didn't go straight down as I had expected, but entered at a steep angle, and I wondered what it was like to be a mole living in such a dark, claustrophobic and lonely place. I pictured myself entering the hole and in my imagination pushed down into the blackness, smelling the musty soil and feeling its resistance against my shoulders. Soon the friction of the sides and the sense of restriction passed, and I was moving freely and rapidly down the spiralling shaft. Before long I was no longer surrounded by earth, but was pushing through thick vegetation and it was daylight. Abruptly, a furry creature seemed to dash across my path. I chased it, and saw a tail disappear under a bush. Then I saw long white whiskers, and finally the large moon-face of a grinning cat appeared in front of me.

'Who are you?' I asked soundlessly in my thoughts.

'I'm your guide.' The creature made no sound, but its thoughts seemed to coalesce in my mind.

'Guide to what?'

'To the lower world.'

'What's that?'

'A place where you can come to ask questions.'

'What sort of questions?'

'Whatever you want to know.'

'OK, when will Ruth come to live with me?'

'Not that sort of question, dope.'

'Alright then. Am I the "One"?'

'That's better. You don't need to know that yet. When the time's right you'll know without having to ask me.'

'That's no answer.'

'It's the best you're getting, chum.'

'Oh alright. I can't think of anything else to ask.'

'It's best to come here with a specific question clear in your mind. Think of it beforehand. And, oh yes, try to make them less self-centred.'

'Why?'

'Well for a start you'll get clearer answers, and secondly it's more ethical.'

'Like… how can I serve the universe?'

'That's the idea. Do you want to know the answer?'

'Sure.'

'There's no simple answer, but I'll tell you how to start. You start by striving without hope of reward and by observing without judgement. Don't leap to condemn people's behaviour but honour, accept and nurture the greatness that lies within each and every one.'

'Then what?'

'Do that first.'

'It's easier said than done,' I grumbled.

The cat didn't respond immediately, but simply looked at me with amused contempt before asking, 'What's so important about "easy"?'

I knew it was right.

'You'll get the hang of how to ask questions and what to make of the answers after a couple of visits.'

'Do you think I'll come back then?'

It didn't reply.

'Well now, how do I get out of here?'

'Same way you came in. Is that all?'

'I suppose so.'

'Cheerio then, see yer.' It padded off into the bushes. I edged back up the twisting tunnel of earth, and before I could think I was kneeling in my garden peering into the tiny black hole.

I locked up the house and went upstairs, uncertain of whether to tell Ruth of my adventure in the lower world. At first I decided to believe that I must have dozed off and dreamed the cat and the lower world, so decided against it – despite knowing it had been real.

'Hi.' She smiled, taking off her reading glasses and dropping the book on the floor. 'OK?'

'Fine,' I said, walking over to the bed. 'I just needed to look at the lights across the bay and listen to the sounds of the night.'

My journey to the lower world no longer seemed like something I needed to talk about. I knew I was not crazy or drunk or had dreamed it. The lower world seemed as normal to me, as I snuggled up to her, as the post office on the corner or her book lying open on the floor by the bed.

*

We'd made no special plans for Ruth's last day, but walked three miles along the coastal footpath to the remains of a church that had been almost entirely destroyed during a great storm in the nineteenth century; then we turned around and walked back. We were walking up the garden talking about how hungry we were, when a familiar figure in a crumpled raincoat approached us from the house looking at a piece of paper in his hand.

'What's he want?' asked Ruth, with a marked lack of enthusiasm.

'I think he's had some grim news,' I said, sensing his mood. 'Steel yourself darling, we may be in for a grilling.'

'Mr Williams,' said Ruth, moving ahead of me to greet the policeman. 'What can we do for you today?'

He gave us each a brief, shifty-eyed glance. 'I wouldn't object to truthful answers to some straightforward questions if you don't mind.'

'Come inside, Williams,' I said sharply. 'The garden is too cheerful for straightforward questions and truthful answers.'

Ruth diverted herself upstairs while I led our visitor into the conservatory. I took a seat with my back to the sun, and gestured to him to sit facing me; but he remained standing, and stood looking down at me.

'OK, Williams,' I said, adjusting my chair and looking up at him. 'What do you want to ask me?'

'When did you last see Mr Verres, sir?'

'About three days ago.'

'Where was this meeting?'

'Pentre Ifan.'

'What did you talk about?' He was uncharacteristically direct, and making more eye contact than usual. My responses matched his directness.

'Our conversation was private, but it wouldn't help you to catch him even if I told you.'

'Are you going to see him again?'

'Probably, but if I happen to know in advance, which is unlikely, don't expect me to inform you.'

He looked reflective so I continued, 'If that's all, I've got a question for you.'

'Thank you for your directness, sir. It saves us both a lot of time,' he said forlornly. 'I hope I can be equally direct. What do you want to ask?'

'There's something troubling you, chief inspector. What's happened?'

He shuffled his feet and looked uncomfortable, shoved his

hands deeply into his raincoat pockets, and pulled out a scrap of paper which he seemed surprised to find. He read it, put it back in his pocket, sat down but immediately got to his feet again and gazed out towards the sea, without looking at anything.

'You remember D.S. Blower, don't you?' he asked quietly.

'I do.'

'His body was found this morning, about ten miles from here.'

A thousand sadnesses came over me. I really liked the amiable and straightforward policeman. 'What? How?'

'His neck was broken and his windpipe ruptured.'

He looked hard at me with tired eyes. His face was full of pain, and I wanted to cry with him.

'Does that sound familiar?' he asked pointedly. 'It's almost unheard of for someone to get killed in this way, especially a strong fit man like him, and a martial arts instructor to boot.' He ruffled his hair. 'In fact, I only know of one other instance.'

'It wasn't Verres, if that's what you're suggesting,' I said.

'You know that for certain sir?'

'Absolutely.'

'Do you know where he was at about eleven o'clock last night?'

'No, I don't,' I said, rising and standing in front of him. I felt his pain, but didn't know how to show sympathy and felt desolated by my earlier edginess. The least I could do was to be civil to him, so I touched him lightly on the arm and said, 'I can't tell you how deeply sorry I am to hear your news, chief inspector. Believe me, I want the culprit caught as much as anyone, and will do all I can to help you. But I can assure you it isn't Verres.'

He looked at me dryly without showing his feelings.

'If I believed he was responsible,' I added, 'I'd move heaven and earth to help you find him. But you have to take my word for it that he isn't.'

'Or the reporter either, sir?'

'What reporter?'

'Oh, didn't I mention the *other* occasion? Last week a reporter from one of the tabloids was apparently close to exposing your friend. He was found dead. Do you know how he was killed?'

'Broken neck?' I asked in a hushed voice.

'His neck was broken and his windpipe half-torn out of his throat.' He scratched his head again, and looked at me with sad cunning on his face. 'I suppose he didn't do that, either?'

At that moment Ruth joined us.

'Can I get you something Mr Wil... What's the matter? What's going on?' She came and stood alongside me, taking my arm, looking at us both quizzically.

'There have been two murders, and Williams believes Verres did them,' I said brutally.

'Who's been murdered?' I felt her fingernails dig into my arm.

'I'll leave you two together.' Williams started shuffling towards the sliding door leading out into the garden. 'I'll go out this way.'

We followed him outside. 'If he gets in touch you must tell me. For his own sake, if he's as innocent as you believe.'

'We'll do everything we can to help you find the culprit, chief inspector,' I replied to the brown-stained back of his raincoat.

Without pausing, he raised one arm and shook a skyward-pointing finger once, a sign of acknowledgement and helplessness.

CHAPTER 29

The Road to Hope

RUTH RETURNED TO domestic life with her husband, who was still acting with generous understanding, and ever feeding her with renewed promises about their impending separation; but tempering them with compelling reasons, beyond his control, for irritating delays. These reasons largely revolved around his book, which had taken over their lives – a reprint, an invitation to talk at the Hay Book Festival, the Archbishop of Canterbury purring whenever his name was mentioned and demanding maximum TV exposure, and his own bishop doing everything to please him short of laying palm leaves at his feet whenever he entered the cathedral. It all heaped fuel on the furnace of her frustration. The greater his success, the more she felt the tentacles of his life closing tightly around her.

Late one evening the doorbell rang. She answered it, and was confronted by Verres.

'Oh my dear,' she whispered, 'I can't ask you in. Bill's here.'

He shrugged disarmingly. 'I know. It's him I've come to see.'

'But he hates you,' she pleaded. 'He'll call the police as soon as he sees you.'

He gently eased her aside and walked into the hallway.

'Is he in his study?'

She nodded.

'Just do one thing for me.'

'What?'

'As soon as I go up to him, make a phone call, and stay on the line for fifteen minutes.' He placed his great paws on her shoulder and looked down at her intently. 'Don't let him interrupt you.'

'Alright.' She knew better than to argue with him but her doubts still itched and she didn't know how to scratch.

'That's most important,' he added, crossing the hall to the stairs.

'Yes, I understand.'

She noticed how fresh he smelt, like washed sheets dried by a mountain wind. He climbed the stairs with soft feet, so that even the screaming bottom tread remained silent. At the top he turned to watch her pick up the telephone, then approached the study door.

Jenkins interrupted her three times during the next five minutes, but she wouldn't relinquish the line; he didn't try again. At any moment she expected to hear an explosion of rage, and see her husband leaping out of his room to demand the phone. From time to time, she went to the bottom of the stairs and listened, but heard nothing. What could she do? Go up and mediate? That would only make things even worse. Anxiously, she fretted about the house, flirted with a duster, tried to read, skimmed through the boring TV channels, walked around the garden, listened at the bottom of the stairs several times until eventually she flopped onto the sofa totally drained and fell asleep without even kicking her shoes off.

It was light when she awoke, and someone had placed a duvet over her and taken her shoes off. Her husband came in from the kitchen.

'Awake at last,' he said lightly. 'You needed that sleep, darling.'

'Oh,' she said rubbing her eyes, 'What's the time?'

'Nearly nine o'clock.'

'Where's Verres?' she asked nervously, getting to her feet.

'He left hours ago.'

'Oh. Was everything alright?' She was wide awake now, stretching stiffness away and fluffing her hair, while they talked, into even less shape than it had been. She had grown it longer at my request; I had told her it made her sexier.

'I like your hair longer,' he said kindly. She couldn't remember his previous compliment about her appearance.

'Yes, everything was alright. Alright at last.' The quiet pleasure in his voice compelled Ruth to believe him, despite his unreliable track record.

'What have you been doing since he left?'

'Thinking.'

'Thinking about what?'

'You, mainly.'

Oh dear! She feared the worst; lately his machinations only meant more chaff to the mill obstructing her hopes and paving his path to glory.

'What about me?' He didn't reply. 'What went on between you two last night?'

'It was quite a night,' he said ruefully. 'Quite a night. Sit down my dear.' He sat opposite her, and started by apologising to her for his recent behaviour. 'I've been unfair to you… but let's start with him coming into my study.'

*

'I heard two sharp taps on the door but before I could even raise my eyes, it opened and he sauntered into the room as bold as brass.

"Good evening Bill," he said, looking around with the condescension of a bishop visiting a country parson, "I think it's time we had a talk."

I put my hands on the armrests of my chair to push myself up. "Verres, what are you doing here?" I blustered, more surprised than angry. My knees jammed under the desk. I must have looked like a duck. He laughed lightly and my surprise turned to rage.

"Don't get up, Bill," he ordered, pulling an easy chair to the front of my desk and settling himself in it, facing me with his legs stretched out in front of him, crossed at the ankles. "And relax. You can get angry later if you feel you should."

"Don't make yourself comfortable, you're not staying," I snapped, finally managing to stand up and glare down on him. "We have nothing to say to each other. Will you kindly leave?"

He met my hot stare with a cool smile. "Sit down." His voice was sharp and commanding yet strangely calming. It took me back to my schooldays, so I plopped back into my chair, which made me even more annoyed. I opened my mouth to order him out again, but again he beat me to the punch.

"What do you believe in most of all, Bill?"

"If you don't leave this instant I'll call the police." I picked up the phone, but you were speaking to someone.

"Is the question too difficult to answer, Bill?" He lifted a bushy eyebrow and spread his hands. "Call the police if you wish, but answer the question first. What do you believe in more than anything else?"

"I'll not answer your foolish questions," I snorted. "Get out of here." Despite my agitation, I wondered what the question was leading to.

"Who or what is your God, Bill?" I picked up the phone again. "Can't you answer that either?"

You were still speaking, so I brought out the stock answer. "My God is my Lord and Saviour."

"Who?" He didn't seem to understand the terms.

"The Almighty, the Lord of Hosts, the King of Kings… err… the omnipresent… the…" The utter contempt on his face drove my fuming clichés stuttering into a faltering silence.

"That's a pretty line in holy claptrap Bill, and you know it." He spoke like an exasperated schoolmaster forced to listen to an especially stupid pupil.

I indignantly blustered to God's defence. "I'm not going to put up with…"

"Who is your God, Bill? Who or what do you put before all else?" His voice was measured, but his eyes were like talons of fire tearing into my anger. All I seemed to have for protection was angry bluster, but he was scything through it like ripe wheat, exposing the stubble of uncertainty we both knew lay beneath.

"The Lord Jesus Christ," I stormed but knew it wasn't true. Yet it was all I could say because I didn't really know the answer.

"Bill," he said, in a kindly voice, "I already know the answers to my questions, so you can't fool me. Why are you trying to fool yourself? Honour your beliefs, even if you despise them."

My hand was trembling as I lifted the telephone again, but you were still there. I'm afraid I shouted at you in frustration, and you rightly told me to stop shouting and wait.

"Who or what is your God, Bill?" The man was tenacious; I felt like a rat cornered by a terrier.

"I don't need to tell you…" I squirmed in my chair, but it was my mind, not my bottom, that was really squirming. I wiped my moist palms down my trousers.

"Tell me!" I was torn between intense loathing of him and a growing doubt for myself, and he wasn't giving me time to decide which was more impressive.

"My faith."

"Ha," he exploded. "Faith in what?"

With anyone else I would have been able to duck and dive, but he was relentless. I'm afraid I completely lost control.

"Who do you think you are?" I demanded. "You, a murderer and a lecher. You, who is determined to break up my marriage, forcing your way in here to question *me* this way? All my life I've…"

Suddenly he roared to his feet like a hurricane hitting a small island. "The truth, you fool!" he thundered. "What is the most important thing in your life?"

I thought of knocking him down, but he was too big. He used my hesitation to offer suggestions and answers. "God? NO." He stepped closer. "Ruth? NO." He leaned across the desk, and I felt overwhelmed by his presence. "Your children? NO," he thundered. "That just leaves one thing Bill, face it man. Admit it."

"Alright," I said. "I suppose you want me to say it's my career."

"At last! Was that so difficult to admit?" He subsided back into his chair, stretched his legs and recrossed his ankles without taking his eyes off of mine.

"Is ambition such a sin?" I asked.

He uncrossed his ankles and leant forward, putting his hands flat on the top of my desk. "I don't care about your hypocrisy, I don't mind your cant or selfishness, but I abhor the way you deny the glorious spirit that is William Jenkins."

His magnanimity broke the spell he had cast over me. I could bear and even enjoy his contempt and rage, but not his approbation.

"You can't go around fucking my wife, then come in here…"

"That's another illusion you have to stop hiding behind." He towered to his feet and seemed to shoot fire out of his eyes into mine. "You know it's not true. Why? Why do you need to believe the lie?"

"It's not a lie. I know it's true," I pleaded, clinging to the last shards of the illusion, because in my deepest depths I knew he was speaking the truth.

I couldn't have passed out but time seemed to jump, for the next thing I remember was feeling soft, warm and safe with him standing behind me; his huge, coarse hands deep into my shoulders, gently kneading the muscles as if he were calming a fretful puppy.

"What happened to you, Bill?" he asked, in a voice from someone else's dream. "As an eleven year old you were bright and open and unafraid," he continued softly, kneading my shoulders so sweetly that I wanted him never to stop. "You were full of sparkle, but so terribly vulnerable. I watched the way you plastered over this vulnerability with your incredible brain as you entered your teens, until by the time you left school you had become a cardboard cut-out of what your parents, your teachers wanted you to be, and what you thought you wanted to be!"

"How do you know all this? Did you know me then?" I asked, turning round to look at him. "Who are you?"

"Who do you think got deepest into your soul when you were growing up?" he asked, returning to his chair. This time he sat upright with his knees bent and waited.

I looked into the wall behind him, and through it into the shuffling crowd of people I once knew. My mother was too consoling, my father too demanding, the church minister too professional, an uncle I was very fond of too infrequent, and teachers too academic.

"Well, I don't know, there's nobody really, but… yes there was one, my old headmaster, a Dr Lloyd." I looked at him and half-smiled at the memory. "Yes, old Ticker, I'd almost forgotten about him."

"Ticker?"

"That's right, I used to feel he saw through me as if I was made of glass, but he always accepted me for what I was."

"What happened to him?"

"Drowned, I believe."

"Are you sure?"

"No, I'm not."

"What would you say if I told you he wasn't drowned?"

"Oh I don't know… it was such a long time ago… it doesn't matter now."

"Look at me and travel back, Bill."

He sat silent and impassive. I stared at him, equally as silent but in turmoil.

Then the words "Twrch Trwyth" left my lips and a tremor ran through my body, as if I was sitting over the epicentre of an earthquake. Verres seemed to change before my eyes in a series of lightning flashes from the man before me, to a creature like a bear with tusks, to Ticker, and back to Verres.

I wretched violently and thought my stomach was being torn out of my insides. I didn't vomit, but wretched again and tasted the bitterness of bile. I tugged a handful of tissues from a box behind my chair and spat into them.

"Breathe deeply, Bill." He came back around the desk, pouring water into a glass from a bottle. "Sip this and let all those years of ache and concealment flow quietly away." I took the glass and did as he told me. "They'll never come back to torment you again."

"Thank you, sir," I muttered, as if the years had peeled back and Ticker was speaking to a gangly, redheaded miscreant with a downy red moustache in the school corridor.

You know, my dear, I've never believed in miracles. I've called them biblical conjuring tricks with Jesus saying "Look, I have nothing up my sleeve", but I can only describe the hours we later spent together last night as a succession of miracles. I don't know how long we sat there and talked, or even much of what we talked about, although my career, my values and my attachments all got airings; we had many years of pain and lost directions to cover. I may have shed a few tears and felt frightened at times, but the overall feeling I had was one of encroaching calm and ease getting stronger as I let go of more and more of the things that have frightened me for so long. I have been living with so much fear, Ruth, and it was such a relief to see them all laid out before me.

Shortly before leaving, he asked about you and our marriage, and if I was able to accept that we had grown apart. I said I could. Then he asked me if I felt able to let you go now. I said I did. "Even at the cost of your career, Bill?" he asked.

I had to admit that that was just a smokescreen to keep you. My career doesn't need you. I hope you'll forgive me, my dear. I haven't been seeing things straight.'

Ruth could think of nothing to say.

'For the last few hours I've been thinking.'

'Thinking what, Bill?' she asked tenderly.

'Two things mainly,' he said. 'First of all, I had to undo a terrible thing I did a few weeks ago.'

'What was that?'

'I can't tell you.'

'Did you undo this terrible thing?'

'No, but I'll keep trying.'

She pressed him to tell her more, but he wouldn't say anything other than, 'One phone call will undo it.'

She looked up at the wall clock. 'Didn't you have an important meeting this morning?'

'I did, but cancelled it.'

'Was that the other thing you thought about?'

'No, my dear woman,' he said tenderly. 'The second thing I thought about was you.'

'About me?'

'About your new life.'

'My what?'

'Your new life. With David.'

Comes through the Mask we Raise

A SUMMER OF record rainfall gracelessly gave way to an autumn of early frosts and boisterous northerly winds, which tore leaves from the trees before they'd started to turn red. September slipped into October, the clocks ticked back to GMT, afternoons became gloomy, and the icy breath of winter chilled the air. Chimneys smoked, central heating boilers thundered, and a scowl of unseasonal foreboding grew daily in people's faces. However, none of this touched Ruth and me who, oblivious of the heaviness around us, gaily danced through the halcyon days like lambs in springtime.

We were not totally out of touch with reality, and during this time learned with dismay of three more murders; another policeman and two reporters all had their windpipes torn out. Verres was universally branded as the killer, and he rapidly gained national notoriety featuring daily somewhere in the media. I was confident that he could outwit his pursuers, but was concerned that someone was ruthlessly doing their best to incriminate him, force him out of hiding and bring about his downfall. I didn't know who it could be or why, and felt impotent to help.

I was now almost blasé about my uncanny ability to anticipate events and people's words and actions, in some cases even their thoughts. I didn't understand it, where it came from, or how to use it effectively and was more reactive to it than proactive. Sometimes I simply 'knew' in my head, at other times a scene, like a vivid 'daydream', came into my mind. With practice, these abilities became more refined; I even found I could to see 'inside' old photographs and surmise what the subjects were thinking about. I read newspapers and knew what really lay behind the misinformation. I learned to understand and even get inside the minds of people by feeling an object they had handled. But no matter how hard I tried to 'see' what was behind the murders, I found myself looking into a void.

I hadn't told Ruth of my encounter with the moon-faced cat down the mole hole, and wasn't going to but, as the weeks passed, I made several clandestine return visits: at first to test it, and prove to myself that I wasn't completely mad. Later I went to find some justification for the existence of the lower world, there seemed to be none that I could discover. The cat sensing my doubt once told me that I should show more respect to him and call him my 'guide' or 'power animal' and definitely not 'cat'. I generally came away no wiser but was starting to grow fond of the absurd creature. In fact, I was starting to respect it and even admire its apparent wisdom when, one evening early in November, it occurred to me that 'he' might be able to tell me something about the murders, so I tried again.

I started in the usual way, passing down the tunnel and entering the bushes where my guide was waiting for me. He was not his usual sleek self but he looked bedraggled, and his fur was matted and unkempt.

'Good heavens, what's the matter with you?' I asked. 'You look terrible.'

'You shouldn't have come. Go back.'

'I just want to ask you one thing.'

'If you ask, I'll have to answer, but I advise you not to. Go back while you can.'

With this negative incentive, nothing on or in the earth could have stopped me, so I incautiously blundered on.

'Tell me who is doing the murders,' I commanded. 'And why.'

'I'll have to take you to the Spirit of the Murders,' he said, with dismal resignation. 'It could seriously harm you.'

There's no fool like an ignorant fool so I simply instructed him to, 'Lead on.'

He led me into the heart of a gloomy mountain range that was no more than a rocky moonscape devoid of vegetation, with a dense layer of black cloud overhead. Here he suddenly left me, utterly alone, although a sixth or seventh sense warned me that something close-by was watching me. I looked around but all was shadows, emptiness and excruciating silence.

Suddenly, a huge black bear rushed towards me out of the gloom. Before I could move, I felt its fangs tearing into my throat and its razor-sharp claws ripping down my flanks. It bore me down and I felt a colossal weight crushing me; blood gushed out of my wounds and the pain was unbearable. The venom in its teeth entered my bloodstream, and I felt it course around my body like a grass fire. Then a smaller bear appeared and said, 'Enough… he's learnt his lesson.' The voice was remotely familiar, then I lost consciousness.

Pain and the sound of my own moans brought me back to my senses.

'Try to hold him still while I give him a jab.' My arm was bared, and someone was trying to inject me with something.

'I can't, he's too strong.' Ruth's voice came from somewhere above my head and I looked up into her upside-down face.

I recognised my own sitting room. 'What happened?'

'Here, get these down.' The doctor put his syringe aside and handed me a glass of water and four white tablets. I sat up, tenderly feeling for the scratches and bite marks around my throat and sides, and obediently swallowed the pills.

'I don't need a jab,' I gurgled.

'It's just anti-tetanus. You should have it.'

'You'd better have it, darling.' Ruth put her arms around my shoulders and kissed a line of stitches on my neck and shoulders. I nodded and placidly looked at the ceiling while he injected me.

'What happened?' I asked.

'Don't you know?' She sounded surprised. 'I heard you screaming in the garden and rushed down to find you covered in blood.' She took a deep breath. 'You had passed out and I couldn't move you, so I dashed next door and got Dr Griffiths and his sons to carry you inside.'

'You were like a bullock,' added Aeron Griffiths dryly. 'It must have been a dog. I'll have to report it to the police. Didn't you see anything?'

'Nothing.' Fragments of my encounter with the bear were falling back into place, and with a heroic grimace I added, 'But whatever it was, I hope they get the bugger.' I knew they wouldn't.

'We must call the police.' Griffiths got up and moved towards the telephone. 'They must catch it before it kills someone.'

When we were alone I turned to Ruth.

'It wasn't a dog.'

'What was it then?'

'It was more a psychic experience.' She gaped at me. 'I did something really stupid.'

'Psychic?' asked Ruth. 'What do you mean?'

'I can't say any more than that for now. Give me a little time to gather my wits.' To her great credit Ruth, though bursting with curiosity, asked no more questions.

Griffiths departed and Ruth insisted that I should try to sleep. I wanted her alongside me so we lay in bed together, not touching or speaking, but awake with our troubled thoughts. I relived over and over again my dreadful encounter in the lower world. My schizoid cynicism had been replaced with the certain belief that other dimensions really did exist alongside ours, and that I had found a way into one of them. Then, the chilling thought hit me with the impact of two meteors colliding: the only way I could stop the sequence of murders was to return to the lower world and confront the bear again.

*

One chilly morning a couple of days later, while it was still dark, I was standing in the garden looking at the lights across the bay when I heard something in the bushes. I knew who it was. 'Good morning, Dana. Playing Indians?'

A familiar voice answered, 'Good morning General Custer.'

We walked to the house arm in arm.

Ruth was in the kitchen. The women greeted each other with the usual warmth, but Dana quickly detached herself and said she had to speak to me urgently.

I knew what it was about and that she would not weaken my resolve but I let her speak anyway.

'You've learned to travel haven't you, David.' It sounded like an accusation.

'To where?' I instinctively knew what she meant but made her explain so I could 'see' it in the cold light of day, so to speak.

'You've learned how to move into other dimensions.'

'What do you mean?' I muttered perversely.

'Don't play the clown, David. You've been to the lower world.'

Ruth could barely restrain her curiosity, and, as I had kept my explorations from her, I was unsure of how to react for the best. Pretending to be confused, I described to them my previous excursions down the mole hole but omitted the last one when I was attacked by the bear.

'At first it was only an imaginative game I was playing, too childish to tell Ruth about,' I said, attempting to conceal my duplicity.

Ruth looked serious, Dana angry.

'You don't understand what you're playing with, my dear man.' She wagged a fierce finger in my face. 'You're running before you can walk, and could become badly damaged if you're not careful.'

'So that's what really happened the other night.' Ruth looked aghast.

'Yes,' I said quietly, and told them about being attacked by the bear. 'But Dana, how did you know?'

Dana looked at me with cold eyes. 'I've travelled for many years and got to know of your… experiments.'

She put an arm around Ruth's shoulders. 'I've learned how to protect myself from malevolent spirits, but I wouldn't dare do what he did. You must stop him now and never let him go there again.'

Ruth looked at me with concern, but my full attention was on Dana. I saw fear in her eyes but the fear wasn't for me, it was for someone else.

'I'm sorry Dana, but I must return. The bear is the key which will unlock the mystery threatening Verres. I have no choice but to go back and confront him.'

'Why, darling?' Ruth asked.

'Because the police are completely out of their depth and only I can stop the killings. They will go on and on until I do, and each death will draw Verres closer to the edge of a precipice.'

We stood in a helpless silence for a minute until Dana said,

'There must be another way, David. Next time you won't be so lucky.'

'What are you really afraid of Dana? Who are you really afraid for?'

'There is no way you can protect yourself, David.' I knew she was shielding someone else, but it couldn't be Verres.

'Yes there is, Dana. You have to tell me.' I gently grasped her shoulders and made her look into my face. 'Why won't you tell me, Dana? Do you know who the bear is?'

'I'll tell you this, David,' she said quietly. 'It is you I fear for and I truly don't know if my words will save you; that depends on you, and how strong you are.'

'Tell me all the same.'

'Before you enter the lower world next time, go to a quiet place where you will not be disturbed and wait until you have shed all the wild thoughts that dash in and out of your mind – until you can't feel the outer world, your senses are stilled and you no longer exist as David Tanner. Then bring one pure thought into your mind.'

'Like stopping the murders?'

'No, it must be a positive thought.'

'Like freeing the killer from his pain and suffering?'

'You're getting the idea, but let it come to you rather than working it out in your head. This is why it is almost impossible for you to do, David. Can't you see that you have to become egoless?'

'Then what?'

She sighed as if hope was draining from her; the lines in her face softened, the tension in her shoulders dissolved and a glow of beauty came over her that frightened me more than the thought of confronting the bear again. 'Keep that thought and nothing else in your mind. If anything distracts you and you get snagged in your ego, you'll be destroyed.'

'Why wasn't I destroyed last time?'

'He was stopped, and probably underestimated you, but he won't make the same mistake twice.'

'Who stopped him?'

'I can't tell you that.'

It didn't matter any more, because I now knew who it was.

'Who is he?'

'I can't tell you.'

'What if I am defeated? What would happen to me?'

'I don't know,' she said icily. 'You could have a simple heart attack or become permanently insane or, worst of all, have your human form taken over by the very being you set out to conquer.'

'What, the bear will return as *me*?'

'It has happened many times, David.' She looked at me grimly. 'And to ambitious people who overestimate their own powers. Many of them are famous people in important positions.'

I noticed that Ruth was silently absorbing every word. I hoped she'd remember them all because I needed her to know and be 'there' for me when I returned.

Dana stayed until daylight and even allowed us to make her breakfast. Nothing more was said about my forthcoming journey or Verres, and much of the time I left the women alone to talk without me in attendance. I was already arming myself for the confrontation, which I sensed had to happen before another dawn. The worldly David Tanner still wondered if it was anything more than a game played by an overactive imagination. The inner David Tanner knew that this was a deadly serious game, which was as real and as dangerous as anything that could happen in anyone's lifetime.

Dana left immediately after breakfast, but her parting words before going out through the gate at the end of the garden were, 'Thomas wants to meet you at Nevern castle at midday tomorrow.'

*

I spent most of the day alone, and ate nothing. Ruth was brilliant, the rock I based my day upon, remaining a presence but without intruding into my space or conveying a trace of anxiety. She kept callers away from me, answered the telephone and created an aura of calm around the house and around me.

Late in the evening I announced, 'I'm going out into the garden, sweetheart. I don't know how long I'll be.' I left without kissing her, but as I passed her she slipped a round, white pebble, about 3cm across, into my hand. 'Celtic women used to give their men a white pebble before going into battle. It represents symmetry, purity and clarity. It helped to protect them, keep them steadfast and draw them back home safely.' She closed my hand around the stone. 'Now go.'

I stood for a long age in the cold, stilling my mind and focusing on my thought. When I was ready, I entered the deep delved earth. I came to the bushes; my guide wasn't there, although for a moment I glimpsed two impassive, deadpan eyes looking at me from the darkness of the trees. I found the stony path leading into the clouds and barren mountain top. I immediately felt the bear was nearby. I ignored the feeling, concentrating only on the one shining thought in my head.

A voice came out of the mist in front of me, 'So you've come back!' I concentrated on my golden thought.

'We don't have to fight,' the voice now came from behind me. I didn't turn. 'We can be friends. Just think of what we could achieve together.' I continued to ignore it. 'All you ever dreamed of.' I steadfastly concentrated on my thought.

Then his voice came from overhead like a clap of thunder. 'If you fight you will cease to exist. You will have achieved nothing, and then nothing can stop me from doing whatever I wish. Perhaps I'll take Ruth for myself. Would you like that?' I felt my thought slipping away, but squeezed the pebble in my hand and its heat brought it back.

Then, with a roar as if from the bowels of hell, it rushed me. Lips snarled back, exposing stained fangs dripping yellow saliva, and curved claws eight inches long with needle-like points extended towards my gut. I turned and held out my free hand towards his throat but, as I grabbed it, the impact of his charge bowled us over onto the hard ground with him on top. I felt a sharp pain as a rock cut into my shoulder, and heard breath being pumped out of my lungs, but I hung on to my thought and his throat. I felt his fangs bite into my forehead and perhaps an eye. My eyes, if I still had eyes, filled with blood and saliva. I could see nothing, but the pain was crippling. I felt a tear down my side and my intestines slither around my buttocks, but still I held on to the thought and his throat. He stood up, dragging me into the air, and shook me so violently my brain became mush within my cranium; but I still clung to the two slim shards of hope in my hand and in my mind.

Suddenly, he let out a scream and started to bound down the hill, tripping over stones and falling to the ground, then getting back to his feet and tearing off in a different direction. I clung to him without hope, without fear, without care. Then I heard him grunting, 'Let go. Let me go.' But I didn't, and felt renewed strength coming to my fingers and my resolve.

He fell over again, but this time he didn't rise.

Holding this throat even tighter I whispered, 'Show me your face.'

'No,' he screamed. 'Pity me.'

'Show me or I will come inside you and find it.'

He went limp and I grabbed the tough, hairy skin covering

273

his skull and pulled. Half his scalp and an ear came away in my hands like tissue paper, leaving exposed beneath me the completely hairless head of a man. I tore away more hairy hide and uncovered the torso of a warrior with hard, thick muscles, a short neck as wide as his head, and scars on his shoulders. He raised an arm to cover his face, but I easily pushed it aside. He turned his head away, but with equal ease I pulled it back and looked down at it carefully so I would recognise him when I saw him again. He had a broad nose, flat lightless eyes and a strangely sensitive mouth. 'Stop this evil,' I commanded.

'I can't.'

'Of course you can, if you so wish,' I said.

'I can't.'

'Then I will destroy you in the outer world as I have destroyed you in the inner,' I said.

'I can't,' he sobbed.

I stood straddled above him, and without pity or mercy tore him apart piece by piece and cast each piece far into the depths of the misty wilderness.

I awoke lying in the grass, my whole body numb with the cold, hoar frost crunched beneath me as I moved, and already a sullen light dragged a new dawn out of the night. I touched my forehead and eyes, then put a hand on my belly, and with immense relief discovered I was intact. I stiffly climbed to my feet and hobbled back to the house, wondering what in heaven's name I'd done. In my left hand I still held the small white pebble.

CHAPTER 31

Untangled Forces

S TEAM FILLED THE bathroom, condensing on mirrors and tiles whilst rivulets see-sawed erratic courses down to nowhere. I slipped deeper under the quilt of bubbles until only my face remained above and looked inwards at the erratic course, to somewhere, that I was on. The water, comfortably warm, embraced me with a luxuriant stringency that soothed and drowsed me into an unshakable acceptance of wherever my course would take me. My first doubtful steps down this road had become confident strides and, although I could see no further than my next footfall, all doubts had vapourized. Downstairs Ruth was murdering Ella Fitzgerald with 'Gee-orgia on my mind'; all was peace in my little world.

'Wake up, honey.'

Ruth had her hands in the lukewarm water, shaking my shoulders. I opened my eyes and dreamily reached out to pull her into the bath, but she knew that game and slipped back out of range.

'We've got visitors. Another policeman was killed yesterday.'

'Oh no. How?' I shot out of the water with a splutter of cold suds.

'The same way as the others, only this time the body was mutilated.'

'Disembowelled?'

'That's right.' She looked at me hard. 'You scare me sometimes.'

All this 'second sight' stuff used to scare me too, but it was becoming part of my new-found second nature. I towelled myself damp dry and dragged on a bathrobe.

'Who's downstairs? Williams and who else?'

'Mr Stoker and a formidable CID policewoman with muscles.'

Williams shuffled, mumbled, scratched and fidgeted his way through the usual questions about the whereabouts of Verres, while the Amazon took notes and occasionally interjected an unnecessary question, more I thought to justify her recent promotion to sergeant than bring light to her superior's darkness.

Stoker stood with his back to us, silently looking out of the window into the garden.

The interview over, Williams passed through the motions of warning us again about the seriousness of the case and the dire consequences of withholding evidence. I felt sorry for him; he was clearly out of his depth, which was evident from his string of unimaginative questions that I matched with equally unimaginative answers. I was more interested in Stoker, and long before Williams had finished, had diverted most of my attention to his expressive back. As Ruth escorted them to the door, I moved over to the window to stand alongside him. We stood without a word for a few moments before he said, 'Of course we both know Tommy isn't responsible for these killings. We must find him.'

'Who, Verres or the man without a neck?'

He slowly turned. 'You don't know who the killer is, do you David?'

'Perhaps.'

'What does that mean?'

'It means I know what he looks like, but I'm not yet certain who he is or why he wants to destroy Verres.'

'Describe him.'

'Build like a wrestler, big nose, flat eyes, completely hairless, neck like a bull, scars on his shoulders…' Stoker stiffened.

'You know him?' I asked.

'Yes.'

Momentarily his composure deserted him. 'How sure are you?' he blurted.

'I've no doubt.' I searched his face for a reaction. 'Now.'

'How did you find out?'

'That's too long a story.'

'How long have you known?'

'Only a few hours.'

'Has he been here?'

'No. Can you tell me where to find him?'

'What are you going to do?'

'Finish the job,' I said calmly.

'What does that mean?'

'I'll know when the time comes.'

*

We were standing close together, talking in the hushed conspiratorial tones of le Carré spies.

'Please try to believe that I love Verres and am his friend…' Stoker whispered.

'I don't have the slightest doubt about it.' I put my hand on his shoulder, giving it a couple of friendly pats. This man was too easy to love and trust for my own good.

'Aren't you going to ask me who this man is?' he asked.

I looked at him in surprise. 'I don't need to know *who*, although I believe I already know. What I don't know is where to find him.'

He studied the empty lawn through the window for several

seconds. 'He's not your responsibility, David. Leave him to the law.'

'The person who can, does,' I said quietly.

He took a deep breath and gently touched my arm. 'I must go. I've got some manhunting to do.'

'And I have some man finding to do,' I replied after he was out of earshot.

*

The scattered stones of Nevern castle stand on a steep-sided spur overlooking the convergence of two small rivers. Virtually unassailable on two of the three sides, the Welsh princes built a stone castle there which the Normans strengthened by cutting a deep ditch in the solid rock between the inner and outer wards. Today, the old walls have become overgrown by trees and undergrowth, leaving only formless shapes huddling in the ground, the deep ditch, the steep approaches, and an overwhelming sense of the monumental events that took place there.

We arrived early and took the steep path from Nevern church, which curved up alongside the river. From the path, we scrambled through the old defences into the inner ward, past the end of the ditch, and continued to the top of a mound that once housed the keep.

'What a beautiful spot,' Ruth murmured. 'Isn't it strange to think of such incredible beauty alongside such incredible violence. How does that make any sense?'

Two men stood on the outer wall about a hundred yards away, looking down with exaggerated interest at something out of sight to us. Hackles rose across my back.

'We're over here.' Dana came up the slope towards us.

'The sweater suits you, David.' She stroked Verres' old sweater affectionately. 'It's a good fit too.'

The girls walked back towards the ditch momentarily, absorbed in their sweet intimate world. Verres had climbed to the top of the mound, so I jogged up and hugged him. 'I'm so pleased to see you again,' I said.

'I understand you've had a little adventure,' he replied with the old twinkle in his eye.

'You mean with the bear?' His eyebrows twitched to give confirmation.

'You went back for a rematch, as I'd expect,' he said lightly. 'I assume things went well.'

'Half the job's done,' I said.

'I believe the other half will be completed soon,' he said, looking around and scanning the two men who were casually strolling towards us. 'I'm expecting Bill. Have you seen him?'

'Oh good.' Ruth joined us. 'I'm glad he's coming. He's changed so much recently. I think he's found himself at last. Did you ask him to come?'

'He was coming down here anyway.' Dana squeezed into the huddle. 'Apparently he had to meet someone called Roberts here.'

'Who's he?' I asked warily.

'Perhaps we'll soon know,' said Verres, looking around, 'if he got my invitation.'

'Invitation? To Roberts?'

He nodded with a grim smile, but didn't explain.

Jenkins appeared in the distance and came striding across the outer ward, waving to us. He had lost weight around his middle since I had last seen him, and his flabby chin seemed leaner, scrawny really. He slowed down near the top of the rise and joined us breathing heavily but still upright. I complimented him on his 'streamlined' appearance and offered him my hand. He accepted it so warmly that the inevitable reservations and doubts I harboured about meeting him again dissolved. Ruth introduced him to Dana, but Verres brought us back to the reason he had summoned us here.

'Now we're all here let's get down to it. Time is short.'

The two men who had been on the bank were getting nearer, inspecting weeds and stones with the intense casuality of men intensely trying not to look intense. They were heavily built, with wide shoulders and rock-like hips. I had a bad feeling about them, and this was compounded when two more, similarly built, appeared to our right, displaying the same extreme disinterest in us.

'Let's get away from here,' I said, leading the way off the keep. 'I'm not happy about those men.'

The girls immediately followed me down the ramp, but the two late arrivals sprinted around the ditch to cut off our only escape down to the river.

'Get back up there,' I ordered, galvanizing my mind into crystal clarity. 'Don't move from here. Bill, they're after Verres not us, if any of them get past me don't let them get to him. Girls, at the first opportunity, get out of here and go for help.'

'Does anyone have a mobile phone,' Ruth asked calmly.

'Yes, I have.' Jenkins reached into a pocket.

Verres was less concerned than any of us and seemed to be looking past the approaching men into the trees, as if expecting someone else. By now the men had reached the end of the ditch and surrounded us. Two more equally hunky men slid out of the trees on the outer ward wall, and hurried across the grass towards us. Verres, who hadn't moved, said 'Aha!'

I followed his eyes and saw the shape of a dark figure, gesticulating instructions from the leafy shadows.

The boldest aggressor was halfway up the mound, leaning

forward to keep his balance when I stepped down and kicked him in the eye with the toe end of my walking boot. I felt the occipital bone crack like a biscuit, and he fell backwards with the eye's humour spurting out of the bloody socket like spittle. His companions looked aghast, but pulled short weighted batons from under their coats and circled the mound like lions stalking a wounded water buffalo, wary but deadly. The battle lines were indelibly drawn.

I followed them from above, watching for their first move. My victim was staggering away as the last two arrived. One of them briefly glanced at him, said something, patted him on the shoulder and came on with a commando knuckle-duster knife around his fist.

'Now,' one of them called, and they charged up the slope. The man opposite me came slower than the others, watching my boots cautiously. Out of the corner of my eye I saw Jenkins aim a wild swinging punch at someone, but before it was midway through its arc he was felled by a baton with a blow to the side of his knee. He collapsed with a squeal.

I left my man and threw myself on Jenkins' assailant with a rugby tackle as his arm went up to finish him off. We both went down as an explosion of air discharged from his body. I immediately bounced onto my feet, and jabbed a thumb deep and hard into his throat next to the Adam's apple. I felt his trachea buckle, but not crack. He gurgled and rolled over, but my follow-up was put off by two others rushing at me, and I knew I hadn't finished him. I met them head-on like a bull. The velocity of my attack upset their timing. I swung the sharp radial edges of my straightened arms into the root of the nose of one, and across the lower ribs of the other.

I felt two stinging but ineffectual blows somewhere on the back of my head; one man went down screaming, holding his nose with blood, cartilage and snot covering his hands. The other was merely bowled over, and clumsily rolled onto his hands and knees where he remained, breathing heavily.

I wasn't aware of the sounds we were making. It was like fighting in a vacuum of silence, but Ruth told me later that the noise was deafening, not of individual voices but one ferocious cacophony of anger and pain. The one sound I did hear was a sharp scream behind me. I jumped sideways and looked quickly towards it. The man who held back from me a few seconds earlier was slumped into a half-kneeling position. He had rapidly gained the top after I had moved away, and was about to attack me from behind when Jenkins, from a semi-reclining position and still grimacing in pain, had clattered a rock against a patella.

Then something exploded in my head. Flashing lights, vomit, dizziness, face in the dirt and dead leaves, despair, helplessness – I couldn't repeat the sequence of sensations that rushed over me, but knew I had to keep moving, so rolled and kept rolling until I had a sensation of falling. I came to rest sprawled in the exposed roots of a tree facing back in the direction I must have come from. The man with the knuckle-duster knife was bounding down after me, his intention clear. He straddled me and paused briefly as if savouring the moment; he raised his cruel weapon, then with bulging eyes, rose into the air horizontally. Verres held him with unwavering, oak-like arms above his head just long enough to take aim before hurling him against a tree with a force that almost uprooted the tree.

'He'll live,' he said grimly. 'Will you?'

'I'm fine,' I lied, slowly getting up and tenderly scrutinizing my vital functions to see which were still performing. To my amazement I didn't feel too bad, and, leaning lightly against Verres until sure of my balance, was able to look around and make a quick survey of the battle scene.

Jenkins was sitting up against a tree, holding his knee,

grinning and wincing. My heart went out to him. He was not a fighting man but he'd got stuck in harder than anyone could have expected of him. Ruth had come down to satisfy herself that I was alright, and was now using Jenkins' mobile phone, presumably to call the police. Dana was going around the injured, occasionally laying her hands on one for a few moments before moving to the next.

'Eye-socket' had disappeared completely; 'knee-cap' was propped against a tree, legs straight out in front of him watching us intently but without hostility as if to say, 'Nothing personal'. 'Nose', who had passed out, had been put in the recovery position by Dana and was breathing heavily through clenched teeth and open mouth. 'Chest' appeared to have some broken ribs, and no wish to do anything other than lie against a tree and glower. 'Thumb-in-throat' was coughing and spitting globules of blood, while my old friend 'knuckle-duster' was still curled up against his tree with Verres kneeling over him tenderly, trying to make him comfortable.

Leaving my oak tree I climbed up to Jenkins. The speed of my recovery was miraculous, and with every step I felt strength returning.

'How's the knee, Bill?'

'I won't be playing football for a week or two,' he grinned. 'Wasn't that something!'

'It sure was something,' I said with feeling. 'You were amazing. I think I understand the term "God fearing" a little better now. He must be scared to death of you.'

'He, she or it!' he corrected. 'You were amazing yourself. Where did you learn unarmed combat?'

'I have no idea, Bill. Would you believe that I've never struck a man before in my life?'

I tenderly explored the mat of congealed blood in the hair above my ear. 'And I deeply hope I'll never have to do so again.'

I felt Ruth's hand on my arm. 'It's alright David, you did what you had to do.' She squeezed my arm, 'I love you.'

'The police?' I asked.

'On their way.'

'Ambulances, too?'

'Of course.'

'Let's see how the other team is.'

Jenkins got up and hobbled after us as we did the rounds of the injured. We dragged, carried or aided them into a hollow at the foot of the mound. None of us felt any ill will towards any of them, everyone involved on both sides had done only what we had to do. They were heavy men and the work was strenuous; for a few vital minutes I completely forgot about Verres. Then, as if struck by lightning, I felt my hackles rise again and, in panic, looked around for him.

He was standing talking on top of the keep, relaxed and loose armed, to the man we had seen in the shadows. His head was bandaged and seemed to grow straight out of his shoulders. His features were already imprinted in my memory.

'Please God, no!' I screamed, leaping up the slope like a panther.

Jenkins followed as best he could, calling one word, 'Roberts.'

As I reached the rim of the mound, the knife sank into Verres' abdomen and he tottered backwards, holding his middle with dark red blood already seeping through his fingers. The knife was raised for the second blow but I caught his arm as it descended and jerked it so hard that the man's shoulder dislocated and both bones in the forearm snapped like dry sticks. I grabbed his throat and thirsted in my rage to squeeze the life out of him, but Dana screamed sharply, 'No David, stop, don't harm him any more…'

My blood-red rage was diverted but not completely

assuaged, so I hurled him away from me. He stumbled to his feet, tottered backwards and went straight over the edge, falling thirty feet into the ditch the Normans had provided. There he lay lifeless, his skull shattered and eyes open, glowering in their emptiness. Dana finished her sentence, '… he's suffered enough.' Stoker crouched on the opposite lip of the ditch looking down in utter dismay at the lifeless remains of a man he had once known.

I turned to Verres, who was resting against Jenkins' thighs and being tended to by Ruth who had opened his shirt and was attempting to staunch the bleeding with pieces of clothing. Dana had disappeared.

'How is he?' I asked.

Verres replied, 'He's not done for yet.' He beckoned me over to him. 'We still have to talk.'

'Where's Dana?' Ruth, with blood drenching her hands, face and clothing, looked around for her friend.

'She went down there.' Jenkins pointed into the ditch.

Ruth continued working on the wound, using her blouse and the old sweater to staunch the bleeding, binding it in place with my belt.

'I think the bleeding's almost stopped, but don't move him until an ambulance arrives.'

'My old friend, I'm so pleased to see you one more time.' Verres looked past us. I turned and saw Stoker, his eyes full of moisture.

'No, don't come up, I'll come down.' Incredibly, Verres stood up, holding onto the bundle of clothing covering his wound. He and Stoker at last came home to each other, and embraced like the brothers they always had been in their hearts. 'Can we have a few minutes alone, please?' he asked.

We walked away to leave the old friends together, and went down into the ditch where Dana sat sobbing with the limp body spread across her lap like *La Pieta*, his thick muscular arms were spread wide, revealing scars on his shoulders. The bandage had fallen off his head, revealing a gaping, bloody hole where an ear had been torn off earlier; I knew when. As I approached I could hear Dana quietly talking to the body.

'Oh Mongan,' she said, 'Why? Why?'

'I know him,' Jenkins gasped, coming up behind me. 'I couldn't stop him.'

'Come on, Dana,' I said, gently touching her shoulder. 'There's nothing we can do for him now.'

She looked up at me with empty eyes. 'He was my son, David. I couldn't stop him. I couldn't cleanse him of his terrible hatred… I've killed him.'

Gently she lowered him to the ground, and with infinite care closed his eyes. Then, as if sleepwalking past Jenkins, she passively received a hug from Ruth and shuffled out of the cutting. She came face to face with Verres and his old friend, and stood before them in defiant contrition.

'There's no need to say anything my dear,' Verres said. 'Come with me.' He looked at Bran for the last time, smiled, put an arm around her shoulder and led her down a path leading into the trees.

'You're not going?' Ruth exclaimed anxiously. 'An ambulance is on the way.'

'Let them go, Ruth.' Stoker held her elbow. 'This is how it has to be.'

'But I don't understand…'

I silenced her by swaddling a coat from one of the assailants around her bare, bloodstained shoulders. 'Let them go, my dear.'

'We'll meet for the last time tomorrow,' Verres huskily called over his shoulder. 'You know where and when.'

We stood around vacantly, not knowing what to do next,

but Stoker did. Peering down at Mongan's twisted remains he sighed, 'Terrible accident.'

'Not an accident, I'm afraid,' I said, standing next to him with my hands limp by my sides. 'I threw him over.'

'I think not,' he said. 'In the heat of the moment you may have thought you did, but I saw everything. After you released him he stepped back and fell.'

'But…'

'That's how it was, David.' His eyes would accept no dissent.

Stoker stayed in charge after the authorities arrived, not allowing Williams or his Amazon more than a few cursory questions. Within half an hour of their arrival we were permitted to leave, with the formal interviews put off for a few days. Our 'opponents' were patched up and eventually taken away in ambulances, under police escort.

Neither Jenkins nor I wanted to go to hospital, but Ruth insisted on calling Dr Griffiths again. He put half a dozen stitches into the wound above my ear, prescribed a packet of frozen peas for Jenkins' knee, and a dozen white tablets for us to share if the pain kept us awake.

Jenkins was almost unconscious with fatigue and torrents of adrenaline by the time the doctor left, so we led him upstairs to the spare bedroom where he immediately crashed out, clutching the bottle of painkillers like a teddy bear. My body, too, was rapidly running down, but Ruth and I sat together for an hour talking through the previous thirty-six hours. Many questions about Mongan and Dana and why he hated Verres so vehemently remained unanswered, but eventually we had cleared our heads sufficiently to let our bodies surrender to the cloudbank of weariness that drifted over us.

We drifted away together and, as sleep overwhelmed me, I had a brief vision of Dana standing all alone in a desolate place and weeping profusely and thinking, 'His suffering is at last over.'

CHAPTER 32

Symbiosis Blaze

Symbiosis is when people and the land give strength to each other. People have to keep the balance and harmony by proper conduct and thoughts.

Native American belief

THE BATTLE OF Nevern castle had depleted me more than I had vainly believed. I collapsed more than went to sleep. Some time later I had recovered enough to be jolted upright by a volcano of light, pain and nausea erupting in my head before spreading to every joint and muscle in my body. Ruth didn't move, but I knew I had awakened her and she would never sleep while I was like this.

'Sorry sweetheart,' I whispered. 'I've got to get up.' Painfully, I started to lever myself over the edge of the bed but she sat up, turned on her bedside lamp, pulled the duvet aside, lay a pillow across her middle and said, 'Come, lie here.' I backed into the cradle made by her open legs and the pillow.

The muscles in my back and shoulders were like iron rims around a barrel, and she started smoothing them lightly with the palms of her hands.

'Breathe. Deep and slow. Feel the air moving… in and out of your whole body…' Her voice eased into my mind and it began to relax. My body took longer.

'That's right, feel the healing breaths moving in and out, gentle, even breaths, reaching every part of your body.'

She kept talking and stroking as my back and limbs gradually adjusted to the gentle hypnotic rhythm of her words. The aches very slowly started to drain away like water seeping out of a sponge, the steel bands around my chest softened. Her hands shifted from my shoulders onto the marble column that was my neck, and her magic touch had the same effect. Finally, her hands came to rest on my temples so softly I barely felt them. The tension continued to drain away until the noises in my head diminished into silence. I started to slip away into a blissful oblivion; she slowly shifted her position so that I snuggled lower in the bed, gently, gently succumbing to a deep, peaceful, dreamless sleep.

A light came from beyond my closed eyelids and I lay without moving, reassembling recollections of the previous day. They were totally unreal, but I dared not open my eyes in case they *were* real. A chair creaked and I peeped out to see the curtains had been drawn back and a fresh morning light was filtering into the room. Ruth was sitting in a chair by the window, fully dressed, looking at me.

'Good morning,' she said brightly. 'How are you feeling?'

I looked at the ceiling, sat up, turned my head to the left and right several times, looked at the ceiling again and pronounced judgement.

'I feel absolutely marvellous.' I stretched, tested a few muscles and groped around my stitches; there was no pain. 'What did you do to me last night?'

'I did what I saw Dana do to the men yesterday.' She came over and sat on the edge of the bed. 'I was at my wits' end with you last night, and thought I'd try anything once.'

'Well it seemed to work.' I swung my legs over the side of the bed and gave my head another test by shaking it vigorously from side to side. 'That's amazing,' I said. 'What did it feel like to you?'

'It was like putting my hands in a fire.' She shuffled up beside me. 'At first the heat that came out of you was almost too hot to bear, but soon it got less and less until you slipped down and went away like a baby. Of course I couldn't sleep then, because the fire seemed to have moved into me. But I remembered seeing Dana shake her arms and hands after touching the men as if she was shaking her hands dry after getting them wet; so I got up and did the same. Lo and behold, it worked. So there.' She jumped up, and, standing in front of me, made a little curtsey.

'I wonder how our guest is?'

'He's gone.'

'Gone where?'

'I went down this morning and the poor man was hobbling around drinking tea and moaning to himself. His knee was up like a watermelon and he hadn't slept all night despite finishing the painkillers. He took the lot.'

'Oh, poor bloke. Couldn't you have done the same thing for him?'

'I tried, but couldn't get him to relax.'

'He knows that Verres wants to see us at midday, doesn't he?' Poor Verres, I thought. 'I wonder how he'll make it; he lost a lot of blood.'

'He'll be there,' she exclaimed confidently. 'I told Bill it was midday at Pentre Ifan.' She intertwined her fingers behind my neck. 'Did I get it right?'

'You're learning.' I groped weakly for her hand. 'Ruth…' I pleaded, summoning all the influence at my command.

'What now?' she responded with mock exasperation.

'There's one more test I need to pass…'

*

We arrived before Jenkins, and walked along the familiar path to the old rocks. It was a cold, clear day, and the sun hung low above Carn Ingli. Even at midday the shadows were long, and overnight frost remained like huddling sheep in sheltered places the sun hadn't reached.

As we approached the great cromlech, Verres appeared abruptly from between the stones; I had come to accept his dramatic entrances without question. He walked heavily, as if carrying a burden, and there was an unusual pallor over his leathery face.

'Is this your portal?' I asked.

He spread his arms. 'My secret door,' he said, with forced lightness. I could see his wound was troubling him, and felt amazed that he was here at all after the amount of blood he had lost.

'You don't bleed in the other world I guess,' I whispered.

'Door to where?' asked Ruth, going inside the chamber and inspecting it as if she expected to find a trap door or trick mirrors. 'Where's Dana?'

'The door leads to Annwfn, the Otherworld,' he said as blandly. 'And I'm afraid Dana won't be coming.'

'Oh, why not?'

He seemed to gaze wistfully into his memories. He looked at me, and our eyes made a bridge of unspoken understanding.

He turned to Ruth with a sad smile, 'She has another path to walk, my dear.'

Ruth looked startled. 'Is she alright? When will we see her again? Is it because of her son?'

Verres placed his hands on her shoulders and looked down at her lovingly, his pain was exquisite but he only showed her compassion.

'Never serve two masters, my dear.' He leaned slightly into his wound to ease the pressure of his clothing. 'Don't let anything pull you in two directions. Not love, not passion, not duty and not conviction. Poor, dear Dana still has to learn this.'

She understood and nodded.

'Has she gone to the "Otherworld"?'

He answered with a barely perceptible shake of his head. 'The portal is closed to her. She has to travel in this world to find another.'

'But I still don't understand… what is the Otherworld?'

He was getting tired, but raised a hand a few inches to stop me from coming to his rescue. 'It's like Avalon in Malory's story of Arthur.'

'So there really are other worlds occupying the same space as ours.' Ruth's face became beautifully radiant, like a child watching a sunrise. 'How marvellous, will I be able to go through the portal too?'

'Of course. Everyone has their own entrance, although it's rare for two people to be able to use the same one as Dana and I once could.'

'How can I find mine?'

He looked at me, grinned and raised an eyebrow inviting me to give the answer.

'It will find you, sweetheart,' I said.

He gave a light nod.

'Have you got much time left, dear friend?' I asked softly, taking his hand as he walked slowly towards a large boulder ten yards from the cromlech. He squeezed my hand; the strength of spirit was as powerful as ever, but I felt the life force draining out of him.

'I'm bleeding inside David,' he said. 'I won't be able to stay here for very long, and I won't be coming back.'

He released my hand and sat heavily on the boulder. 'So let's get it said and done quickly.' He turned his ear towards the gate. 'I'll just wait for Bill; I can hear him coming.'

A few minutes later Jenkins appeared around a bend in the path. He waved and limped gingerly towards us, leaning heavily on a stick. 'I'm sorry…'

Ruth put a finger to her lips to hush him.

Verres called her over and she moved alongside the great man, and, closing her eyes, placed one hand on his back and the other on his abdomen where Mongan's knife had entered; his eyes shone. Jenkins and I sat on smaller stones in front of him. A clear memory came back to me of the last time we had sat like this in front of Ticker, on the cliffs above Porth Clais many years earlier. Jenkins looked at me and smiled, as if we were sharing the same memory, but I could see his mind had moved away from us since we'd fought together.

Verres' voice was soft and gentle, yet also deep and strong. 'You can't force a seed to grow,' he said slowly. 'You can help it with water and warmth and nutrition, but it will only grow if something inside it urges it to. It's the same with people, and my mistake has been to try to force people into growth; so I must move aside and make way for others who are wiser than I.'

'David?' asked Jenkins.

Verres didn't reply, but continued thinking aloud. 'Also, my main weapon has been my fine words; they are not enough.'

'Then how do you help them, if not with words?' asked Jenkins, struggling hard to understand. 'With messages between the lines?'

Verres shrugged. 'Actions – positive actions – inspire, Bill, words confuse. That's a recent lesson I've learned.'

Jenkins looked puzzled, fretful.

Ruth shook her hands vigorously, then replaced them. Verres looked first at Jenkins, then at me. I knew what he would say next and was grateful.

'There is no particular "one".' He coughed and winced.

'You all have qualities that the seed needs.' He produced

three hessian envelopes. 'I have a gift for each of you, to help you remember.'

'For you, young Jenkins, once you stop talking about yourself and start *showing* people how to discover their own self-love and self-belief – if they so wish – thousands can be transformed by your example.' He handed him an envelope tied with straw. 'You will bear the shears. You've already become a great communicator, and will become an even greater mover. You are ready to stop seeking power for yourself and to start bringing life, giving moisture to the seed.'

Jenkins tentatively took the package and looked down at it as if it concealed a venomous snake. 'I know,' Verres whispered. 'There's no need to say anything, Bill. We both know how difficult you are going to find it. Just believe in yourself, my lad, and be true to who you are becoming.'

He turned to Ruth and handed her a similar gift. 'I don't have to tell you what you've become in the last few days, my dear.' She raised her chin proudly and shook her head. 'You have earned the comb and become a healer. You have no idea yet of how great a healer you can be, but it will come to you more and more as each day passes. People will revere you, and be inspired by your healing powers and the way you live your life. Many will want to be like you, and in trying they will discover who they already are.'

I noticed that blood was seeping through his clothing and spreading over the boulder. Ruth saw it too. After respectfully placing the package in her shoulder bag, she shook her hands again vigorously before kneeling down and wrapping her arms around his middle. 'You, my dear, provide the warmth the seed needs.'

Finally, he shifted his gaze to me. 'David, you are my son and I bequeath to you the razor.' He passed the third hessian pouch to me. 'Through you I will live and continue to love.' I looked up into his pale face and tired old eyes and felt happy for him, because his tortuous worldly journey was almost over and he knew he would find his ultimate fulfilment through me.

'Everything will be brought together in you. You will weave together the worlds of the spirits, of magic, of fable, of enchantment, of dreams and of the solid earth. You have already made tentative explorations into them and soon you will travel between them as easily as a bird flies from branch to branch. Your work is with the land and the spirits who inhabit and nurture it. For you there will be no acclaim or worldly recognition, you will do the work the old boar used to do before he was trapped and banished. You will help make the world a fertile garden that nurtures every seed that lies in its soil. You provide nourishment for the seed.'

Abruptly, he slumped sideways into Ruth's arms and gasped, 'I can't say any more. I can't stay any longer in this place. I mustn't die here.' I leapt up to add my support, and between us we held him up until some strength returned.

'But what if the seeds don't want what we have to give them?' Jenkins was kneeling in front of him and touching his feet and blooded knees like an infant, impotent to help but frantic to do something to save a dying parent. 'I'm sorry, I'm being selfish... but what can we do?'

'Seeds fall where they will, Bill.' He smiled weakly. 'Stony or fertile ground. There's nothing you can do for those on stony ground, except wait.' I felt his weight slump against my chest and thighs. 'I must go now. Help me to the door.'

Ruth took an arm, but couldn't hold his weight. Without a thought I picked him up in my arms. He was a brutally heavy man, but in my arms he felt like a sleeping child. With Ruth on one side and Jenkins the other, I carried the great man slowly and lovingly back to his portal.

A yard from the cromlech he said, 'Put me down now.' His

face was drawn, but he hadn't finished with us. 'The One?' he asked, 'Who is "the One"?'

Ruth and Jenkins looked towards me, waiting for me to speak.

'We all are,' I said.

'Now! There's time for one last small indulgence lady and gentlemen.' He looked admonishingly at us. 'A quarter of a century ago, not far from this spot, I asked you something, and didn't get a response. Remember?'

'Was it to do with something Daniel Defoe wrote?' asked Jenkins, thinking hard.

'Well done, Bill.'

'It was, "All men would be tyrants if they could." You asked how we would have behaved if we had been in Arthur's boots. I've used it as a theme for a sermon from time to time; now I remember where I first heard it.'

'So you have your answer ready?'

Jenkins grinned sheepishly, 'Of course Defoe was right, although I have always denied it from the pulpit.'

Ruth looked thoughtful. 'I think he was wrong. Tyranny is part of the dirt we pick up from the world; it is not an intrinsic part of us.'

Verres nodded and turned to me. 'David?'

'He's neither right nor wrong.'

'Trust you.' Ruth laughed lightly.

'The statement implies lack of control. We are all capable of tyranny, but very few exercise it. We all have choice and control over our actions. Only those in desperate need choose that path.'

He nodded again; then Ruth came forward and slipped something into his hand. 'This is my little gift to you.'

He opened his hand to show us a small white round pebble.

Suddenly I felt heat coming from Jenkins, something was

boiling inside him. Then he blurted out angrily, 'This is all utter nonsense.'

'Bill!' Ruth gasped, shocked.

'Shears mean nothing, they are no help to me. Life-giving moisture and seeds deciding when to grow are empty metaphors. Saving thousands? Senseless humbug. You're speaking gobbledygook.' His eyes blazed with rage, but Verres, leaning against the great, wise stone that had stood in that place for five thousand years, listened kindly.

'Bill, nothing is impossible if you have proper conduct and thoughts. Things are only impossible if you believe they can't be done.'

'Proper thoughts,' Jenkins muttered bitterly. 'What's proper…?'

Verres looked at him with exquisite tenderness. 'Oh Bill, how I love you. I love your doubts, your vanity, your ambition, but most of all I love the ability you have to give them all up.' He patted Jenkins on the shoulder, while the patch of blood got bigger as we watched. 'One day all these doubts and uncertainties will be faded memories.'

He stepped around the stone, and disappeared from our lives for a second time.

*

None of us could say a word as we shuffled away from the stones. Jenkins seemed still unable to understand, and looked back over his shoulder two or three times, almost willing Verres to return.

'Let's see what he's given us.'

'Not now,' I said.

'I'm going to,' said Jenkins, undoing his parcel.

He found a pair of black, iron sheep shears.

'Is there a point?' he asked. Ruth looked at me with disappointment on her face.

'What's in yours?' He tried to snatch Ruth's bag, but she pulled it away from him.

'Bill.' She stepped back, shielding the bag behind her back. 'What's the matter with you?'

'What's the matter? What's the matter? Have you forgotten yesterday we nearly got killed; I had my leg almost chopped off, all Verres' violent past caught up with him and David threw Roberts off a cliff. He was a scoundrel, but he hardly deserved that.'

'Didn't his words, his life, his parting gift mean anything to you Bill?' Ruth grabbed his arms and started to shake him. 'Don't go back Bill, you've come so far. Don't go back.'

His head slumped to his chest as if it had become too heavy to hold upright.

'I'm lost, Ruth. I'm lost.'

'Oh Bill.' She kept hold of his arms and shook him. 'Believe in the Boar. Believe in what we can help bring about.'

'I need to think.' He dragged himself free from her hold. 'I'm going now. I'll try not to let you down…' He started to limp back up the path to the car park, and didn't look back.

Ruth's preoccupation broke the stillness. 'David.'

'Yes.'

'Bill's frightened.'

'He's got a hard struggle ahead, but he'll come through it – in his own good time. Trust me.'

'What do *we* do now?'

'We could go home and have some lunch,' I said, looking back at the cromlech and the outline of Carn Ingli behind it as if on guard. 'But first perhaps we both need to spend a little time by ourselves.'

She nodded.

'I need to stay here on my own with the stones for a while.'

'I need to walk,' she said. 'See you... when I see you, my dear.'

We basked in a brief embrace but the stones, the trees and the wind were calling me with an urgency I couldn't resist. I watched her bobbing hair and swinging arms, her hips and shoulders swaying to the rhythm of her stride as she disappeared down the path. Then, I turned back towards the old stones. They stood stark and hard against the outline of the dear old hill, and I felt a vibration come from them; it spread over the land around, as far as Carn Ingli, and into my entire body. I stood for a long, deep moment, feeling the timelessness.

Nothing's changed here, I thought. Not for thousands of years. Except now everything is back to normal. Balance and harmony is returning.

I stood for a blissful age with my hands feeding off the stone. Then I turned and started walking back along the path. Something moved in front of the sun behind me, and I was walking in a shadow; a shadow that seemed to move with me at the same pace, the same undulation. Then I heard a rustling in the dead grass and bracken behind me, followed by a grunting and snuffling sound. The musty smell of damp skin and animal sweat filled my nostrils and salty tears stung my eyes as I felt completely at one with the presence. The sounds and the smells and the huge humpbacked shadow were all at one with me.

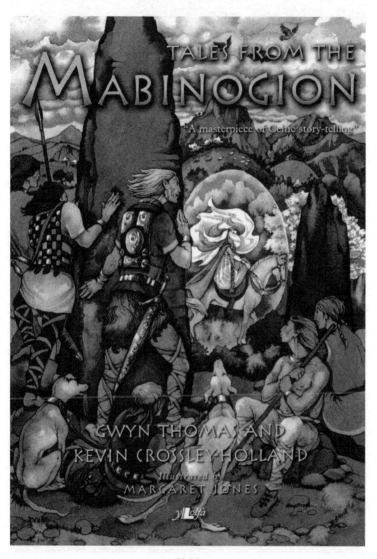

£9.95

ROB GITTINS

INVESTIGATING MR WAKEFIELD

y Lolfa

£8.99